PRAISE FOR *CLUB CONTANGO*

"*Club Contango* is an increasingly rare thing: science fiction with both a brain and a heart. With this worthy follow-up to last year's *Other Minds*, Boey shows that she's one to watch."

—Edward Ashton, author of *Mickey7*

"Eliane Boey is set to immerse readers in a world full of intensity, yearning, and moody beauty, and the human spirit finding its way despite the all-consuming grind of hypercapitalism. *Club Contango* will make you hear faraway music and see the glimmer of distant neon."

—Samit Basu, author of *The City Inside*

"With fully-realized worldbuilding and kinetic prose, *Club Contango* is a dazzling cyberpunk tale that will grab you by the heart and won't let go. Full of twists, thrills, and the coolest characters I've read in a long time, this is an assured debut from Boey, and you can bet I'll be reading anything she comes out with next."

—Victor Manibo, author of *Escape Velocity*

"Heartfelt characters, imaginative worldbuilding, and a unique yet eerily plausible vision of the future."

—Lincoln Michel, author of *The Body Scout*

"A crackling, nostalgic cyber-noir, brimming with voice and atmosphere. A future lost in time for a generation still looking for a home."

—Aubrey Wood, author of *Bang Bang Bodhisattva*

Books in "The Tracerverse" Series by Eliane Boey

Other Minds

Club Contango

CLUB
CONTANGO

CONTENT WARNING

This book has content on maternal depression and suicide ideation, both resolved. Reader discretion is advised.

Edited by Rob Carroll
Book Design and Layout by Rob Carroll
Cover Art by Nickolej Villiger
Cover Design by Rob Carroll

ISBN 978-1-958598-57-3 (paperback)
ISBN 978-1-958598-77-1 (eBook)

darkmatter-ink.com

CLUB CONTANGO

ELIANE BOEY

For CX.

And for the losers and the dreamers.
Don't stop playing.

PART 1

DEAL

AFTER

WHEN I THINK about Chance and our time together on Freeport Station, I remember the birds.

And I remember Chance pushing me over the edge.

I hadn't thought of Chance much since then. I wouldn't have now if it weren't for this door, light and sound filtering through its cracks. I had stopped on my walk because my shoelaces had come undone, but it was this sound, this classic Shanghai jazz that led me into the alley and to this door. *"The Scent that Comes in the Night."* No, that's not the song. Not that it matters. Memories press against the skin of reality, notes testing the tension. The door identifies itself as "Sanctuary to Spacefarers." In subscript: "all are welcome." A different Sanctuary, on a different station. But the messaging works. I feel its hooks dig into me. *All are welcome.*

The remastered strains of Bai Guang's "Waiting for Your Return" becomes part of me like gold dust. There is no one around to ask if they hear it, too, so I must assume its not a dream. I remember another sanctuary. A place. A point in time. A slim, beautiful, androgynous person as fluid as memory. The day the birds returned, sulking on the counter at Tanuki, on the viewing gallery of the Freeport Embarkment Terminal, threatening to tear us apart. I imagine stroking my kid, Sticky's, plump little hand for comfort, and I kiss it.

This is the way I remember that day:

Chance first lifts the empty glass off the coaster, then Chance's boots are atop the barstools. *Had those boots always been at the crossroads of distress and perfection?* A skip, and Chance is on the counter, five stories above the frantic bustle of the departure hall below, where an extraordinary crush of Contractors and a few remaining Settlers scramble to leave the station It's a mean drop from the gallery to the concourse. Not a sure-to-kill you drop, but a sure-to-make-you-not-want-to-try.

I know because I lived it.

But my eye goes to the table, to Chance's boots.

The glass in Chance's hand is like a drop of water.

I feel cold condensation on my hand.

Rosewood. That's what the counter at Tanuki was made of. Real goddamn rosewood, stripped from some spent tycoon's heirloom, nineteenth-century bed-and-divan set. It warms beneath Chance's palms and releases oils that were embedded deep in the heartwood. The mother-of-pearl inlay of peonies is still intact. I'd forgotten about those.

Only good things happen at Tanuki.

"Don't do it," I say.

"Tell me what I'm doing," Chance says.

I tell Chance it's about having the option, even just to hold and never use it.

Chance half-smiles. There is a sadness behind the expression. I can see that now.

"I said that, didn't I? Do you think I meant it?"

Chance had taken the small, safe life that Sticky and I had, and destroyed it. I had begged Chance to destroy it. I had welcomed Chance with open arms like Chance was our savior, our very own Sanctuary.

The Commission's lock-down procedure has the elevators inactive, but the thunder of combat boots draws closer anyway as they stomp instead up a long, spiral staircase—another historical asset salvaged from a once-wealthy family's library back on Earth and reconstructed piece by piece here on Freeport, humanity's first multi-national frontier station in space. I wonder if the family used the expensive donation as a write-off on their relocation tax.

Try harder.

I say, "It isn't us that they want. I can give them what they need."

Chance says, "You are not going back to what you were."

The boots reach the top of the stairs. All that sound for just two men. But we are also two. For now.

I always used the stairs, even when the elevators worked. Climbed them with eyes toward Tanuki, so I wouldn't lose sight of Chance. Thinking about it now makes me laugh at myself, teary-eyed.

There's a clink of chopsticks on porcelain from within the restaurant. Two Sparklers have been hiding behind a table of stiffened dumplings since the restaurant was cleared out and the Embarkment sealed off.

Did I know them from somewhere?

A party, most likely. At my flat, thrown by Chance, where I would have squeezed past them from the galley kitchenette on my way to the only bedroom, where I would check on Sticky. If they recognize me amid the experiences they are streaming behind their privacy shades, they don't make a sign. The privacy shades cover the top halves of their faces and depict early-century pixel-art renders of cute, cartoon fox faces.

Any moment now, I'll see the Teacher. A red shimmer catches my eye, but it's only the mascot of the ubiquitous Red Unicorn Group, which came out of nowhere four years ago and now owns every third thing on Freeport. No human has stepped out from behind the avatar of the mischievous horned red satyr, but Red Unicorn's rise did mysteriously coincide with the time Hong was sloughing bad debt onto Alchemy. Shaking it all off, with me attached.

To say I'm distracted is an understatement.

If I'd known this day was going to be our last, I would have watched more closely. Would I have seen anything different? Would I have stopped Chance from pushing me?

All this time. Everything we've done. And I still can't own it.

The satyr twirls. It's a lonely, manic dance above the departure hall—a ghastly send-off.

I haven't thought of what I will say to the Teacher. In a different timeline, or on a different station, we might have been friends. Shoot the breeze about organized crime, diaspora friendship networks across a solar system, the gray spaces between the two.

Focus.

They say the biggest set-up for failure is the failure to plan for growth.

What happens when you plan to fail and—against all odds, logic, and history—you grow? So big that you're pressing against the walls of your former life. Crushing everything in the way. Perhaps it doesn't feel like I've won, because I'm about to lose the only thing I want.

I say to Chance, "The world we left behind doesn't exist anymore."

"Connie." Chance winks, uses my name as only Chance can, like a lure, an admonition, a weapon. "Nothing bad could ever happen at Tanuki."

An announcement booms through the departure hall. The last scheduled shuttle has left. The next shuttle docks in six hours. The pushing crowd below erupts in a renewed surge of anger and confusion. A loud crack is followed by muffled grunts as three people fall over each other. A child wails over the music-box tinkle of a plushy chiming an old tune: "You Are My Sunshine." If anyone was holding back from pushing to the front before, they're not holding back now.

No Contractors ranked below L3 are leaving the station today. Not until the Enforcers have found and rounded up whomever the Commission thinks started the fire in the dome.

The blaze grows brighter.

WHAT DID CHANCE say as the sting of the shock weapon ripped through my flesh?

Burn it down.

"Help me," I say. "I can't."

One of us was never going to walk out of here.

Do it, or I will.

Had I always known?

Chance throws the glass over the edge just as the Teacher reaches us.

And the birds lift their wings.

What does it feel like to be pushed over the edge?

WHEN I THINK about Chance now, standing outside this hidden door in a different alley, on a different station, a familiar song playing—outside this Sanctuary for the lost—I don't think about how Chance found us, but how I invited Chance in. How I thought I was lost, but really, I knew nothing.

I was wrong, Chance. The world we left behind still exists.

We just couldn't find our way back to it.

This is a story about last chances and trading the future.

It's a story about losing to win.

BEFORE

I KEEP TRYING to start the story on Freeport, but really, it began on Earth, with Jerry and I sharing a desk at Reliance Marine, peering into Hong's glass office. It began with me at the Imperial Resort and Conference Center, standing speechless before the people I was supposed to represent, carrying the shame of my parents' disappointed gaze.

It started with everything in my life that had led to me to the booth seat across from Jerry at Auntie Wong's Dim Sum parlor, sweat pooling under my ass on the red vinyl.

Jerry had been Bad Luck Jerry for as long as I had known him, which wasn't super long, but long enough that I always broke my fortune cookie with him, since he never failed to remind me that I started with the larger piece.

With twenty-nine minutes to option maturity, I can tell I'm winning.

But I can't win.

The bets against me at Club Contango far out-strip those in favor. Thank Doris the prediction AI for that. The house winning should be a good thing. Stars know we need the coin. But in reality, the way a micro-casino keeps its players coming is by making up for what it lacks in size and legality with high levels of trust and opportunity. Contango gives its players enough small wins to keep them coming back for more. But a house win this big will pull the rug out from under the players, out from under us all.

Unbothered, Jerry Sit hinges his chopsticks. He reaches for the shrimp dumplings and touches one, the droplet of soy sauce transferring from chopstick to translucent dumpling skin. "Crystal skin," it's called, and it holds fast to his chopstick. He pulls back, reaches for the chive and mushroom. Jerry isn't just unbothered, he's the epitome of delight. A sloppy grin pinches the corners of his lips as he shakes his head at our luck.

Today's bet at the club was supposed to be a sure thing for those betting against, just like it always was for bets on my personal outcomes. Because I, Connie Lam, am a loser, with a long track record to prove it. I never win. I've never even won a free oil change for Lucky 48 Extra-Terrestrial Chandlery's rust-bucket minibulk hauler—the one I pilot for deliveries. And I certainly don't win at life.

But there's Jerry across the table from me, a big smile on his face. I thought we were meeting so he could pitch another one of his start-up ideas, or to inform me that the long arm of the law has finally fingered him for tax evasion, and he's giving me up to the authorities as part of a generous plea deal. But instead, we're meeting about something else, some-thing unexpected from Jerry, the recovering fintech bro who had always been weak on the tech part and strong on the creative accounting.

Jerry knocks back a cup of tea to wash down the dumpling.

"A windfall like this makes up for everything that's gone down since the '70s. I couldn't have done it without you, Connie. You *are* Echo."

Jerry's been on the hustle circuit since the 2070s, forced to squeeze every contact and eavesdrop on every conversation for something to get in on because I put him there in the first place. In the '70s, we shared a desk at Reliance Marine. A lot of people were losing their jobs due to the retrenchments of the '70s, and neither of us made it out unscathed. I barely lasted longer than he did, but Jerry never let me forget who "blew the whistle" first.

Was it just another excuse for what we did?

Not that it matters now.

I do know that the Jerry who came asking for a favor—to train his AI in sales pitching—isn't the one sitting across from me now, telling me he'll split us sixty-forty. Telling me, "It isn't how good a product you have, Connie. It's who you know who'll buy it off you. People are breaking down my door to get in on Project Echo."

This version of Jerry knows people.

He talks about transferring coin to me. Sixty-forty in his favor, because we go way back from Earth days. I imagine myself flipping the tower of hot steamers in his face.

Sixty-forty? It's my trading model that I uploaded to train your AI, Jerry. Hours of videos of my face, my voice, presenting it from all angles. I should be cutting you a commission from the stack, Jerry. 2.75 percent. Not the other way round.

But those weren't the odds I played.

Chance is not going to like this.

Jerry says, "Of all the little ideas we've cultivated over the years, who would've thought this would be The One?"

Who would've thought that Bad Luck Jerry would be the one who would, with one hand, lead the first properly successful project I'd ever worked on, and with the other, deliver a blow to the only project I love: Club Contango?

Twenty-six minutes until maturity.

The restaurant conveyor belt delivers a train of five steamers, and Jerry hits pause on his spiel to lift all the lids and inspect. He breathes heavy, contemplates the soft rice rolls and the fluffy white buns. I picture droplets of his warm breath landing on the tacky white skins. He covers the steamers, and the train rolls along.

"Of course, I won't see the gains right away. They'll pay every quarter, making sense of transfer costs and all. What I do have is the starting bonus. The rest you'll get when I do."

Who's they?

Between us, the translucent skins on the shrimp dumplings are drying out from the recirculated air—which by late afternoon in Auntie's means the scents of steaming rice flour, and stale farts. The acrid sting of kitchen grease wafts in on their tail.

"What's the payout, Jerry? You say you licensed Project Echo for a fortune, but I'll be damned if it gets paid in crumbs over forty years and shot straight to our NET account, which neither of us will see until we're seventy-five. Right after blowing up my projections for Contango."

Jerry reaches for the egg tarts, and a discrete ring on the table under our teacups glows white with a prompt:

<<Add tea, 0.03 SG-Bit.>>

"You're running a projection now? Against yourself?"

"It's a club week. And game night or not, we keep Doris running the projections. The AI gets sharper the more it's used. You know that."

I didn't say that today was the one day I called a win on my future outcome, to be realized this week. Because, why not? Let the house lose now and then so it still looks like chance. Make some personal coin. But today, Bad Luck Jerry is holding up a mirror, and when I look at him, I see myself.

Twenty-two minutes.

The table behind us opens a steamer and removes it from the belt. Inside are rice rolls with *char siew* barbecued meat of unspecified organic composition. Delicate and trembling under soy sauce and sesame oil. Wet with droplets from Jerry's breath. The table digs in.

Jerry says, "Hong wouldn't recognize a unicorn like this if it kicked him in the face. Not for all the pyramid schemes and hack jobs he's been pulling for years."

It's me. I'm the unicorn.

I push away from the table, but the clatter doesn't register above the din. When Auntie Wong's opened, with its teak-colored walls and sliding doors edged in gold, it was a dim sum parlor like the ones you took your Zoomer grandma to on her birthday. But then dynamic short-term visas happened to Freeport. Auntie tried to hold on to her old servers, but eventually she had to put in the conveyor belts to replace them. Now the elegant dining room is shot through on all sides with steel belts that groan like an aging diva on life support.

The table warns me as I get up:

>   <<*Please pay at the counter before leaving, or your estimated expense will be deducted from your NET, with a penalty fee.*>>

Jerry's eyes pop as he points at me with his chopsticks. The meal's on his profile, against his NET. But according to him, coin isn't going to be a problem for us now—once we get to the next quarter's payout, that is.

Sixty-forty.

It's Jerry who's in coin, not me, so I leave him with the bill and head back to the club.

I head out through the heavy doors that only open if you put your shoulder to them, because Auntie doesn't really want your business, and I step out into the filtered dome air that's at least lighter on the scent of grease. If I take a left and stay on Beach Road, head past the hotels, casinos, and boutiques until I get to Delta Road, I'd get to Lucky 48 fast. But a flop in my gut tells me to avoid the main boulevards of the station, so I keep to the alleys instead.

I skip over a tarp displaying 3D-printed power tools and bulker parts for sale, do my best to avoid the eyes that look up at me from all around. It's five hundred meters to the back of the bulk food emporium, but if I turn, it's two hundred meters to the slip road, which leads to the bleakest roundabout in all of terraformed space: Pioneer Ring.

Pioneer Ring is a loop around the sprawling dorm complex of the Pacific Mutual Company. It also boasts the only trees on this side of the tracks—a perk of being an indentured employee at the fastest growing corporation with extra-territorial powers. The outer circumference of the ring houses the Contractor quarters of lesser corporations like Red Unicorn, and the work-life centers like Raintree. It's where I spend most of my days when club nights—or my former ward, Trace Pereira—doesn't keep me at the Lucky 48 Chandlery.

Fifty meters to Delta Road and Lucky 48. Here, the buildings are squat and narrow and already show the first signs of aging a mere five years after the first Settlers turned the keys on their penthouse apartments on Beach Road, or on their townhouses on River Valley Road. At the fork in the alley, I turn onto Delta—Beach Road's poor cousin—where the hustle isn't dressed as charisma, and where business isn't conducted in private rooms upstairs. On Delta Road, tenants pay by the half-month.

I skim my palm on the chipped edges of the walls and feel fragments of it break away and lose themselves under my fingernails.

Finally, I'm scanning in to Lucky 48 with the ID tag of an ex-employee who left long ago for a better contract on a Tier-2 station. I use the back door, because I can't face Trace's misplaced admiration before I know how bad it is inside.

I head down the stairs to the storeroom just as the option reaches maturity.

CONTANGO

THE MUSIC FINDS me first. It's is a mix of retro-synth-meets-ragtime—something only Chance knows how to cut into a lightheaded dervish that echoes every period of music history and none at all, to create something entirely new. It's played off a memory sliverfilm permanently adhered to the side of speakers that were torn out of a first-generation inter-station cruiser. They belt out the music with enough power to force the beat of your heart, which is good, because when you launch yourself into space with nothing but your carry-on allowance in Contractor class, you make sure to pack the feelings that pull the strings of memory, the ones that bypass the dull ache at the back of your skull that says relocating stationside was always a bad idea. Chance was big on physical media for this reason. Couldn't risk losing the only real connection to Earth.

At the bottom of the aluminum stairs is Club Contango—my domain. It's where I take fate by the collar, turn it upside down, and shake it on behalf of the person it wouldn't let me become. On behalf of Chance and the other lost souls who have joined us tonight—twenty or so this evening.

The skin of my throat eventually unsticks, and I find my voice.

"I don't know how Doris didn't see this coming," I say to no one.

I don't know if Doris the AI registers my remark, because she doesn't say anything, not that she would—it's not her job to quibble, only predict. She takes my life, and the lives of any players who want to be "it," and spits out three randomized scenarios of the near future, along with their respective probabilities of occurring.

I've never *not* been a failure, so why would Doris have thought differently today?

In this moment, I'm extra-glad that I chose to house Doris in a vintage robocleaner, rather than inside a humanoid casing, or as part of a smart hologram like the ones you see on the side of the Circle Finance building in Enterprise Square, because the last thing I need right now is to see another judging face. The walls feel like they're closing in on me as the players all turn to look at me in their various stages of grief.

Behind them, straddling a chair atop a stack of shipping pallets that act like a dais—radiating munificent impatience—is Chance. All the players assume Chance is in charge. An observation that Chance takes no pains to correct. To Chance, I'm just another thing inside the club that needs managing—like the drink list, or the occasional brawl. To the players, I'm just nervous-smiling Connie, who stays on the periphery and only speaks up to timidly greet you—tells you to make yourself comfortable, to grab a drink, to place a bet. It's a charade Chance and I play at the club that's bled into our life outside of it, but I never find the right way to address it. At this moment, Chance the whip serves us both, then pulls up the chart of outcome positions and values by projecting them upon a cracked concrete wall.

Beneath the projection is a list of bettors and their wagers.

When we started the pool, I wanted to call it Boiler Room, in homage to an old film from the twentieth century that my Popo watched on bad days to remind herself that she'd had good days once, too. She also liked the one with the man named after a lizard, and another one that used wolves as a metaphor for stockbrokers. But *Boiler Room* was her favorite.

Chance was dead against it, though.

"A bit on the nose, isn't it, Connie?" Chance had said, with a shiver of the shoulders.

To Chance, the name was a reminder that we were committing two crimes in the eyes of the Freeport Commission's Justice Department, and that one of them was criminal and punishable by deportation back to Earth.

I guess I should mention that Club Contango is an *illegal* micro-casino. Illegal here on Freeport, because even in outer space, at the tail-end of the twenty-first century, the greatest crime in the eyes of the government is still tax evasion by the little guy—the ninety-nine percent who can least afford the clawback by Territory and Company. The second greatest crime on Freeport—which Club Contango is also guilty of—is not maintaining the minimum balance of coin in your NET account required to keep your legal status and the privilege to remain stationside. The minimum is a hard floor to maintain for old-money Settlers who aren't tycoons, let alone a single-mother Contractor like myself. I'm either tight on funds or illiquid, just like everyone else on Freeport.

Thank goodness for the combined fiduciary powers-that-be, for it is they who even things out by loaning us back our own money with interest. When everyone's in debt, the sin isn't borrowing more than you can return, it's not making more promises you can't keep.

With all that hanging over everyone's head, it's not surprising that mind-altering drugs are not only legal, but encouraged. It was always going to take more than virtual simulations inside Lion City to help the first migrant generation forget everything they'd left behind on Earth. But since chemical drugs mess you up extra in space, most users have moved to audio-neural drugs that offer a much cleaner high. They do, however, scramble your ability to pinpoint your place in reality, but who doesn't have bigger problems? A few Sparklers—the rich kids of Settler-status parents—tried making chemical drugs and even organics popular again, but that fad faded faster than the pen-and-paper revival.

Club Contango aims to please, so of course it flows with booze and is flush with sliverfilms of every electric dream—from the nasty "Loop" to the sweeter "Delight." We never make the entertainment license payments on time, but we eventually make it right with interest. When we don't, we get busted—sometimes by real Enforcers, sometimes by bunch of goons just dressing the part. It happens.

"All bets are final," Chance says.

Someone new to the club speaks up. "You're not serious. Wasn't that one a simulation?"

Weak laughter collects in the room, but doesn't touch Chance.

"You said this was a fun round," said the new player's friend. "It cleared us out more than expected, and we're not liquid now."

They're new, all right. New money, too. It seeps from every pore, every hidden stitch in their bespoke printed clothing that is too strikingly fashionable to be worn by anyone from the old-money, mining-empire families. And their privacy shades are too gauche. They obscure the top halves of their faces with pixelated cartoons. One presents a dolphin wearing a black hat, and the other a squirrel with a Cheshire cat's grin. They're limited-edition live filters—one of one. No others like them throughout the entire solar system. Sparklers love them for the exclusivity. They don't seem to mind that one-of-one exclusives make it easier for Big Surveillance to track you.

"Are your names on the positions list?"

Chance is asking, but the dolphin and the squirrel are looking at me, because it only takes two seconds for anyone to figure out that between Chance and me, I'm the good cop.

The dolphin speaks. "I'm Roar Wang. We met at the Great Eastern, remember? This is Mazie. We're Zetta's friends."

The smile on the squirrel's face turns upside down. "We just put coin down on the Red Unicorn launch. It'll be a full quarter at least before we see anything." Cartoon tears form at the corner of the squirrel's eyes.

Chance speaks past me. "I didn't ask for names. I asked if they're on the board. If they are, Stiff will show you to a quiet corner, where you can radio your parents for the transfer."

Stiff is Club Contango's accountant. He approaches the two Sparklers and stands ready with his ancient tablet.

"We were at your party," the squirrel whines to me. "You like us. I made a model ship with your kid. Remember? We made it out of chopsticks."

Mazie the squirrel's thin, pale arms *do* look familiar, and maybe I *did* see those thin fingers of hers sifting through a pile of chopsticks with Sticky, and Zetta *is* a friend of the club—she contributed a significant sum to keep us afloat while Arcadia went after us with their own predictive gaming room—but none of that matters now. Not when Chance is standing right next to me. I can't waive the debt or put them on margin as long as Chance is close enough to breathe whiskey-laced breath against my earlobe.

Chance watches Mazie with dark, deep-set eyes. They're beautiful and luminous beneath slick-backed bangs that end in an undercut. It's a look that shifts the room and sucks the air out of you, forces you to recognize that you're in the pull of a dominant force.

But Roar and Mazie are quickly forgotten after another player, Visala Kumar, shouts a string of curses and kicks a chair across the room. When I look at Vis, I see someone who used to be my best friend and who I miss. When Vis looks at me, she probably sees three years wasted—time she wants to forget.

"Vis, I didn't know—" I begin.

"You could have told me," she says. "Not the outcome. 'Respect the club' and all that—fair enough. But maybe, just maybe, you could have told your oldest friend on-station to *not* put three of the Hands' seven coins down. Something like, I don't know, 'stay home today, Vis,' might have been helpful enough. Wink and nudge. Anything."

By 'the Hands' coin,' Vis means the collective cookie jar of the HaboHub Logistics Contractor's association—an informal and secretive club, because the third greatest crime on Freeport is organizing. Vis has gotten in with them in a bad way, and she's been trying to play her way out.

"I had no idea it was coming. Nothing I do with Jerry is ever investment grade. I still can't believe he made the sale."

Am I lying?

Chance waves her along.

"You rolled the dice, Vis."

Vis sets her jaw. "I'm calling margin on that."

I step between them. "Vis, the club is all out of buffer. We started this cycle in the red. Today's win barely puts us in the black, and that's assuming sixty percent of players even pay what they owe. If everyone calls margin, it'll take the bottom out of Club Contango."

I don't tell her that Stiff has already added the numbers up, subtracted them, weighted them, and still can't balance the books. I never thought the club would make us rich, but I also didn't expect to be a single Sparkler's wager away from insolvency every cycle.

Stiff looks up from his tablet with a frown, but I turn away before he can see me staring. His reaction says it all. He's honesty personified.

"Except you're personally flush now, aren't you, Connie Lam?" Vis says. "That's why we're in this shit. If you cared as much about keeping your friends as you do keeping your club and this game of yours going, then *you'd* plug the gap."

Vis doesn't have to say, *you owe me as much*, but I see it in my memory of our first year on Freeport, back when we shared a corner of the MAM resettlement hostel after sharing a berth section on the shuttle out. Other Contractors have become life partners from less. Instead, I left the dorm as soon as I had enough savings in my NET to qualify for a basic housing loan, with a little help from the Pereiras of Lucky 48. Even though it meant moving to Pioneer Ring, I had to go. I packed Sticky's bag and mine while Vis was at work at HaboHub.

Don't hide behind that deep breath. Say it.

"Not this time, Vis. Club isn't liquid. I'm not liquid. All this expected revenue we're writing doesn't even pay until at least a quarter or two later."

"Bullshit! You've been making bank all year. We can all see the scores."

My answer for Vis is on the tip of my tongue. It's not about the scores or what I can or cannot afford in coin, but what Club Contango is and what it needs from everyone in the pool—not just Chance and I—in order to survive. *Keep playing. Don't stop. Because as soon as you do, your losses find you.*

That's the easy part. But Chance and the club players who come here every fortnight to mock their failures and mine—to own their disappointments—see Jerry thanking me on my livestream. See his smile, like he and I knew we were always going to win.

If I look up now, I won't see the large black birds circling. But that doesn't mean they're not still there.

Truth is, I've already paid down all the coin I earned into Freeport stakeholder bonds, bought and managed through a discreet broker, a mutual friend of Stiff's.

Stakeholder bonds are the most precious NFTs in the Greater Belt, which means I'm a little bit closer to investing enough in Freeport to renew my Contractor visa through appeal—to remain stationside, legally. To hard underline my status as my own kid's resident guardian. I can't risk losing her again. Stakeholder bonds are a mean system of luck and exploitation of the weakest, and they don't guarantee I still won't be deported once I come out in the open to appeal to MAM, but every year that I don't try increases the risk of me being separated from my kid. I can't take her back to Earth. She needs to grow up galactic. Any coin that isn't kept liquid for Sticky's present needs is locked away for Sticky's future. That means Club Contango is illiquid. Chance doesn't manage the earnings. Chance's purpose here is vibes.

There's movement at the foot of the stairs, where jeweled ballet flats become a tiny black-and-white outfit that's not so much a dress and lining as it is strategically-draped lace. A privacy mask beneath bobbed black bangs presents a cartoon cat with large watery eyes. The cat dips its curious head.

"Rude of you to start without me," says the cat.

"Zetta. I didn't think you would show."

"What? And spend another night at Arcadia, sweating at the foot of the DJ platform, waiting for Suziebaby's new face to glitch?" The rosebud lips beneath the cat's nose show the slightest curl and twist.

Suziebaby is the owner of the Arcadia, the grand old club and casino that nearly put Club Contango out of business. Zetta's remarks about Suziebaby are meant to be in the club's defense, since Zetta is the one who saved us. They're also meant to remind Chance and I what she's done for us. We owe her.

Roar lifts a finger off a coupé glass. "Lucky of you to miss a cleaning!" His drink sloshes from the glass as he speaks, and I'm certain he's flying high on Delight.

The weepy cat eyes on Zetta's mask brighten, and Zetta drops the mask for a half-second—just enough to flash a wink at me from an elven face, sharp and pointy, with a little upturned nose. The cat face reappears as she walks over to join us.

Zetta's as mercurial as a magnetic storm over Saturn, and she has a large margin account that she doesn't always remember to draw from, but will play in full if reminded. She's also the only player in the club who will take things up with me instead of Chance, because she knows the truth of who's really in charge. It's too bad she didn't play today. She doesn't always bet against me.

On the wall, Doris the AI continues to run a slow-motion replay of its projection in an effort to see where it had gone wrong. It had predicted that I would run out of coin by the end of the month, lose my home, my status, and custody of my kid, but none of that came true.

"It's *your* outcome, Connie," Chance says to me. "Own it."

My shoulders feel heavy. The circling birds have landed, and they refuse to fly away.

Chance mouths the next words to me: *Live it.*

Can I outrun the future I made for myself? The future I bet time and time against? *Fail to plan, plan to fail.* That sounds about right. Except no one tells you what happens when you plan to fail and instead you succeed. I can't come back from this win. If tonight's windfall for the club drives the regulars away, it'll be a long slog to acquire new ones, and the club will be forgotten in the next wave of new bar and casino openings. It isn't about the coin. Coin that Jerry tells me I'll have coming soon…when he gets it.

Club Contango is everything.

LUCKY

WHEN YOU STEP into the Freeport Embarkment terminal, you breathe the filtered air that is fragranced with atomized essence of wet grass that smells like an hour after a rain on Earth. Years of psychology research says this will calm you, and it does.

Your pay hits your account the second your foot meets the ground—minus, of course, the whopping seventy percent of your coin that is immediately locked away in Freeport's NET pyramid scheme—*I mean, retirement fund*—leaving you with thirty percent for a sleeping capsule, a few rounds of synth alcohol, a handful of sliverfilms of Loop (or one precious stick of Delight), and some pocket change for a night out at the clubs on the corner of Delta and Lower Beach Road. It's been months since you've had to find your own food and capsule, and the variety, the very existence of choice, is intoxicating. You can be anyone you want in this town, so long as you don't break status.

Freeport soon stretches, grows, and escapes your ability to comprehend, but it's the reason you're on Freeport to begin with—to remember what it feels like to live in a city, to feel this alive.

You walk past vending machines that bleep like a pachinko parlor, and stroll past real shops that sell things you can actually purchase and take home. Nearly every shop and vending machine is owned by one of the same three chains, but they get points for at trying to appear unique. If you want to buy something from inside, you'll have to pay with forward commitments through your NET, which will help continue the debt trap for years to come.

Beach Road looks like a waterfront city from the turn of the twentieth century, forgotten for decades, then reopened within the past five years with new technology and a determined effort to restore the lost age of hope. Here, the frantic pace of the space commodity race meets the desperation of second-lifers needing a place that doesn't know them.

The architecture and attitudes here are pre-Great Depression by choice, only wilder, faster, and more determined not to go down without a flash of Delight through the brain—a lesson learned during the Second Great Depression.

From the gilt-edged casinos, to the tinkling of the Great Eastern's prized 1930s Blüthner piano, to the wail of dance electronica on the floor of Arcadia, to the Industrial-Revolution-themed clubs that look like abandoned warehouses, everyone here parties like they're part of the next great economic miracle.

As you approach the neon lights of Enterprise Square, see the Deco curves, you realize that Freeport is an empty blend of styles and cultures, inspired by aesthetics, not meaning. Here, the glamorous pre-war years of the Shanghai Bund and similar cities of the West mingle with 1980s long-boom hedonism, together resuscitating the times when people either didn't know what dangers were around the corner, or didn't care to look.

You head to one of the clubs and order a drink, gulp it down while looking at your reflection in the mirror behind the bar. It takes two more draws before you remember. You're here because you've run out of reasons to tell your folks why you couldn't make it back on Earth.

Maybe it's something about the way you down your drink without a grimace, or the way you blankly ask for another, that tells the bartender—their name is Bel—that you're looking for a new adventure, that you have nothing left to lose. They hand you your next whiskey sour and say, "Finish that, ride the tram for three stops up the strip, and walk toward the Charter Warehouse until you see a place called Lucky 48."

So, you do just that.

A young woman named Trace Pereira is watching her favorite shows on stream from behind the Lucky 48 counter when you arrive. She works here because her parents own the joint, but she keeps to herself, doesn't try to kick you out. Tonight is club night, which means all are welcome, even newbies.

With a polite wave that Trace ignores, you head down the stairs into Freeport's deepest basement. The Pereira family were some of the first Settlers on Freeport, and one of the first things they did when they arrived was commission a comparative analysis of upwards and downwards real estate in a fixed dome that's built upon an asteroid. "Downwards" won, and the next day, they started digging before the Commission could run more tests on the rock's core integrity, which would have led to them being shut down.

Now in the basement, you squeeze past shelves of floppy instaheat bags of Shipmeals™ until you reach a small, crowded room of gamblers. Those in the know call this place Club Contango. Everyone's manic. Some are riding the high from a win, while others are weathering the gut-punch low of a loss.

Two Sparklers, Zetta and Roar, scatter sticks of Delight to the uproarious crowd, drunk on the liquor of their choice. Rice wines and whiskeys and cheap bottles of synth line the shelves behind a makeshift bar.

At the head of the room, the club's co-owner, Chance, holds court from a throne atop a dais of shipping pallets, watching odds update in real time, thanks to the projections made by Contango's AI oddsmaker, Doris.

Chance says to the crowd, "Place your bets! The only way up is down!" Then after the bell rings, Chance climbs down from the throne and paces through the crowd. "So, you lost. At least you *feel* something now, and that's what you came here for. Own it. Punch the wall. Curse your existence. Just make sure to play again. You will never feel as alive as you do here." Chance has no pronouns. Chance is Chance.

Chance reels you in as the bets fill up on the board. You chase the version of yourself you want to be and place a bet alongside the rest.

While you wait for all the bets to come in, you learn from a fellow gambler that gaming isn't hard to come by on Freeport, since legalized gambling was never outlawed. The Commission knows that when you're this far from Earth, vices help. You throw your hands in the air for the only species that derives joy from self-sabotage. You're also told that Club Contango is different than the rest—better. Contango was the first and only gaming club to combine intelligent prediction, futures hedging, and real life into something you could bet on.

Until Suziebaby, owner of the Arcadia, opened a new gaming section just like Contango—one that promised more than the cheap, decorative games of luck. The game room overlooks the golden balcony above Arcadia's mind-shifting dance floor, and it uses predictive AI and takes bets on the actions and outcomes of Freeport politicians. The Arcadia's copycat nearly put Club Contango out of business.

Chance tells you it's a full rip-off of Contango.

I had hoped Arcadia's success would have driven new players our way. It's cluster economics. Let Arcadia drizzle the honey. The blacklisted, the credit-red, and the un-statused will be filtered out and come our way. But I had been wrong. Soon after opening, Arcadia was pulling all the bets off our table. Then, right before Contango was toast, the bots doing the damage were called off until further notice. It was as if Suziebaby had simply lost interest in the takeover. Or perhaps, she'd been told to lose interest.

Look around at all the new faces in the club. You recognize them—all of them—because they're all versions of you. Every one of them is a disappointment to their parents, an under-achiever to their employer, a deadbeat to society. They're wasted chances, lost time, and bitter memories personified.

You've never felt so at home.

LOSER

THE SINGER'S VOICE strains through the speakers in the Hazy Halia, along with the resonance of an electric guitar. I can't make out the words, but the melody of the song fills me with a coy enchantment like a memory I wish I could call my own. Like the warmth of the sun on your face, seated on bleachers over green grass on Earth. Before the migration, before the same sun grew scorching hot and vengeful, pushing humanity to its first extra-terrestrial cosmopolis, built upon a hub-and-spoke of asteroid assets. Back when I thought that failing on Freeport was less visible and embarrassing than failing in SE3 back on Earth. I thought the frontier nature of station life would hide inequalities, but here on Freeport, with its Settler and Contractor divisions, clear lines have been drawn between classes—lines that are easy enough for all to see. Still, it's a good-enough town, and there are more opportunities for me here than I have on Earth. It's why I stay.

The light in the dome warms from a cool pinkish-amber to a blue-edged gold. Most stationsiders no longer notice these things. The beam from the lighthouse breaches the windows of the Hazy Halia just as Zaqy Ibrahim flicks the spotless linen torchon off the shoulder of his white muscle tee and onto the counter, then turns up the volume on the speakers.

The singer croons how his baby lied. *Lied, lied, lied.*

I swallow a yawn and blink to pull up the time: 8:00 a.m.

The tram that goes up-station from Pioneer Ring to Delta Road—the one that bypasses Hub City and Beach Road on its way to the Embarkment—passes me right on schedule. Fifth tram of the day. Sticky should be at Junior Academy by now, but it's rehearsal day for the graduation dance, so she pleaded sick and I allowed it, instead of pressing her about her reasons for wanting to avoid the rehearsal. The teacher insists it's stage fright, but I know it goes deeper. Sticky can make up new moves to any song on the fly. Ask her to repeat them, and you will never get the same move twice.

Smiling, I look over at Sticky, who is having fun beating on a vintage taiko drum set. It sits beside an early-century electric guitar kept safe inside a glass case that Zaqy unlocks only for the worthy.

Two Sparklers in the booth behind me are still high on whatever they were experiencing last night, riding out the tip of the dragon's tail while slumming it at their personal shopper's favorite all-day joint on the other side of the tracks. Giggles float on the air like bubbles, then pop into peals of choked laughter, which starts to become actual choking. Hands over mouths. Muffled snorts. One of the girls tries to speak, but can only grunt and cough some more. Most Delta Road establishments, are filled exclusively with Contractors, but Sparklers regularly flit into the Hazy Halia during the lean hours of the morning to cap off a night of revelry just as the Contractors punch in.

A Contractor is anyone who doesn't make the minimum coin savings or station investment to buy in as a stakeholder—or anyone who can't hold down an L4 job for longer than two cycles. That's most of us, and our right to remain stationside is tied to our contracts.

The Settlers are the 0.0008 percent—the top-210 out of the 250,000 registered inhabitants on Freeport, not counting the thousands of illegals living on the edges of The Seam.

"Delight messes with their interface audio when they've got those boxy masks on," Zaqy says, planting a cold, tall glass in front of me. "For the rest of us, it's too early to be laughing or crying into an empty glass."

The glass is a tall pour of chilled *teh halia.* Strong black tea, stem ginger, sugar, condensed milk, and more sugar. The ginger flavor comes from a powder. The slice of dried root is just for nostalgia. So, too, is the "ice" bar, which is really just a cooling cylinder that looks like ice, sounds like ice when you shake the glass, but will never actually be ice.

"Thanks, Zaqy."

"On the house."

"Really?"

"Your tab's been running all year. What's one more?"

"I'm going to close it one of these days, Zaqy."

"I know you will. And when you do, tell me the name of the rooster to bet on. I could use a spot of luck. MAM's playing roulette with our visas again, and I can't schedule people at the counter or in the kitchen if they don't know where they'll be next week—on-station or deported to Earth."

"Whatever I have is the exact opposite of luck. But that's a story for another day."

Zaqy shrugs and raises his hands, like honest men don't need to know.

"Speaking of work, when did you start pulling the dawn shift? What happened to Yusof?"

Zaqy tightens his lower lip, draws it into his face as he considers what he won't say. "He's on strike, only he can't call it that. Yusof's got no beef with us, but he won't punch in here as long he and the others from HaboHub are organizing. They can't let themselves be seen at their second jobs. You're the labor rep. You know the terms."

"*Was* a rep. And not a career rep either. My folks pushed me in front of them because I was the kid with the advanced grad degree from Southeast Academy. On scholarship." *A rep who never practiced again.* "But let me guess: Freeport wants to make Contractor work stoppages illegal. Must explain the wave of unexplained machine and bot breakdowns. Today's *teh* is exceptionally good, by the way."

"The intern made that. Are you saying he makes it better?"

I pretend to wince and smack my lips. "You know, now that the undertones are hitting, I'm detecting a bit too much bite in that ginger."

Zaqy points. *Got you, Con, you spineless pleaser.*

"Yusof's group calls themselves the Free Hands. The big issue on the table is HaboHub using gameware to make work addictive."

"With respect, I don't see how you can make bot management addictive. All they do is stack containers in the dark."

"You should see the interface plug-in when the filter's active. Makes the warehouse look like you're inside a virtual reality arcade game. It pits the workers against each other, but they don't know who they're competing against because IDs are masked. Lessens the chance of infighting."

"The Hub workers don't know who they're working alongside during a shift?"

Vis still works at HaboHub. I do remember her telling me she had no work friends because most of the time she didn't know who she worked with.

I remember thinking it couldn't be true.

"Workers don't even know what the real job looks like. All they see with the filter engaged is some dance game with flashing lights." Zaqy opens a tin of tea dust and breathes deep. He opens his eyes, draws a level spoon and taps it out into a filter bag. "They also use low-grade audio-neural stimulants, like diluted Delight. Shouldn't be legal, though. Not how they force-stream it all shift. That kind of stimulation can't be good for the brain."

I push the reusable straw down on the slice of ginger. It's too long-petrified to release any flavor. "Those games are the grandchildren of the viral dance apps from the early century."

"People can't do fun things in private anymore without corporations devising new ways to take away the fun and control them in the process."

I crush the ginger again. "Those games were never private to begin with. Users were unknowingly feeding the machine data points, like what makes them jump, shake, or bop. My Popo refused to believe it, but I knew better."

"Anyway, Yusof says he has to set an example. Which reminds me: Call Vis. She's waiting for an answer. Hands need all the help they can get."

"I saw her yesterday," I say.

Let Zaqy take what he needs from that.

After trying to make good on a useless degree in nineteenth- and twentieth-century literature, I got a license in labor representation—formerly labor law—before it was kneecapped by various "standardizations." Even that didn't make it any easier for me to stand in the conference room of the Imperial and face Walter Woo, PR rep of Dash, my parents' employer. Didn't keep my hands from shaking, keep the key arguments we worked though weeks in advance from slipping from my mind, from hearing someone stutter in desperation only to realize it was me. My labor rep career ended after my first case.

Behind me, the table of Sparklers bursts into another peal of distorted laughter and muffled coughs as the girl with a cartoon lemur on the top half of her face tries to speak.

"What's their excuse when they're not on Delight, eh?" I say to Zaqy. I look down the counter to Sticky. "Time for school," I tell her. "Mama's got to get back to work, baby."

I open my digital wallet and blow breath through my nose in relief when I see that Jerry has, in fact, transferred a fifth of the coin he said he would. Blink. Swipe. Tap. Pay my Halia tab in full, with a large rounded-up tip to cover interest. That makes a noticeable dent in the coin Jerry's handed over, but it's the least I can do for Zaqy, especially when he's short on help.

He can't believe his luck.

It feels good to be generous. But then I'm back in my interface, looking at overnight messages from Chance on the club channel. Chance is calling in all the coin that is due to the house, but all of the old-timers—which on Freeport is anyone who's been stationside for more than three years—are borrowing against their losses to double down.

That's no good. Club Contango is supposed to challenge losing, make it dance for our entertainment. It's not supposed to create a greater circle of debt that turns Chance and I into a private bank. I know from personal experience that being on either side of debt never works out well. Not unless you're Gary Weng, popularly known as Wengzai, with an army of goons to enforce your dues and no friends that you care to lose because you're one of Freeport's founding Settlers.

People unfamiliar with Gary Weng might think his business is nothing more than debt collecting, but they would be the people who pay their bills on time. Debt collecting and debt purchasing may be a simple old-fashioned business, but Freeport is a rocking town of Settlers looking for new ways to kill time, and Contractors hoping to double their money and shorten their shift. Between the luxury boutiques, the experience parlors, dance clubs, casinos, supper clubs, and restaurants, there's no shortage of ways to spend money you don't have. Wengzai profits off all the spending by buying up all the debt—by owning you. It's a simple and unevolved practice, but terrifying, like a big dumb beast that will rip your head off for fun.

I get a ping through my interface, which I nod to preview. It's a newsletter from a non-profit called Sanctuary. The rest of the organization's name is hidden in the preview. Sanctuary for Cats in Copacabana, for all I know. I could use some sanctuary myself. From the voices inside my head. From the birds on my shoulders.

Blink to delete.

I knock back the rest of my drink and call out to Sticky again. On my interface, the Halia's job board icon, which Zaqy has been maintaining for three years as a service to the Contractor community, glows green with new opportunities. Zaqy only hosts the board, doesn't moderate it, so I silence the alerts. I'm not searching for honey and finding live bees again. I've had enough stings.

I look down to find Sticky at my side with big eyes that can only mean one thing.

"No, baby, you can't play the claw machine. It's expensive, and what does it do?"

"Eats our coin and leaves us with nothing," Sticky repeats from memory, with a sulk in her sweet voice. "But I'm going to be lucky today."

"Not today, baby."

Zaqy bends down to Sticky's height and smiles. "Let her have a go. Two tries, on Uncle Zaqy." He looks at me for approval.

"I can't. I just got done paying you back."

If I were a Settler, or if Alchemy had gone the way Hong said it would instead of imploding in our faces in a black hole that gouged out what little NET credit I had left, I could keep borrowing forever. But I'm not lucky like that. I'm just Connie Lam.

Zaqy waves me silent. "Give the kid the chance to believe in luck, would you? I have to take a delivery out back, but I've already put two free-plays on the machine." He winks at Sticky. "Remember me when you strike it big."

I throw a two-fingered salute to Zaqy's retreating back. "Don't wait on it."

Sticky runs to the claw machine, and I settle back into my seat. I wanted to do the school run and be back at the chandlery early, but I suppose that can wait.

Across the road from the Hazy Halia, the sharp light of the morning sets Lucky 48 in relief. Contractors crowd the streets, many of them running errands for cheap employers who don't employ enough bots.

The chandlery maintains one bot for heavy lifting and one bot for engine repairs. Papa Pereira checks their activity logs remotely from his retirement community back on Earth.

I am not looking forward to cleaning up from yesterday's club night by myself.

KING

THE BASEMENT IS a mess. Turns out players deep in margin don't care much to stick around and help clean up. Most club nights, the regulars stay back after the game and stand around holding a stack of disposable cups, ranting on the night's minutiae. If it's a bad night, or a holiday—when shifts pay double—the players quickly disperse and the cleaning falls squarely on me and Stiff. I've never seen Chance clean, ever.

The sight that greets me this morning, seasoned and untouched from the night before and left to marinate, is a poorly lit room of kicked-over chairs, empty cups reeking of souring synth alcohol, and the stale leftovers of Chance's bizarre canape selection which runs from soy-pop-crunch to stiffening chive *guotie* from Tanuki.

I reach behind a shelf for a mop and bucket, disrupting the balance of assorted objects that are not all part of the chandlery's inventory. Above me, a bar of white florescent light flickers. A year ago, if I told you I ran Contango, I would have done it with an affected shrug and calculated disinterest. Now I know better. Every job, even the one you dream of, eventually boils down to cleaning, because in reality, everything in life is a mess. The severity of the mess is all that separates one from the other.

A ping on my interface vibrates. I blink to read the preview, half of me hoping it isn't Vis holding me to a margin I can't fill, while the other half of me hopes it isn't Hong.

<<Can't ignore me forever, Connie>>

It's from Hong. Swipe off-screen, <<*Unread.*>>

Jobs used to require skill—any Zoomer who's lived through two pandemics and the Second Great Depression will tell you. I'm a lucky Midlennial. I took my first steps on Earth, but was still young enough to jet off-planet to Freeport as part of the new frontier. The last entirely Earth-reared generation. We don't have the excuse of early-station education deficiencies, or the excuse of floundering unemployed between the post-depression and pre-scarcity periods on Earth.

Many Zoomers say that the in-between, anxiety-driven Midlennial generation reminds them of their parents, the Millennials, who were caught between two worlds of their own: analog and digital. But Millennials had the option to log out of the simulation if they wanted, had the option to remain on Earth. They didn't have to risk their life's savings on a one-way ticket to Freeport because off-planet was their best chance to survive.

Freeport is Sinatra's city, high on its own supply. If you can't make it here, you can't make it anywhere. Jobs are invented every week that didn't exist five years ago, and the lead-time for new Contractors is at least half an annum—unless you're lucky to catch someone rotating off an asset.

Despite being unsuccessful in a lot of ways, I actually like it here. I like how Freeport's limited choices greatly reduce my opportunity-cost anxiety. I like the dull repetition of human-proof, space-age jobs that smooth the edges off the quiet desperation of station life (doubt is our collective sin). I like how people party on this rock like there's no tomorrow, as if it could go up in a cloud of cosmic dust any second—which, let's face it, the scientists have never actually ruled out. I like knowing that this station is my last chance for making something of my life, and Sticky's best chance to succeed where I failed. I don't run from the unknown anymore. I run toward it. No one belongs on Freeport, which means everyone does. It's the one thing we all have in common.

Besides, I can't go back to Earth even if I wanted to. It has to do with Hong burning through Alchemy's seed money and owing more than the company raised—with my name as CFO and Financial Controller on the holding company back on Earth. I showed up to work one day to find the office empty without warning. If I went back to Earth now, I would be wholly liable for Alchemy's debt, and a I would have a lot explaining to do to a lot of angry people, many of whom I don't know are after me. Hong didn't even give me the courtesy of renewing my station visa for a new term before he vanished.

Another ping from Hong, requesting video.

> *<<I wouldn't call if it wasn't urgent. You want to hear this.>>*

Why did I put myself in such a position? Because I couldn't resist seeing the shiny "Director" title beside my name. Or hearing my father's surprise when I told him that Kin Hong and I were striking out together after years as Senior Analyst at Reliance Marine and Investments—a job I needed Dad's union affiliation to land. After two wasted years of labor law that I don't like to talk about, Alchemy was my first time step up. I wasn't just working for Hong anymore. We were partners.

The ping jolts me again, this time with maximum urgency that I thought I'd blocked on settings. Hong must be paying a fortune for a custom comms plan. Then again, he's a Settler. A status I imagine he's holding on to by the skin of his teeth— through investments and unrealized assets, not coin.

I flip through the auto-answer options and send:

> *<<Can't talk now.>>*

A video clip lands in my inbox two minutes later—without a read receipt, which shows that Hong knows I don't care to talk to him even when he can see I'm online. *It's only a video.* A video can't unravel my sense of stability. *It's only Hong.* He can't bring back the birds to roost on my shoulders.

I open the video.

Hong's hair, which is usually neatly combed, is a rat's nest. *Was his hair this gray when I last saw him? Has it really been that long? Two years already?*

<<*Connie, we need to meet. This channel isn't secure for what I have to tell you. You have your reasons for not wanting to see me again, and I hear you, I do. But this is bigger than you and me, and I won't breathe a word on Alchemy if you don't want me to. I can meet any time. Your soonest convenience. Just tell me where.*>>

Hong won't breathe a word on Alchemy?

If I don't want him to?

I don't care what Hong has to say unless it's about clearing the Alchemy debt from my name.

Swipe, delete.

Blink.

It's only Hong.

Hong, whom I hitched my wagon to as a trainee at Reliance, the reason I kept my job as long as I did. Logistics still relied on human supervision despite automation, and I was a top-ten in one of the least sexy industries. Kin Hong's office was the glass one at the end of the corridor on the commercial floor at Reliance Marine and Investments. It was always open. The day the universe spun around and threw us together, I was getting a public dressing-down from my newly-minted middle manager, who was five years younger than me and incompetent.

Kid Manager said, "Never tell a client their claim will go through. They'll expect the check in the mail."

"I heard old Cheong's refinancing loan will be approved by National Re." Reliable sources had told me the Cheongs were turning the corner. "Reliable sources" was Daffy Cheong, who had been popping bottles at Zouk Club all weekend.

"Get this into your head, Connie. A claim's not cleared until it's cleared."

He didn't call me Connie, of course, but the name I used to go by on Earth.

"Soon as he gets that money, he's expanding the fleet. And he's going to get it covered by a protection club that didn't clutch the purse over ten thou."

After the scolding was over, Hong leaned on his glass wall and said to me, "You care about your work."

I said, "I just don't want to waste time fighting over something we'll be begging to give away next month."

Buried on the ground floor in ops and claims, I didn't want to be mistaken for someone who actually *cared* about marine insurance.

"You're a humanist, but rational," Hong said.

Later, I would find out that Kin Hong wasn't even in claims, but was a consultant specialist in marine investments. When Reliance made me redundant, I dug him up on an old industry networking site the Zoomers used. I should have been more cautious and seen the red flag when he was happy to hear from me and offered me a job as a director. Together, he promised, we'd carve out a new niche in hedging spaceship bunker fuel.

"All you'll have to do is clear the inbox and be the young face smiling for the trade papers. You won't have to leave Earth. You won't even have to leave your flat if you don't want to. You can spend every minute with that cute kid of yours. Take in the trees."

"I'm waiting for the 'but.'"

"There is no but. Everyone wins."

"You're letting me be the fiduciary boss of your company out of the goodness of your heart."

Kin Hong, not yet "King Hong," rubbed the inner corners of his eyes, near the bridge of his nose.

"My ex…"

I waited.

"What else is there to say? Bettina Awyong is all the answer you need."

I blew my breath. "Is she still doing that real-food influencer thing?"

"She trades antiques now. By the looks of her clients, if you turn them upside down and give them a shake, or take a hammer to them, you'll get a surprise. Like a Kinder egg you need to keep away from the sniffer dogs. Remember those? Kinder eggs? Of course you don't. Anyway, between my ex-wife wanting to take everything from me and you only wanting to take some, I feel more comfortable betting on you."

Sticky and I were happy on Earth, but after spending years painfully untangling myself from a spouse who had long tired of what we never had, and who resented my decision to not waste the rest of my life pretending to be what I wasn't, I was looking forward to some stability.

Ultimately, it was the threatening messages from debt collectors on notes that I never signed off on that eventually led me to Freeport. Notes that became like graffiti on my door, which then led to a goon being stationed across the street from my apartment. Kin Hong welcomed me to the rental on Beach Road with open arms, like I was a prodigal daughter. He had nothing to hide, he said. The debtors? Never took a thing they offered. Never signed with them.

"Connie, look at me. This is nothing more than the usual first-quarter lull. Okay, it's worse, but only because Astra pumped the market with too much fuel reserves right after Q4 closing. The bastards. But they'll run through it like butter. You can trust me on that."

"I, too, believe in the second coming of the market correction." Palms together. "But that's not the point. You're absolutely certain you didn't take a little help from your friends to float Alchemy? Jog your memory. I came all this way."

"Aside from the Jain Brothers." Hong wagged an index finger at me like I was the one with the explaining to do. "Don't start,

Connie. That was a profit-sharing scheme. Wholly legitimate and structured. I took Amit Jain and his brother out for drinks at the Oriental after."

"And Lee and Lee, you told them it's a profit-sharing venture, too?"

"You don't get to build anything worth remembering without asking for help. You can't do it all yourself. That's something you proud kids need to learn." Hong's face droops. "I had to. We were being raided by some black pool fund based out of Whiterock. I needed the funds to buy our own damn company back, and I'm still trying to trace them."

"You signed loans with my name. *IN* my name."

"Let's not get personal now, with the you and the me. It was for Alchemy."

"You signed as me. You committed fraud."

Did I expect that Hong would see what he'd done and repent?

"Tell me, Connie, about the fiduciary duty you perform for Alchemy. This is what you signed up for. Have a little faith, my dear. We've made it through turns in the market before. Prices will correct next quarter. They can't sustain. There is pent-up demand, and the shipowners can't hold back forever. They'll restock. And when they do, we can pay it all back. Because this will be a whopper. What's mine is yours."

What's mine is yours.

Twenty days later, he was gone, the office cleaned out, and all his debt was mine. The market didn't turn for another quarter, and by then, Alchemy had bled out. The buying hold *was* sustainable after all, thanks to oversupply from the previous quarter.

I paid the most menacing of Hong's "friends" immediately from my own savings. But after that ran out, I hid behind the insolvency declaration and changed my and Sticky's names. I didn't feel bad about hiding the last hundred coin to prepay Sticky's preschool fees for the year—with full board—so no matter what happened to me, she'd still be covered.

Look at Freeport, and most of the time, you see the promise and industry of a new frontier. But you don't have to pull up much carpet to see the underemployed and the no-longer-young, many with irrelevant Earth degrees, clinging on with the one skill they have left: hustling. And there are thousands of us, which is a lot of dead weight for a frontier.

We are the disappointments. We spend coin and get high. Whatever it takes to get by. Like energy, the disappointment transforms.

When you're in the basement of Lucky 48 Chandlery on a work night, with a dozen other Contractors trying to forget the same problems you are, the feeling of being a failure becomes an asset.

Bet against it, or bet with it. Doesn't matter which. Harness your failure, turn it on its head, and tell it to go fuck itself.

We'll pay you for the pleasure.

CON

"THIS IS SMALL Claims at Thevar and Tann Protection and Indemnity. How may I assist?"

The amber icon on my dashboard turns green, and an angry male voice launches into me, already mid-sentence. I blink and swipe with a finger, out of habit. The T&T dashboard minimizes, and the voice drops to a whisper above mute.

That's me: Small Claims.

I pull up a personal folder, bring it to front-of-view, and open the first video in the queue.

> *"Submitted towards a vocational teaching certificate with a specialization in Classics. This thesis argues that themes in Victorian literature have begun to emerge in our generation's media, from a sample of the top trending streams on ViewBucket."*

I sigh, like released steam, through my nose. This should be interesting. Coaching and giving feedback on thesis defenses and other academic examinations is just one of the ways I shake the tin and collect enough to keep Sticky in Junior Academy. The other ways are working here at T&T (full-time at temp-pay), covering for Trace at Lucky 48 when she needs me, and monitoring ship-bunker price trends to sell as tips to Jerry.

A lifetime ago, I thought I'd seen the last of the brain-swamp that was shipping insurance—terrestrial or otherwise. There's Dad, shaking his head. *Never say never.* No thanks to Kin Hong and Alchemy.

But at least T&T is a job I can get by reverse-auctioning myself as the cheapest option with modest experience in the field. The work isn't demanding. It mostly involves spending the day logged onto the Thevar and Tann system from my rental in Raintree, or at their premises on Delta Road, above a personal mining tool and mobility device shop. Most days, I spend my shifts screaming into the silence of my skull, but some days—like today—when I've maxed out my bandwidth dealing with the messages and missed videos from the club players, the mindless work at T&T actually becomes a relief.

Another call incoming.

I send it on to the voice bot, but it only flashes assertively and refuses to minimize. My breath catches for a moment. It's not Thevar, is it? No. The sole living partner of Thevar and Tann can't personalize his menu at his resort-style care center in the French Alps. There's no way he learned how to send a priority message. Someone has pulled a low-grade hot-wire hack on the T&T dashboard to send me this message. That's all the more reason not to hit <<*Accept*>>, but I can't resist.

I accept. Voice only.

Heavy, ragged breathing on the other end of the line says the caller has bad lungs. Sounds like he's been running and just found the nearest, semi-private spot nearby to make a cheap voice call free of eavesdroppers.

"I saw you on Beach Road, Con. On the corner of the Mandarin and the Circle Finance tower. In a nice suit." The last part he shook like an insult.

"Circle Finance on the Square, near the ViewBucket HQ? Not my scene."

The voice belongs to Stephen Widjaya. His lungs are live-embalmed with clove-infused vape smoke, so his telephone voice is always this sexy. Stephen, pronounced Stiff. Stiff works the day-cycle in operations for a lightering company that also does bunker supply runs out to the farthest reaches of the Belt. We met on opposite sides of a chain of small claims lodged with T&T after he busted my ass for a metric ton of discrepancies only he was talented enough to spot. I used to go offline, endure full days without media distraction, just to avoid his calls. Stiff was exactly who we needed to run our accounts at Club Contango.

Three years ago, when the pool started growing, Stiff protested, said that what we were doing was going to blow up in our faces, and that he could no longer serve as our accountant. He wrote as much on untraceable paper stationery that he slapped on the table in the basement of Lucky 48. I signed a corner of the paper, acknowledging. He came back to work for the club shortly after and hasn't spoken of the protest letter since.

"I hate to break it to you, Stiff, but if you went home with someone you picked up outside the Mandarin, it wasn't me."

"You were hustling greyfield mining bonds like a get-rich-quick scheme. Very unsubtle."

"How plausible does that sound when I can't even get myself rich?"

Stiff coughed up half a lung without turning away from the receiver.

"Stephen. I was at home with my kid, managing the minutiae of my life."

"I know it wasn't you, because when I went up to it, I discovered the truth. It was a holo, Con. Trained on your likeness, I'm sure. What're they paying you? One coin each time a holo loads and pops up on a street corner? Extra four coin each time you convince some drunk mining tech to put all his coin into a new retirement fund?"

"I don't know what you're talking about, Stiff. Honest."

"Okay, be that way. But know this: If the club players catch wind of your new hustle, you're not going to have a club left to manage. Contango is already in bad shape, Con. If we lose the regulars, have to rebuild the player list, we're done. The house winning big like it did was bad for business. It said to the players that the best is over. This side hustle of yours will surely be the final straw."

"Whatever you think you saw, it wasn't me. I don't know anything about any holos. And let's not forget, Club Contango is a gambling den, not a country club. The players need to grow up and own their losses."

A silence hangs for a beat before Stiff speaks again.

"I'd never bet High Excel on you, Con. Never. It would be like tossing coin down the drain. But you bet High Excel on yourself. And you didn't just beat the AI models, you destroyed them. Players taking losses is one thing. They know the risks. But this time is different. They saw the holos of you and Jerry, Con. They know what you two did."

"Are you accusing me of insider trading my own future?"

"I know you've been slicing the top off the club earnings for yourself, but I don't say anything because it's yours anyway. As long as you keep me in my share. Besides, I get it. You need the coin to stay off MAM's radar. It's the only thing keeping your illegal ass here. But rigging the bets? Selling your image to a holo company? You're crossing lines. I hope Jerry is treating you well, at least."

Jerry? Is Stiff talking about Echo?

Echo is a fintech training program. That has nothing to do with holograms. Least of all holograms that look and act convincingly like me. Maybe Stiff has spent too many late nights doing the accounts while on Loop.

"What does Jerry have to do with this, Stiff?"

"Just head down to Enterprise Square tomorrow. See for yourself."

Now I'm laughing. So hard it hurts. *We both thought we were helping each other out, didn't we Jerry?* I sat with Hong and pitied your failed projects and startup scams, while you pitied me for living off pocket money from Hong. Poor Connie, with a new baby. Here's a project for you. Pays a day's rates. Poor Jerry, I guess I can help you this time.

Stiff's voice forces its way back into my awareness.

"You fucked us over, Connie. I could deal with the illegal gambling so long as we were honest with our customers. But this? This is too much. I trusted you."

I try to explain myself further, but Stiff cuts the call.

It's when I'm left staring at my inbox, that I notice the missed call from minutes ago.

Hong again.

After he emptied the Alchemy office, I tracked him for months, haunted the building he last lived in, the clubs he most frequented, the alleys around our office in case he came back for something he forgot. I was in a panic about the Alchemy debt, my expiring visa, and Sticky's future. Even thinking about Hong now reminds me what an idiot I was to ever have trusted him. Call me a coward, but remembering that time brings back the birds, and I don't want to think about the birds.

<<Connie. Don't ignore me. We need to talk.>>

Blink, ignore. Mark *<<Unread.>>*

<<I'll wait for you at Lucky 48. Contango's slipping into backwardation. You are not ready for this.>>

Blink, delete.

Blink, close all windows.

In the half-second between tapping out of my interface and the real world flooding my hyper-stimulated senses, I'm holding on to the last wisps of an already forgotten dream behind closed eyes. I'm not awake, but not asleep. Four times out of five, I imagine I'll open my eyes to my old bedroom in my parents' house. I'm fourteen years old, and my feet touch the foot board of the twin bed they keep promising to upgrade. Mom's up, and I can hear her in the kitchen through the door. It wasn't much of a privileged childhood—what, with all the steps forward and back just to keep us above water—but at least I had two parents to rely on. Parents who mostly knew what they were doing. How many years will it be before Sticky realizes that all this while I had no fucking clue?

Open your eyes.

I am not in my parents' home. I'm in a studio in the Raintree Work-Life Complex, where rent is higher than the average take-home earnings of its target occupant. It's the size of a bathroom on a luxury space cruise. I got lucky with timing, migrating on the third ship. I wouldn't be able to afford this place now. I *won't* be able to when the rent gets adjusted next quarter. I've done away with the bed frame and laid the mattress on the floor to give us a few inches more inches to move. A half-wall partition is all that separates the bedroom from the tiny living room. Still an improvement from our first capsule on Pioneer Ring. I work at the table on the other side of the partition. I'd love to keep Sticky at home more, but at Junior Academy she at least has a yard to run around in. Despite the namesake, there are no trees in Raintree, or on this side of the dome, for that matter.

"Mama, Mama."

Sticky was a big baby. I don't remember how heavy she was. How do other parents remember? What I do remember is how round and red she was, like a Chinese birthday bun. And so beautiful. But it was the chord that tethered her to me that I couldn't look away from. Purple-blue and thicker than I imagined. Then the chord was cut, giving Sticky a cute little belly button. I saved the stump but lost it somewhere between Earth and here. In that chord's place, a string emerged from my heart and found its way back to her.

"Go back to sleep, baby."

"You were looking at me first, Mama."

"Sorry, baby. Did I wake you? I'm just working."

Sticky flops and lolls on the bed like a fish out of water that knows it's too cute and small for you to keep—you'll toss it back into the sea. Also, she's not going back to sleep.

"Mama, where will I go after you die?"

Okay, neither of us are gonna sleep now.

I blink my interface away and move around the partition to sit on the mattress with her.

"Back to your life after the funeral, I should hope. Why do you even ask? What brought this on?"

"Jiayi's grandfather died. He was on Earth, and Jiayi's mother is going to see him, but Jiayi's staying."

"She probably has a lot on her plate."

"Why do people go to see people when they're already dead?"

I'm trying to put a explanation together, one that will adequately explain the rituals of death and respect to a pre-schooler, but I can't think of an answer that doesn't raise more questions.

A hairline crack appears on the wall that's held all day between me and the roaring tide of exhaustion. A wall that takes all my strength to hold.

The first bird comes and lands on me, flexes its wings.

I put a smile on my face…for Sticky.

"Alright, get up. It's fix-it time."

IT'S WAY PAST Sticky's bedtime, but we're awake and sitting on the mattress. Sticky crunches on her "fix"—chocolate-dipped Pocky sticks—chewing with her mouth open and littering our bed with crumbs I try my best to ignore. I hold her while she eats and breathe in deeply her artificial, honey-scented shampoo. In my mind, she smells like a newborn baby again, even though it's been six years since that day.

My "fix" is a small bar of chocolate. Not what I really wanted, but it's what I'll allow myself. I can't slide, not now. I still need to get to the bottom of what Stiff just accused me of. Figure out how to keep the club afloat without losing players. And now Hong is back from hiding and most definitely wanting something I shouldn't give. Just adding it all up brings back the birds and their sharp claws. My breath quickens, and I feel the familiar tightness in my chest.

I do not want to talk to Kin Hong. I don't care what he has to say. I'm not thriving, but I'm getting by just fine, and Sticky's happy. It wasn't easy making it here. But I can deal with my own disappointments now, even trade them for a profit.

Hong isn't going to mess up my kid's life and expect to come crawling back.

Blink, *block*.

HANDS

TRACE PEREIRA HAS sampled every retrowave, neuevintage reboot of every classic TV series my grandmother grew up on, and she takes great pride in teaching me useless nuggets of pop-culture history, for what she calls "my improvement." She doesn't care to mind the chandlery, but it's where she finds herself. Her black hair is dyed a more intense shade of void, and she wears cat-eye glasses that her generation brought back in style. She's also cat-like in the way she prefers to wedge herself in the little nook behind the counter of Lucky 48.

The chandlery sits at the apex of Delta Road, where one branch of a T-junction heads right at it—enough to give any feng shui master a heart attack. Trace told me it's why her father, Joseph Pereira, named the chandlery "Lucky." Trace is nineteen years old, but she already has a Midlennial's nostalgia for old tech and cultural icons she didn't grow up with—another Gen-D fad, I'm sure. Witness the projector she scowls at, the scene cast on the opposing wall that's frozen in the still of a woman about to jump off a building.

Like every Gen-D kid who hypes indie remakes of twentieth-century TV shows when she isn't watching the top trending ViewBucket and Streamy programs, Trace believes compelling dialogue and creative plotting died the moment AI programs like Streamaker made it possible for anyone to produce and upload a film or series by using the licensed AI likeliness of old actors speaking bot-generated dialogue from a spec sheet that lacks proper spelling and grammar. As a result, she watches the same five mid-century remakes over and over. Occasionally, when something really gets to her, or if you drop inside references about it often enough, she starts a new one, which she's likely to abandon after a single episode. Right now, she's parked herself at the service counter of Lucky 48, relieving me of my usual shift because the connection's more stable on the ground floor than in her cozy living quarters upstairs.

"What's the point of having a library of every series ever made," Trace growls at the projector, "if the universe fucks me over when I actually want to watch something new?"

Don't let go of your physical media. Chance is right.

I step up to the counter and help myself to cold brew kopi from the mini fridge.

"Which of our devices died on us today?"

"*Forever Rangers* is gone from ViewBucket."

"You hate *Forever Rangers*. Twice remade, and it still hasn't aged well. Did you check out *Electric Supernova Seven*? That's more Gen-D. Even if Lux Chan is holding onto that teen role by the skin of her teeth."

"Some days, I wish I were five again."

"You're too young for dome life to get you down, Trace."

Trace does me the honor of not cringing. "My streamer or the projector, please."

"I'm on it," I say as I slide over to her side of the counter and fiddle with the micro projector like I know what I'm doing. Neither of us really needs to be at the shop for service. The chandlery isn't exactly bustling, and most of our buyers ping ahead anyway. But there are only so many hours you can spend in your capsule or studio, and neither of us are Sparklers able to pay for full days out on Beach Road. We've come just far enough in life to hide in the comfort or our work and hobbies.

Trace cranes her neck to look over my shoulder.

"Also, could you tell your club guys to go down in shifts from now on?"

"Say that again until it sounds like it's supposed to."

Eyelashes flutter. "Okay, gross. All I'm saying is my dad is going to see the hustle on the relay and come up from Earth himself to have a look."

"Not Papa Pereira."

"Seriously. He hasn't said anything about sending me back for a while, and I want to keep it that way."

"I get it. But if your father sends you a long-overdue one-way shuttle ticket to Earth, it won't be because of me."

"Thank you," Trace says with a hand on her heart. "Don't forget, I won't be here for your next club thing. I'm going to the ViewBucket Experience on Enterprise Square."

"You know that's just holos. The Rangers don't exist."

Trace sticks out her tongue. "Hey, keep your cynicism to yourself, old lady."

"Now she chooses to be a kid," I say with a wink.

"Say you'll cover for me. Please?" She widens her eyes for effect. Cute kid when she chooses. "We still have the consignment for the Maris fleet to fill, and that's probably going to float back to the surface by then."

"I thought it was a basic CVE? Load and launch?"

"You would think. Except Bobby Singh sends orders that are half-factoids of the market he expects to buy into. The other half are questions. I can't fill that order. There is no order. There is only chaos."

"Maris has a stationside rep, a third son or cousin."

"I've tried, and the call goes unanswered. The Sparkler's probably laid out at POPPY. I expected more reaction on the Maris order."

I flash a hearty thumbs up. "Good one."

"You're an asshole."

"I'm a big sister. It's my duty to be unimpressed." I give the projector a shake. "I'll handle the Maris order. Enjoy your holo show."

There was a time when Trace wasn't just my chosen kid sister, but also my ward. The Pereiras had had enough of station life and wanted to return to Earth. They missed the trees near the rewilded district where they lived. Lucky 48 was supposed to be left to hired Contractors to manage, but then MAM pulled the visas. Fifteen-year-old Trace found me at the hostel cafeteria four nights before her flight back down and begged me to step in. She didn't want to go back to Earth. Station life *got* her.

The morning of her flight, we spoke with her parents, told them how Trace wanted to stay stationside with me, and by afternoon, we waved the Pereiras off on their one-way shuttle back to Earth. That was four years ago. Becoming Trace's guardian came with full access to Lucky 48, and the place became my soft landing when Alchemy blew up in my face. Trace is no longer a minor, and my guardianship has expired and dissolved, but a part of me still feels like I have two kids—one age six and the other nineteen.

I give the projector another shake for good measure and a motion picture flicks to life on the far wall.

Trace nudges me away, and she resumes her shrimp-like position behind the projection.

"I'm heading out for food. You want dumplings or noodles? Roast and rice maybe?"

Trace nods. "Yes."

"All right. Wherever has the shortest line, it is." I point above her as I leave. "And tidy that overloaded shelf above the counter. Avalanche of boxes. Not a good thing."

She nods, mouth agape, while rewinding the movie back to where she had previously lost connection.

I salute her on the way out.

I STEP OUT of Lucky 48 and onto Delta Road right as a tram passes, which blasts me with a cloud of dome dust. It's as pleasant a day as any on the working end of Freeport, so I walk up to Auntie Wong's. It's located on the sharp elbow of Delta, which makes it close enough to Beach Road to bask in some of its shine, while still taking advantage of Delta Road's lower rents.

I wave at Zaqy through the window of the Halia, but he has a faraway look in his eyes as he dries glasses by hand, so he doesn't notice me. No one's noticing me at all.

Auntie's has a curbside service counter like most of the popular joints on Freeport. Contractors may be far from Earth's toxic work culture, but they're still always in a hurry.

Curbside at Auntie's is beneath a yellow-and-red awning that hangs over a window that looks into the kitchen, where two sweaty humans do all the cooking in singlets, boxers, and Wellington boots. You can order anything on the menu to go, except for the soup noodles, which Auntie says are never good past ten minutes, swelling in a closed box. I get the *har gao* and *siu mai* to go, mostly for Trace, with a couple for myself. I'm not hungry, but my stomach's feeling empty.

"You wait," says the skinny kid who wraps the dumplings.

A large fellow who I can only guess is Uncle Wong, commands the wok.

I'm not going anywhere. I lean on the wall and listen to the sounds of the kitchen. Auntie's gets into the swing of breakfast service, and I let myself slide down the wall until I'm half squatting—but mostly sitting—on the street. It feels entirely appropriate for how I feel about my life.

Then comes a voice: "Last stop before we move in. Does everyone have the graphics loaded on their interface? On my count, project them on the buildings as we pass."

I look up to see a small crowd of about ten people led by someone who looks like they're barely out of Junior. But he's got the attention and loyalty of his crew, who now collectively swipe the air in front of them. Holo signs map onto the buildings as they pass. Cheap pixel masks snap onto their faces to hide their identities.

<<*No to gamification.*>>

<<*Work is not play.*>>

<<*Just pay fair.*>>

It's the first Contractor protest I've seen on Freeport. It's polite, shuffling, and terrified of its own shadow. I pull myself off the ground, and the person closest to me pings me with a drop-set of graphics and slogans, edited for easy projection. Independent labor organizations are illegal on Freeport. Contractors are automatically registered with the Manpower and Migration Agency (MAM), as well as the Welfare Associations of their respective employers, which are really just outsourced human resource departments. Belonging to any other association is legal grounds for dismissal, which on Freeport, also means deportation.

The Hands, which is who this crowd must be, are Vis's passion and purpose. I haven't the heart to tell her how labor movements died at least fifty years ago. Second lives on Freeport are only for disappointed Settlers. I don't want to tell her about the town hall meeting at the Imperial, ten years ago. Vis needs the Hands the way I need Club Contango.

"Remember the Secretary General's warning. On no account do we obstruct business, or it's over for us."

An older protester grinds his teeth. "I remember when that was the point of strikes."

"Just map your signs and say your line. We're marching from here to the Circle building, where the Habo execs will be on-station for a meeting with their bankers. We don't know when they're flying up again after this, so this is our one chance. Don't blow it."

"Habo is due for their annual safety inspection at the end of this cycle," another protester says. "If we keep the pressure on, there's a higher chance they'll give in."

A voice from the back takes the cue. "The Free Hands reject compulsory interface updates! From HaboHub, or from anyone!"

"End dynamic MAM visas!" pipes a voice from the front.

The crowd is hesitant. It loiters at the fringes, hangs on to the security of the surrounding buildings. It's ready to flee at any moment.

DAD USED TO work on the docks while Mom marshaled harbor traffic and made sure the bots didn't malfunction on the job. They dedicated their lives to their work. But just as they were starting to plan their retirement vacations, union management was taken over by a human resources subsidiary of new ownership company, Dash. Before then, no one knew that ports could be purchased from the nation and privately run as enterprises.

Dash came bearing gifts. Employee meals were free and tasted decent. The company buses ran at greater frequency, and the new dorms had enviable rec rooms. But Dash also took productivity targets and kept pinning them higher and higher. Workers began pulling longer hours, and started competing for more shifts to make the same amount they did before. They pushed themselves to the limit just to keep their jobs, make enough to pay their inflated bills. All the free, whole-bean coffee in the world wasn't going to inspire them to run themselves ragged for the sake of bloated corporate margins.

But Mom and Dad didn't panic. Not at first. But then one night, after finishing my shift as an unpaid intern at a video archive, I came home to them bent over in their chairs, hands on their knees, expectant, hopeful smiles painted over strained faces.

Mom said, "We met their targets, even after they raised them. Took fewer days off—"

"There's nothing left to give. No slack," Dad said.

Mom put her hand on his knee, gave it a loving squeeze.

"It wasn't easy, but Dash has agreed to a town hall with the employees," she said.

"That's what they call it, anyway," said Dad. "They'll probably just send a suit to talk down to us, but what matters is they'll listen. "

"That's where you come in."

What hurt most then—and even more now—was the absence of doubt on their faces. They trusted me. I was the overeducated Midlennial with a foot on both sides of the bridge they needed to cross. I could help them.

But as it turned out, I could not.

THE HANDS RAISE their voices. Cries of "End dynamic visas, let Contractors settle!" and "Gamification is abuse!" break from the group and ripple through a small number of onlookers who have gathered. The rallying cries grow from thin, hesitant statements to loud, confident demands.

That's when the Enforcers spring their trap. They pour out of an office building that hosts a number of mid-tier commodity prospectors and auxiliary services in the mining industry, and sprint toward the protest. They had been expecting the Hands.

Behind me, the kid in Auntie's kitchen hits an aluminum plate against the wall to signal that my order's ready.

Hurry up. Take it.

The boots close in on the small group of Hands who are suddenly too petrified to move. But once the Enforcers start swinging their shock weapons, striking those nearby, the protesters become frantic and start to stumble and fall over each other in retreat. A few brave protesters attempt to hold the line, hold it like they've never held something before, but the pained voice of their leader shouts at them to disperse.

"Fight another day! Don't let yourselves be caught!"

It's smart to run. Getting caught means visa termination and deportation.

So, I run.

Live to fight another day.

As I run, I think back to a similar incident, fourteen years ago on Earth, at the Imperial Resort and Conference Center. It's late afternoon, and the sun's rays are long and low through the blinds of the conference room, casting stripes across the perfectly tailored suit of Walter Woo, the Dash representative. Walter Woo is confidence. Walter Woo owns the room. He does not have to stare me down. I'm not worth his attention. He's talking directly to the crowd of harbor workers that includes my mom and dad.

"Hunger," he says, "is what pushes us to do better."

WHERE DO OUR dreams go after we give up on them?

When we're children, we imagine grand futures for ourselves, where we're famous explorers, inventors, and entertainers. But as we grow older, the futures we imagine for ourselves grow less fantastical, less ambitious. We no longer expect to cure diseases or command colonies in the Belt. We imagine being good enough to get a job, to afford a capsule, maybe afford curbside service at Auntie's now and then. We imagine being enough to survive.

BACK WHEN STICKY was born, Alchemy occupied a 300-square-foot office on Marina Bay that was walled off from a neighboring office by three sheets of gypsum board.

"Privacy is the mark of success, Connie," Hong told me. "Our clients need to see that."

Still, the "conference room" was always empty.

One day, while waiting for Hong to get off the phone, he paused his call and said to me, "You don't have to pull a full-day, Connie. You don't have to prove something to me."

"Thank you," I said. "But I'm proving it to myself."

Hong's smile melted into a frown. He glared up at me over the top of his glasses. "Connie, is this about money?"

"It isn't, but it should be."

Hong rose from his desk and took my hands in his, as if preparing to lead us in prayer.

"I value you, Connie. I will stand at the bourse podium and tell the world that I couldn't have brought Alchemy into being without you. You are the sharpest trader I've ever met. You still don't know how to command your talents, but when you unleash them, you're a genius."

"But—"

"Genius needs the guidance of patience—and learning. Alchemy isn't off the ground yet, but you can have the money right now if you want it. Just say the word, and it's yours."

He moved to open his desk drawer, and I nodded for him to proceed. I thought maybe I would show Hong I was made of better stuff than workers like Jerry, who only hustled to feed their greed. But unpaid "exposure" wasn't enough to raise a kid.

"If you do this, you're buying now at the price of later," he said.

I couldn't stand up for my parents against Walter Woo and Dash. How was I going to stand up to Hong, who only wanted me to learn and bide my time?

I decided against taking the money.

A week later, I was sitting across from Jerry at Al-Azhar.

THERE ARE TWO types of people on Freeport: Settlers, the top fraction of the one-percent, and Contractors, the rest of us. You qualify for Settler status either by accumulating enough wealth, measured as equity in Freeport and the Belt, or by being appointed to a high-level executive position, equivalent to L4-status and above in the Territories. As a Settler, you have access to everything that was once taken for granted as citizenship rights on Earth. Freedom of movement, freedom to work or not work as you please, freedom to vote on matters of local governance, priority status for pioneer shares in the Pacific Mutual Company, and pre-launch stakes in its growing mining assets in the Straits—shareholder value worth more than the total GDP of certain developing nations back on Earth. You'll also be granted permanent residency on Freeport—free to remain stationside for as long as you wish, regardless of employment—and be granted permission to travel anywhere within the Straits and beyond, like the Great Road and the Western Ring.

Settlers live in generous apartments on Beach Road, or in gated communities in River Valley, where they have enough space to own things and raise families. All the coin in a Contractor's wallet can't buy a single week's rent on Beach Road, and even if it could, they better hope it's not a cash-rich, asset-poor year, because MAM will just tweak the investment requirements to keep them out. Contractors are tied to the jobs they ship to the Belt for, usually for a mining asset or as a city worker.

Corporations, and that includes the Freeport Commission, reserve the right to cancel contracts at any moment, and when your contract's terminated, so is your visa, and it's back down to Earth with you until your next job out. Only the cream of the corps is allowed to pay passage in NET credit against your future earnings. The rest are left to sort themselves out with the various snake-head crews. And if that wasn't enough, the non-project-specific work visas for Contractors are dynamically needs-based. Needs that are continuously assessed and re-evaluated by MAM. Essence of dynamism. The nimble station gets the best talent.

Say you're an accredited airlock maintenance tech, or a solar panel development engineer. Freeport Commission decides they're short of your specific skill. Lucky you. MAM releases visa slots at 0100 hours SE3-time, which are usually filled by 0104 hours, via reverse auction. Reverse auction means that Contractors compete to price themselves the lowest, based on total contract value. Fixing total contract value up front is another way Contractors are shortchanged, because you get paid the fixed lump sum for your entire contract period, quarterly. No extras, no overtime, no bonuses. All before NET deductions and your shipping-out expenses. As soon as Freeport Commission deems your skill set no longer in demand, the skill set's essential status is dropped. And with it, you. It's the skills that are needed, procured, and protected, not the people.

Drop your bags on the shiny vinyl floor of the Embarkment that's printed to look like checkerboard marble, squint at the recessed lighting doing the real work of illuminating the arrival hall—behind the antique chandelier for show. Take it all in.

Why ship out to the Belt at all? Because Earth, after decades of denial, is truly on its last leg. One generation after another heaved a sigh of relief as they passed a barely functioning Earth to the next, until the Zoomers finally killed it. But it wasn't their fault. They just broke what was already breaking.

Earth is now too hot to be outside most evenings, and we've lost a few island nations, coastal cities, and plant and animal species to the rising tides. Jobs are so scarce that many are forced to sell their political voice in exchange for basic income. Only the wealthiest, like the Pereiras, can afford to live a bearable life.

Pick up your bags and step out of the Embarkment and into Freeport. *Welcome.* Life as a stationside Contractor is slightly less horrible than being unemployed and unhoused on Earth.

People like Chance and I, we know we'll never make Settler. We are always going to be living on the crusty rim of space-set society. And by "society," I don't mean the glamorous, Delight-laced, diamond-frosted degenerate, hanging on the edge of the bar at the Mandarin.

That's where Club Contango comes in.

Every fortnight, Chance and I, and up to about thirty-three other punters at any time, run simulations on our own futures and bet for or against ourselves in the worst possible outcomes. Call it a hedge, if you will. Call it insurance. But it was always about taking that disappointment, staring it down, and owning it. We started out with the three fleet managers who lurked around the back room of Lucky 48. Somehow, through word of mouth and the enthusiastic interest of Bel the bartender at the Mandarin, we've grown.

As I said before, we came dangerously close to having to shut it down once, in the second quarter of last year. The house took a bad position, and we would have lost it all had the biggest winner—someone who never lifted their privacy mask all evening—had not chosen to walk away from the pot.

Club Contango is the only den where I have any ounce of control, where the takings don't depend on the graces of an employer or a sage partner, and where my failures don't seem so crushing.

And when the going is good, it's fucking great.

SPARKLE

THE WRITER'S BAR at the Great Eastern Intergalactic Hotel and Casino is named after a nineteenth-century colonial hotel back on Earth, located in Territory SE3. Once upon a time, when the peacock of the British Empire plumped its plume and strutted the green lawns of its brave new home away from home, far flung literary stars lounged in woven rattan chairs and read aloud sketches of tropical traipses, and letters never intended for private appreciation. In its current iteration, the Writer's Bar is anything but a literary salon. I pass the prized traveler's palms on the checkerboard floor. I would keep walking just to hear the click of my shoes on real tile, but I'm stopped by a pair of charcoal-gray trousers with pressed creases down the center of each leg.

"How may I be of help…Madame?"

It's the third time this quarter Nadir Hussein has seen me, and still he forgets me—or chooses to show that my person has no place in his lofty memory. White-gloved hands fold over themselves atop the polished golden bar, elegantly freckled with age spots at the corners. Nadir is the night manager of the Great Eastern. It's no longer nighttime, but neither is it the lunch hour, so Ed Choy stays in her top bunk in the staff dorm in the warren beneath the hotel, slurping noodles from a mug until precisely eleven in the morning, while Nadir stares down the last of his shift.

"Cut the pretense, Nadir. I'm here with the two hundred gallons of tomato concentrate you need to restock the kitchen and bar."

White-gloved hands flit to the level of his chest, and Nadir looks around and behind me.

"*You* were sent by the chandlery."

"Yes, my man. Commissioned by Trace Pereira."

Nadir's eyes narrow. "Where's the...*product*?" he says, as though naming food ingredients outside the kitchen is too much for the delicate ears of the Writer's Bar.

"With the delivery bot, waiting to unload. Just needs your acknowledgment. Same as always, right? The bots load it in the back. You know this. It's your job. You're not being paid to just mooch the front of house." I wave and drop a receipt in his interface.

Why are you *here then?* the arch of his eyebrow says.

But Nadir is in a charitable mood and forgives my unnecessary presence, accepts and acknowledges the chit.

Here's a secret of the food industry, unique to station conditions: When you're light years away from a source of real food that isn't vat-grown or precious hydroponics, the swiftest source of supply in an emergency is from a ship chandlery. If Lucky 48 can hold a large enough standing stock to victual a ship set for the far ends of the Greater Belt, they can provide tomato concentrate à la minute for lobster bisque at a resident's reception. For a price, of course. And only if you ask nicely.

These service runs are the reason why, despite living in the rusty depths of Pioneer Ring, I've seen the inside of all the hotels and clubs of Freeport.

I'm listening to the click of my shoes on the tile when familiar voices pull me back.

"Connie, dear, you saw us."

Click, click, click.

Keep walking.

"Are you really pretending we're not here?"

"She absolutely is. This is about that club of hers, isn't it?"

"Darling, it's settled. Remember? Have breakfast with us."

I don't remember their account being settled, but if Chance settled it without me—and by settled, I mean collected and not forgiven, because we can't afford that, not until Jerry transfers the rest of the coin he promised—then nothing's stopping me from turning around.

Bite, swallow, and reel me in.

The lure of the Sparkler-set led by Zetta and Roar is, after all, why I'm inside the Writer's Bar and not in the back where I belong. It's a force I can't resist. Neither can Chance, I suspect. Chance acts like nothing matters, but Tanuki is our special place, and it's bejeweled with sparklers.

Zetta is the other reason.

A year ago, Zetta walked away from her wins on a particularly rough night for the house. I'll never forget that night. Zetta wore a Chinese dragon pixel-mask and a bright fuchsia dress printed with peonies. I never saw her face, but I knew it was Zetta from the way the dragon nodded as she disappeared up the stairs.

Zetta blows me a kiss that floats on scented wind. Like a little gold bug with humming wings of film. It flits around my head, and I resist the urge to reach up and catch it. It loses itself far above me.

"I suppose I could use some breakfast."

"There's our gal," Zetta purrs. "She wants a tall Bloody Mary, no ice."

Roar laughs over his shoulder at Ming, already reaching for the hot sauce and rolling his eyes with his whole face. The two other sparklers on either side of Zetta are dressed in sheer black mini dresses in the style of their queen, with face filters on that feature a black-and-white hyper-feminine cartoon from the silent era of film: Betty Boop. When privacy masks were first launched, they simply blurred or pixelated the wearer's face. They were mostly used by administrators on business they'd rather not discuss, or by traders walking into a dark-pool deal. Or criminals. But now, the number one use of privacy masks is as a decorative accessory adored by Sparklers, and many graphic designers pay their bills in full by just designing limited-edition masks.

"You're not bringing those back, Zetta. They're foul."

"She brought the tomato juice, didn't she? Ming dear, step aside. Your spritzes are perfect, but I make the best Bloody Marys."

"Only because no one drinks Marys. Nor has anyone seriously liked them in the history of cocktails. They were more of a hangover cure," says Ming. There is a palpable sulk in his voice. He is not insulted by Zetta's assertion that he doesn't make good Bloody Marys, but by her taste in them. Old school bartending, replete with shaker flips and juggles, is still just a temporary visa-ticket for him. Ming came out to Freeport after answering a ViewBucket casting call. The audition went great, he said. "Floored them." And it wasn't just his ego speaking. He saw it in their eyes. Saw it when they held him back and used every minute of his day's rate to record him. He was Detective Sneezy on a pilot for a cozy mystery. They thanked him for his time and paid him a day's work. Ming didn't get the role, but his image is now licensed for eternity for use as supporting characters in ViewBucket pilots. Real stars are shuttled in from Earth for big launches, as needed. Meanwhile, Ming shakes daiquiris and stirs martinis behind the bar of the Great Eastern, his back to the large antique mirror that reflects debauched, drug-hazed parties from midnight until dawn. He smiles dourly when every so often, someone points at with a raised eyebrow and wonders aloud where they've seen before.

Zetta slides off the golden stool, glides around the side of the lacquered bar, and pulls a ribbed glass from beneath it, already filled with real ice.

"Bloody Mary's had an awful reputation because of the ratio of vodka to juice."

Roar lifts a finger. "I thought it was something, something… and a murderous queen. Jazzy would know. He was the history head. Say, I wonder what that boy's up to these days?"

"Right, that's what the tomato juice is supposed to stand for." Zetta pours red juice from a container at the back of the chiller labeled "Reserve."

"Dreadful. How do you know these things?"

"Education, dear Roar, is how one knows things of the world. You need equal parts vodka and juice. Not one to two. Equal."

"And that, children, is why Zetta's never good for anything in the mornings."

"Darling, I'll be nothing without them. And it isn't the drinks doing me the green this morning. It's that bad Delight from yesterday."

Roar is beside himself. "I got it from the host at Arcadia. She was at Wen's pad pushing trays of canapes, and then some."

"What did she look like?" Zetta picks up real ice with silver grips.

"Giant shades? Black-and-pink something… Oh, how would I know, honestly?"

"I hope to never be murdered in your presence."

Ice in the glass over the mixture.

"I'll take a closer look next time you send me out shopping."

"No, you are not going back. That was some bad Delight. My head hurts, and it's only because I streamed a quarter while mixing and saved the rest for after the drink was ready. If I'd streamed it all, why, who'd be mixing your drinks now?"

Sauces. Squidge of… *Is that real lime?*

"Unfathomable. We'd be Zetta-less. No means to cocktails. No breakfast."

"You laugh. The next time you pick up the Delight, get it from the usual guy at the Oriental. The one with the woolly hat."

Black pepper from a silver mill.

"That would have been my first choice, bunny, except the man's vanished."

"Vanished." Zetta rolls her wrist, swirling the drink around.

"His boss at the Oriental says the guy's name didn't show up on the visa-approval lists last week. Got picked up protesting against Habo. Can you believe that? He's probably on a shuttle just past Yokohama Wormhole by now."

Zetta purses her lips. "Tommy-something, then. The pianist at the Oriental. Someone must have taken on Wool Hat's supply."

Pours the mixed drink into a fresh glass.

"You don't even know our regular guy's name?"

"Roar, pay attention. For all we know, the old baby's had a rheumy eye on Connie's little club and wants to rake it in by knocking us all out first."

"That's pretty grim," I say. I try an unfazed laugh, but it sounds like I need the washroom. "She's welcome to drop in and talk about collaboration."

"Connie. Dear. Suziebaby doesn't do collaboration. She's a crook. She's, what, a hundred years old? And a discharged bankrupt. The baby consumes and dominates."

Of all the charges, it's bankruptcy that makes Zetta cringe.

Roar's slapping his knees. "Okay, kitty. No more Delight from Arcadia."

"I mean it. I'm not streaming anything the baby's stuck her claw in. She saw me leave my cruiser at Lucky the other day, did I tell you? She knows we're players."

Zetta stirs the drink with a stick of celery and slides it to me. I sip and hold my face.

"It's a good pour."

I didn't notice how the salt got on the rim.

The other sparklers burst into laughter. Ming, leaning against the supply cabinet in the back and swiping through casting calls from Earth, cocks his head around but doesn't return to his post. Not when Zetta Zhang is playing at mixology.

"You're horrid, Zetta. Stop teasing her," says Roar, three fingers curled around Zetta's shoulder. His other hand reaches out to me like a life raft. "You absolutely don't have to finish it. It's foul, and she's pushed it on us all. But we love our Zetta in spite of her appalling mixing skills."

Zetta flicks his hand off her shoulder and pats her temples with her fingertips.

"It's the Delight. I can still feel it sitting on my head, and I hate it. Truly, Roar, something was up with the sound on that film of Delight, and it messed up my interface. Now I have a mean headache, and I'm seeing glitches."

Zetta demurs with a pout and engages her privacy mask. The pixelated cat with large weepy eyes appears and obscures the top half of her face. The girls on either side of her turn on their masks, too. Two foxes lean in and kiss the cat on the lips—details obscured by the blurring of the pixels. Roar raises his hands in mock annoyance before joining them.

I, meanwhile, have become a large, bright lamp post, so I knock back two more gulps and nearly drain the glass before I remember that I have less than an hour before I need to pick up Sticky from Junior.

"Thanks for the drink. I, er, have to head back to Lucky. Help Trace audit the bot's inventory."

No one cares about the soundness of my excuse. I nod at Ming, making a weak show of posing a finger for coin transfer. Hoping he doesn't stand and wait for it. He cocks his head at Zetta. *It's on her tab.* Thank the sparkling stars, because a drink at the Great Eastern will erase my dinner budget. I turn heel and soften my steps across the tiles. My brain is untethered and swimming around in my head.

"Come find us the next time you're running a tight pool," says Zetta, lips parted over her drink. A large, yellow stone glistens on her middle finger, the one that clutches her drink. Hers isn't a Bloody Mary. It looks like a whiskey old fashioned.

"Don't let anything get in the way of *us*, Connie."

Roar winks. "It's only money."

"Don't insult her, Roar. The club's rolling in it."

She waves, and a glittering pink-and-purple sliverfilm appears in the palm of her hand, which she tosses at me like a blown kiss. How could I not catch it?

"Don't stream it all at once," Zetta coos.

"See, *that's* an insult."

I leave the sparklers to their liquid breakfast and their poor estimation of my sensitivities, and make for the street. There is a determined cheer and abandon about them, like the bright young things of the 1920s and '30s, and the hustle hard, party hard young capitalists of the 1980s and '90s. Youth on the cusp of a new age. It's the second industrial revolution and we're not even planet-bound, baby. Nor bright.

The canteens and clubs of Delta and Pioneer are less tethered to the artificial dawn and its sharp tug on the leash of work. Less tethered by NET contributions and bills. Think about that tomorrow. Today, the third sons and elder daughters of the aging Gen-A magnates have youth and money, and don't want to be reminded that they have but crumbs waiting for them back on Earth. Stretching their days on Freeport from cocktail breakfasts to audio-neural drug-fueled nights on Beach Road. The frantic excess declares that there is no tomorrow.

ENTERPRISE

I STILL HAVE yet to tackle the small claims that landed in my tray this morning, but that's what sleepless nights are for. When you live in a climate-controlled dome, on an asteroid station beneath an artificial sun, you don't get good days and bad days as much as you get a colorless, bleak stretch of sameness peppered with the occasional freak storm which you see more than feel through the dome. Still, today feels like it can be a good day, and after sending a quick apology through the communication channel of the Junior Academy to let them know I'd be forty-five minutes late—swiping to acknowledge the immediate addition of a payment for one session of guided language tutorial—I get on the tram to Academy and hop off three stops later at Enterprise Square. I need to walk the rest of the way to sober up.

I'm barely off the tram when holographs the size of mining haulers compete with interactive displays to attract my attention. They advertise sales on the latest companion app, two-for-one shots at a speakeasy-themed bar, unbeatable rates at capsule hotels if you check out by two in the morning, tickets to e-sport challenges in exchange for three hours of your time spent filling out customer satisfaction surveys, and free side dishes at the new dinner theatre, where you can watch a somewhat authentic Cantonese opera that guarantees at least half the cast are real human actors or your coin back, guaranteed.

My shoulders roll in, and I can feel myself hunch, make myself smaller. I usually take pains to avoid Enterprise Square, but I march on anyway, grab a bitter-tasting coffee from a street machine not because I need one but because my face wants something to do. I slurp on it, and it burns my tongue.

I'm trying to blow on my own tongue when I see her across the street, standing near a snack machine in the shadow of a luxury hotel chain's budget option. She's smiling so hard my hand rises to my own face. That's a sharp suit. I could never afford to shop in a place that sells something like that.

She says, "Is your NET sitting in your company reserve account, earning a pitiful 0.01 percent? Why keep coin in your wallet, when it could be working for you? Buy a piece of the future with Endeavour's greyfield portfolios. Buy-ins to suit every budget!"

Her face is my face, with high cheekbones the likes of which I haven't seen in the mirror in eight years. The effects of parenthood and moving across the solar system airbrushed away. That smirk on her lips is my smirk, tweaked to speak to the wry humor I like to imagine I have, and less to my exhaustion. But anyone who's ever seen me in passing won't be able to tell the difference. She *is* me. Drawn with a kind squint, no doubt from a template of choices. You can tell from the soft edges as you approach that she isn't corporeal, but she's rendered with enough detail to fool the distracted folks on Freeport, who are always gazing over each other as if they're street obstacles. This version of me must run on Red Unicorn's latest holo tech—the kind that's not publicly available yet.

She catches my eye, and thinking she sees a customer, continues her sales pitch about greyfield assets, no recognition evident. I allow myself the indulgence. Maybe this isn't as bad as it looks. It would be worse if she was aware, wouldn't it? Then I'd truly be fucked. Maybe she's just someone who looks too much like me. Except I'm looking into her smiling eyes from a few feet away, and I know better. The denial doesn't stick.

What is she? How did she get here?

Then I think about Jerry and that little favor he asked of me a while back. Just a small job. It'll pay for the baby's needs until you find yourself on solid footing. "Come on, Con. I wouldn't ask you if I didn't think you were the best."

Stiff was right.

A groan rips through me, and I'm riding a shredder straight down to hell.

This other me says, "You don't look like someone who would turn down a good deal."

"No. I mean, yes, I can analyze a deal all right. But what I'm not doing is falling for this shit. Not from you."

And just like that, I'm talking to myself.

"Proud of yourself, are you?" a voice from behind me says.

I spin around and meet the eyes of a man who looks like he hawks illegal upgrades from his tent in a Delta alley. What's a guy like this doing in Enterprise Square during the daytime? Doesn't he know that MAM scans the street cams for drifters?

"Excuse me?"

He points at my holographic double. "You must be. Only reason I can think of as to why you'd want your face plastered everywhere across town."

"Everywhere? What do you mean?"

"Counted at least six more of these holograms today alone. I'll take you on a tour to see them…in exchange for a fraction of some coin."

"No thank you," I say. I start to walk away.

"You're a real selfish lady, you know that?" he shouts after me.

Behind him, Not-Me latches on to an unsuspecting passerby and second-guesses their investment decisions. It's like watching my own public character assassination in real time.

I'll later come to learn that it's not as bad as it looks.

It's actually much worse.

PART 2

CHECK

OWN

JERRY SCRATCHES HIS hand and winces. "It's nothing like how you put it."

"You asked for a favor. 'Train my AI, Connie, please.' And for almost nothing compared to what you would have had to pay any other trader. You could have told me what you really wanted: to sell my likeness."

"License, not sell." He catches his breath and glances off-camera. "I would never sell, even if I had the right to. You must appreciate this. Red Unicorn, the licensee, is in talks to sell the rights to Pacific Mutual. Those guys are on their way to owning all the Belt between Yokohama Wormhole and the Eastern Gate. Project Echo is our way of sitting at the big table."

"Oh, it just keeps sounding better."

"The Mutual Association extended Pacific Mutual's operating license indefinitely. Right pocket to left. Soon they'll be the top buyers on the Greater Belt—of everything."

"I didn't ask for the trajectory of Pacific Mutual. You said you wouldn't sell."

"Yes, but I *did* pay you for the work." Jerry's left hand floats to obscure his face. Talk about a tell. I see a scab hanging off the edge of a partially healed cut, which he's just scratched off. A fresh drop of blood.

"You compensated me a day's pay on consulting rates."

He breathes into the speaker. "I can top you up retroactively."

"Don't insult me."

It just keeps adding up.

Jerry softens his voice, and I can feel him change tracks, where he can come at me from a different angle.

"We had nothing then. We *were* nothing. This was our one shot. And look, we made it. We did this together. We *won*."

"*You fucking sold me* to the Unicorn, and to Pacific Mutual, and to whoever else they're in bed with. Why not make me open-source code, upload me to the galactic free library while you're at it? My consent obviously means nothing to you."

On the video call that I'm casting onto the store counter of Lucky 48, Jerry appears to be in a comfortable-but-average business traveler's hotel, high-class enough to have its own shuttle dock. And that looks like real carpet on the floor. He'd mentioned the name at the start. Rock-something or something-Rock. I must have missed it. Did he think I wouldn't find out? Or was he planning on making it a surprise?

"This is revolutionary, Con. We are right there with the big players on the edge of innovation. The Echo project is what Red Unicorn and Pacific Mutual have been pushing their tech teams to develop, and we delivered it. Why don't you look at it that way instead?"

"That is exactly the sort of shit Hong would've said." The words are out before I regret them.

"And you'd drink it up from Hong. Don't lie."

"Not everything is about your missed chances with Hong."

Was Jerry right? Maybe it's all I ever was with Hong—a lost child seeking a mentor. So much that I loathed to push Hong for a raise, or a bigger cut of Alchemy after Sticky was born. Afraid to break the spell of master and disciple. Instead, I went to Jerry for a side hustle. There's your hat, Connie. Try it on. It fits.

"Let's start again. I agreed to train your AI in sales pitching. Nothing more."

"And part of the training involved the walkthrough demo. You gave it everything it's using now. Nothing in that source file isn't there without your consent. You know this."

"No, Jerry. I did not know that. Nor could I have extrapolated to the Nth degree the extents you would go to monetize everything."

"I didn't want to say it…" Jerry pinches the bridge of his nose as if this is harder for him than it is for me. "But you might have left it out in exclusions, Connie. You signed the contract as is. Full Ts and Cs at the back of the receipt for the day's consultation. No comments or amendments. I have it on archive."

Fuck. Me. I'm grasping, but there's nothing to hold on to. Jerry's saying he's sorry, but I know he's only sorry that I found out.

"You're no coder, and I know enough just to fix things," I say between deep breaths. "Between us, we're no match for Red Unicorn teams. How did you manage to do this?"

"I didn't do any of it. I gave them access to the source material, and they put it together. They just needed a willing seller, what, with the red tape around the AI ethics memorandum review."

"And the only reason why they hadn't done this yet was the need for a legally licensed lifetime of data on one person. From all angles. They could have done it with what they collect on the networks, but it wouldn't be permissible. And willing trainers were holding off until the revised memorandum on AI ethics. You asshole. You crossed the line."

"Listen, this isn't the only reason we're meeting. I have a place on Pioneer Ring that I was going to flip, but with the sales talk ongoing, Red Unicorn won't pay until next quarter. Why don't you and Sticky move in? It's perfect. And I don't need the space. I'm going to be off-station for a while."

"Perfume on shit, Jerry. You sold me so the Ethics Committee couldn't get its teeth in Red Unicorn. And now you want to pay me off with lodging in lieu of wages."

"And you'll take it won't you, Connie?"

Jerry looks comfortable, ensconced in a giant armchair, fully occupying the space instead of perched at the end. There is weight in his voice. Jerry today isn't the same bleating loser he was when we were both working small claims at Reliance.

If I unspool my memories of the last years, be honest with myself this time, Jerry hasn't been the same for a while. Not since Sticky and I left Earth and tried to remake a life for ourselves on the pretext of chasing down Hong to make him clear his own checks. Meanwhile, Jerry sniffed after Pacific Mutual's trail, chasing the big-time, ready to sell whatever it bought.

Jerry's an asshole acting in bad faith. But allowing it to happen because I'm careless with my relationships—and my contracts—that's on me. I underestimated my harmless desk buddy, and I shook off a friend I used to be inseparable from.

When I flex my cramped shoulders, there it is. The returning weight of the birds.

We did this together.

"I SLEPT IN my own room!"

Sticky runs from the bedroom, excited, pattering like a large cat to where I sit at the kitchenette counter, pulling a coffee from our very own machine. Little paws on the counter. I nudge the cup of warmed soy milk closer to her, near the Auntie's takeout box of steamed *cheong fun* with soy sauce, sesame seeds, and sweet sauce. We're still on the Ring, but we're not capsuled in Raintree anymore. Jerry's spare flat is the top shelf of Contractor accommodations, where Pioneer Ring forks into Delta Road on one side and an express trunk road to Hub City logistics park on the other. Real estate agents have been marketing it as DelHuPi, and in the last year this two-square-kilometer space finally caught on and is now called Delphi by upwardly mobile hopefuls. As good as it gets without being a Settler.

Our building looks down on the courtyard of the Pacific Mutual dorm campus. If you tilt your head and squint over the tops of the buildings, you can almost see florid blue surf crashing on the recycled-plastic boardwalk of Beach Road.

"I'm going to paint the walls!"

I did not hear that.

The flat is huge. It's better than any place we've lived in since moving to Freeport. Plus, the coffee from the machine is low on acidity and tastes like it's more than fifty percent real-bean coffee, so I sink into a chair and let Sticky indulge in nest-feathering. I don't have to deal with everything at once. I can let myself enjoy this moment, even if it is earned with the ill-gotten gains of my licensed not-self standing in Enterprise Square, selling the promise of manifold returns on rocks unexplored. Because whether I like it or not, it's happening.

How did I not pick up the signs five years ago? I *thanked* Jerry for the day's pay. He didn't even flinch at the consultancy rates, higher than his last salary at Reliance.

"It's nothing," he smiled generously. "You're doing me the favor."

The only good to come from that meeting is that Sticky now has the chance to live someplace that isn't a capsule. The flat likely belongs to some uncle of Jerry's who wouldn't recognize him even when he shows up to the clan's annual Lunar New Year dinner. I'd sooner take the money, but Sticky is so happy. I don't have the heart to tell her we're moving out as soon as I find someone to sublet this palace to, and realize the coin. This is your brain on parenting.

A notification buzzes on my interface, and I blink to preview. It's Hong again.

>*<<We need to speak as soon as possible. In person, if that's all right, Connie.>>*

When Hong says "if that's all right," he means that is what he needs. I blink the message away, hard. Scrunching wrinkles around my eyes to show Hong my displeasure.

"Can I put my drawings up on the wall, Mama?"

"Yes, you can, baby."

Sticky's pulling on my arm, but in my head, I hear Stiff.

You fucked us over, Connie.

It's wind on the ear, but I can't shake it off, and it sits on my shoulders and folds itself over me like a large crow that's too heavy to fly, and unwilling to leave. When I get like this, I just want to fold myself away and sleep.

"Mama, sorry. Mama, I'm sorry,"

I pull myself off the floor, and the world is overfull, sloshing against the inside of my skull and nearly throwing me back down again.

"Sorry for what, baby?"

"I spilled the glue on the floor."

You fucked us over, Connie. I trusted you.

We did this together. We won.

"Mama, there's no more glue."

I don't want to listen. I don't want to think.

I throw myself on the bed, and the enormous bird flaps its wings and follows. I don't want to think about how I'm sometimes Happy Mama, sometimes Sad Mama, but mostly Fail Mama. Sharp-taloned feet tap on my back. This is a dream. My eyes are closed. And when I don't see, I can be anywhere. I'm back on Earth, and I'm not a mother. I'm not a failure. If I don't open my eyes, memories of Sticky—of Hong in his glass office—slip away. Maybe Hong never leaves the office to touch me on the shoulder. Maybe I never go home with that stranger from the bar.

The door pings a shrill chime. I'm hearing it for the first time. It's the middle of the afternoon, and I'm on my stomach on fresh sheets in a new bed. It can't be dinner delivery. I haven't thought that far ahead, even though I should have.

The bird on my back ruffles its heavy feathers and shifts its weight across my shoulder blades. The only way to shake it off is to get up, so I stumble to the door, which disarms at my approach.

I don't remember telling Chance about our new pad, but I must have, because in comes Chance, swaggering tall. Chance is dressed in Chance's signature every-style-and-none-in-particular that says "anything might happen tonight," and Chance is dressed for it.

Chance sniffs the air.

"I smell a fresh steamer of plump little BUNS!"

That's my kid, running to her second favorite person on Freeport, if I'm even still her first. She runs into Chance's wide-open arms.

"I'm going to catch and eat them all!" Chance says playfully.

Sticky turns and runs away screaming, and I raise both hands and press myself to the wall to let her pass, happy in defeat.

I wish I could be Happy Mama always, to be how Chance is to Sticky. The two of them even have their own language. Chance has a full set of nicknames for Sticky that I don't dare appropriate. The same way I don't dare question how Chance always knows when to show up for us, especially during times like this, when I'm too exhausted to bear anything more, and I'm overcome with fear. Fear that my next failure will be one we can't come back from. Fear that Chance will take my place with Sticky. Fear that Chance will leave me, and I will fall.

That day atop the Embarkment, I was supposed to fall.

I fear that I'll find myself at the Embarkment again, looking up, looking down.

BODY

THE BACK DOOR to Lucky 48 is ajar.

That's the door that leads to the basement and down into the club.

I don't want to be at Lucky 48 today. I don't want to risk the chance of a few of the players skulking around the back, waiting to talk me into extending margin. It shouldn't be this hard for me to tell them that they knew the rules, and that margin limits are limits, that the house isn't as solvent as they think it is, that collectibles don't equal income—they're assets with assigned risk. But when have people ever waived their right to be aggrieved? I only stopped at the chandlery today to swipe a pot of old-fashioned paste-glue for Sticky's interior improvements, and now I'm looking at what appears to be a break-in.

The front door is closed and locked to the outside world, armed by a sophisticated security system. It's a smart system that if triggered would have Trace's dad pinging Trace and I on our interfaces, begging us it shut the alarm off before it he has to pay for the security company's response. The back door, however, is a basic keypad and PIN. Wouldn't want to wake Papa Pereira every time we prop the door open for the early morning deliveries. And if it doesn't log the comings and goings on club nights, or Trace's nocturnal movements on most nights, that's all right with us, too. To help Joseph Pereira sleep at night, the camera facing the back door has been streaming a loop for months now. *Pity.* This is the one time we could have used a proper surveillance and security system for the back.

Then again, maybe it wasn't a break-in. Maybe I had forgotten to close the door myself.

Don't be a coward, Connie. This isn't Earth. There are no senseless violent crimes up in the Belt. The worst that awaits me down there is a debt collector on Alchemy's trail. That, or the Commission has finally come to pay us a visit about Club Contango. Either way, I can't walk away and leave Trace to deal with whatever's down there.

I push on the door and descend as slowly as I can. The bright white-blue lights come on as I pass mid-level. Before I touch ground, I can tell something's wrong.

For one, I see feet. Not standing feet, soles down and ankles slowly appearing as I approach. These soles face me, with the rest of the person coming linearly into view.

Another step down.

The smell. It's like days-old liver soup. Worse. A heavy, meaty scent, ripening to the salt-sweet stench of decay. And a pungency of something that smells an awful lot like piss.

A part of me is still deciding if this is better or worse than being held by a Commission Regulator. A knee-capping fine and time in the lockup for illegal business practices and tax evasion might be preferable to what truly awaits.

Two more steps.

I can see the body attached to the feet.

It's Hong. He's lying on the floor of the basement of Lucky 48, in the dark.

I step softly forward.

"If it was a room you needed for the night, you could have called," I say with a thin laugh.

No movement. The feet are perfectly still. So still. Like I've never seen with Hong. He's always fidgeting and shifting. The only reason he'd be this still…

"If you didn't want to stay with me, I could have booked a room for you and charged it to Jerry."

I squat down beside him and suppress a gasp with a sharp draw of air. There's no point reaching down to touch Hong's blue skin, or to lift his head on his twisted neck and inspect the point where a blunt object pierced the back of his skull. Liters of spilled blood mix with a pool of urine on the floor.

King Hong.

"Who's caught up with you?" I whisper.

I hear the clatter of the door above, and the sound of Trace singing along to the retrowave soundtrack of *Forever Rangers*. I smell coffee. I would love some coffee right now.

"You're early," Trace calls to me down the stairs. "I didn't get you anything, but you can have half a *youtiao*." Chewing noises. "Well… A third of one now."

I'm reaching for something to say.

Hong is dead.

What's the name for this catch in my throat, or this tightness in my chest? It can't be a stifled cry. You were never that to me, were you Hong? Just business. Just partners. Just my damned mentor complex. All those years I looked up to you, but the man you were was long gone. Or maybe was never there.

To Trace: "Yes. I mean no."

The sound of Trace's pacing stops.

A ping through my interface jolts me, and I blink away the reminder to renew insurance on my minibulker. When it disappears, I'm left with a view of my inbox. Messages from my father that I've left on <<*Unread*>> beyond the twenty-word summary.

And at the top, that message from Hong I left undeleted.

>   <<*I'll wait for you at Lucky 48. Contango's slipping into backwardation. You are not ready.*>>

The message floats, not like cream, but like a dead fish. It looks like I had planned to meet Hong here. Like I killed him.

Contango being past its good years would be assigned to me as motive. And no cameras to prove I didn't do it.

Trace's footsteps advance down the steps.

"Don't come down! I'm not hungry!"

She's singing, *"Go, go, Forever Rangers!"* under her breath—a high-pitched loud whisper—which means she's listening to it in-interface and can't hear me.

"I promise I didn't bite the end off. I just tore it," says Trace in regard to the *youtiao.* Her boot steps stop. "Oh. Shit."

"I tried to tell you not to come down."

"That's…your partner. Hong."

"Former partner."

Trace goes pale for half a second before the color returns to her face, and it drops back to its cool slackness.

"Formerly-alive former partner, you mean. I think I'm going to be sick."

"You didn't happen to see anyone come in here last night, did you?"

Trace shakes her head. "I wasn't here. ViewBucket Experience, remember?"

I stand up and move away from the body to join her at the foot of the stairs.

"I'm so sorry I dragged you into this, Trace. I'll deal with it."

"My dad's going to have such a fit."

I thought I was done with Jerry. I want to be done with Jerry. But it's not like I can just walk my visa-lapsed self into the Freeport Commission to report a murder either. I might as well pack my bag and take a shuttle back to Earth—without Sticky. I need to make sense of this, and Jerry's the only other person I can call who also knows Hong. He's already sold me. How much worse can he do?

Trace and I head back up the stairs. At the top, I pause to look back down at Hong.

<<You are not ready for this.>>

My hand tightens on the rail, white knuckles bulging. *Not now, Hong.* A sigh as my memory of him leans back in his chair, behind his desk at Alchemy. Sticky is six months old, and Alchemy is as much a baby as her, struggling to roll off its back.

"You can't advance me now, fair enough. But I need to know this is going to last."

"It's my responsibility to take Alchemy to market and feed us, and you can hold me to that." The memory of Hong stabs a finger on the desk. Or did he point it at me? "Tell me, are *you* going to last? You painted your ship in our colors. Finish the voyage, no matter what happens. Leave the navigation to me."

We carried each other, is what he meant.

Why did you want to meet me here, Hong?

What am I not prepared for?

COMPLICATION

TRACE RETURNS UPSTAIRS to the counter, to curl up, arms around her knees, in front of her projection. *Forever Rangers* is a good security blanket when there's a dead body in the basement. It also keeps the appearance of business as usual at Lucky 48, while I step out to place a call to Jerry. This is not the type of call I want picked up by bot censors through my interface, so I initiate a virus sweep, followed by an update on my interface that "accidentally" makes it go offline. I then fit on a scrambler mask, a cheap but convincing copy of a trending accessory that Trace bought on a whim at an alley sale.

Trace pauses the Rangers battling another band of masked teens. Once-over eye sweep. "You're going out in that?"

"Right." I pull off my practical pants. "I'm borrowing those leggings." I point to her sheer leggings printed with miniature monsters from another vintage-revival cartoon. *Pocket Monsters?*

"These are my favorite pajamas."

"Off with them. You'll get them back. Laundered."

I toss my pants over the counter, and Trace reluctantly hands her leggings over, muttering about dressing my age. Now it looks like I have little yellow manga spots on my legs. On the shelf behind Trace, shining coils of copper catch my eye. I pull a few of those down and throw them loosely over my neck. Trace tries not to laugh out of respect for my age.

Such a Midlennial.

I'm headed to the Mandarin Hotel. It's too soon to go back to the Great Eastern, and the Mandarin has just changed all their lobby staff.

I get off the tram at my stop, check my mask for fit, and there she is. There *I* am. She steeples her fingers and cocks her head of perfect hair at me. She is not me.

She says, "I'd like to see you say no to a 0.5 percent guaranteed yield on greyfields."

"No thanks. I like to keep my coin in my wallet."

Do I look as self-assured as she does when I smile?

"You'll be back. You have questions, and I have answers."

Did she speak off-script?

Did she recognize herself in me?

"Pretty wise for a copy. What questions do I have?"

A flutter at the corner of her eye. "Why, about your interest in the maximum yield on a one-percent stake in our elite class asset, Taman Central."

"Fuck off."

She shouts after me, but she does not follow. "You can do better than that, Connie. Or are you just bullshit promises without the nice clothes?"

I keep walking. I activate the mask, and a pixelated image of a cockateel wearing sunglasses appears over the top part of my face. I don't stop until I reach the pretentious early-century revolving doors of the Mandarin. *Look normal. Act normal.* The weighted turn of the revolving door approaches its interior opening. The tips of the bristles at the edge of the glass door frame resist the door with a muted sussurance. I am a Sparkler returning to roost from the night. Not Connie Lam, desperate to fix the fraying ends of her life.

In a bar styled after an ancient inn from conflicting periods of the Qing dynasty, a self-playing piano plays a classic, accompanied by a qin. Settlers are already lounging, or have never left. They're like slow-moving, shimmering lizards draped over their breakfast cocktails and miniaturized buns with imaginative fillings. Not one head turns to look at the oddball in the cockateel mask, distressed T-shirt, decorative wire necklace, and cartoon tights.

In the hotel's business center, at the back of the lobby, I pass an irate couple trying to communicate with their staff back on Earth, and I enter a privacy booth to call Jerry. The mask and its built-in firewall prevents ID-packet queries and automatic uploads. That—combined with the privacy guarantee of luxe hotel business centers, which are as hush as fiat Swiss banks of the former world—means that no bots will trawl my conversation for trigger words. No alerts will be sent to the Freeport Commissioner. Granted, the hotel's records will be there for the asking, and I doubt it'll take many turnings of the screw for the Mandarin to release my data, but still, this buys me time.

It takes two attempts at connecting before Jerry picks up. He's in another nameless, equally forgettable hotel room.

Hong is dead.

No. Don't start with that.

"When was the last time you saw Hong?" I ask.

Jerry looks off camera. "Last annum? I think it was spring festival. Small business owners' party at the Residency. Hong had too many martinis and almost fell down the stairs. So, a typical evening for him."

"Where are you right now?"

"Whiterock Station. Flew out after you ditched me with the bill at Auntie's."

The plush beige backgrounds of classy off-station hotels all look the same to me. Jerry's been off-station a lot. If he's not greasing his chin at the noodle shops on Freeport, he's usually somewhere else in the Belt. But Whiterock is news to me. For one, it's not exactly an open station for tourism.

"You don't mean the Red Unicorn product development campus."

The connection is startlingly clear coming all the way from Whiterock, but that's Red Unicorn 8G connection for you. I would have missed the pause if I hadn't been waiting for it.

"Meeting some people about a thing. Circle Finance is here, too. Two birds, one stone."

"I hope that thing involves Circle Finance paying us what they promised ."

"Whoa. Circle doesn't have anything to do with Project Echo. Forget I said that."

So much to unpack. Mostly how I think Jerry is lying, because I know he's been trying to establish a Circle Finance credit line for years. But Hong is lying dead in the basement of Lucky 48, so I really don't have the luxury of sidetracking.

I turn sharply to a resounding slam of the door, but it's only someone vacating the next booth. The couple outside have left. The late-morning light warms the cherry-wood-colored screens of the bar. In the cloak of amber glow, it looks like a period film set during a more creative time, when extras from every location let their real selves breathe. Stolen seconds before the cameras roll again. All we ever are is extra.

"Something's happened to Hong."

"Whatever it is, he had it coming."

It's on the tip of my tongue, and then I'm stopped by a loud rapping of knuckles on the glass of the call booth. I look to see Chance leaning on the panel and beckoning with an index finger.

"Not this bad, he didn't." I think I said that aloud.

Jerry shrugs. "I might need to look him up when I'm back. Something about the flat."

"The flat." I'm looking at Chance, head shaking at me through the glass. "You don't mean the one you gave us."

"No, it's not that bad. Just, I need Hong to sign it over to me so that it's officially in my name. He gave it to me to flip, practically said I could dispose of it, but it was a verbal agreement at the time."

Two things: Jerry isn't as remote and out of touch with Hong as he says, and…

"The flat my kid and I are squatting in, Jerry? The flat you flipped to me as a favor? It doesn't actually belong to you?"

Jerry's measuring out his words like he doesn't want to say what he must. "Why does that bother you? You and Hong literally share a bank account."

That's one more connection to a murdered Hong that I don't need. My mouth's still open, but there's Chance lifting chin with a swift jerk. *Hang up now.* Chance's finger draws a line across the neck, then points at me. *Now. Close your mouth.*

"You're not making sense, Connie. What're you saying?"

Chance opens the booth door, brows furrowed, elbows pressed against the frame.

I blurt, "I've got to go," and I fall out of the booth and onto the chair beside it.

Chance hops up to sit on the table.

"Hong's dead," I say, soon as I hear the click of the door close behind me.

"Hello, Connie. I thought you'd never stop blabbing to Jerry."

"He's dead. Blue when I found him. The blood from his head wound was already dried and thick. Like unset pudding all over the floor. Fuck."

Chance crosses a leg. "What kind of pudding?"

"Fuck kind of question is that?"

"Where's the body? Did you move it?"

"Basement of Lucky 48. And no. Hell no. I did not move it."

A pop, like a sucked cheek released.

"Good. Leave it. I know someone we can call to help us out."

"Hold on. We're skipping ahead to 'I know a guy'?"

Chance is already off the table.

"Thank the stars you kept this between us, didn't ask Jerry—of all people—for help."

I take my face from my hands. I shouldn't have done so. Now I feel naked and seen.

"I was calling Jerry to get the story straight before I contact the Commission. I had to ask him if there's anything I needed to know. Jerry's been sneery about Hong, even more so since he struck gold selling me."

"You don't trust him. But if you're fishing for a confession, you won't get one. Besides, Jerry's off-station." Chance bends to the level of the table top and scratches at a crack in the veneer. "You might want to rethink going to the Commission, seeing as you're an unlicensed casino owner and an illegal overstayer."

I groan as my face goes back into the waiting cup of my hands. "I'd be walking myself in."

"You almost lost Sticky once already. Do you really want to risk that again? The Commission is friendly to Settlers and Sparklers. It won't be friendly to you."

I almost lost Sticky during my second year of migration, right after Hong shook me off and left me with more debt than I could earn in a lifetime, let alone pay back with interest. My NET account was bleeding, and deportation was a real threat, so to survive, I took any and every job I could get my hands on. But in my desperation, I took a job from Zaqy's job board that I shouldn't have. I put my hands inside a trap.

I must have said something aloud, because Chance raps on the desk to get my attention. "I'm making the call."

"Are they a professional, like in the films? How does one even know these people?"

"She's done a few jobs. Not quite the same as this one, but same skill set required. Look up from your hands for once, Connie. When you do, you'll find that people can surprise you."

"I need a drink," I say into the web of my fingers. I've had enough of surprises.

"Pit stop at Tanuki after this." Chance sniffs. "What else don't I know?"

"Trace is the only other person who saw the body. But Trace is cool. You know her." My eyes narrow. "Your professional had better act like that kid doesn't exist. Anyway, she was at some ViewBucket event the day before, so she wasn't around when the actual murder happened."

"Go back and hang out at the Halia in case my expert needs anything. She shouldn't, but better safe than sorry."

"You don't need me to let her in?"

"It's my club, too, Con. I've got this."

Thank you, Chance. Thank you, emphatically.

Only Chance isn't waiting around to collect thanks.

I stride out of the Mandarin with the momentum of the revolving door hurling me back onto the street. I hold my hand up to block Not-Me from my sight, but she tries her luck anyway.

"You can't ignore me forever, Con. I won't cease to exist just because you don't want me to."

MOST OF THE trams headed to the Embarkment and HaboHub beyond make their last stop on Delta, across the street from Lucky 48. Crowded express trams trundle filled with exhausted Contractors are always trundling by, so it's not a terribly good vantage point to watch for foot traffic into Lucky 48. Not unless I rubberneck around the heads of commuters. I leave the stop and head down to street level.

And that's when I see her…again.

Another Not-Me stands at the Hazy Halia, not five feet from the curbside service window, where Zaqy takes morning orders. She has her back to me, turning away from a customer who's crossing the road to avoid her.

As I cross the street to Lucky 48, I realized something. This Not-Me has a clean look at the back door into Lucky 48. How long has she been outside the Halia? Was she active the night of Hong's murder? Could she possibly be a witness?

Back inside Lucky, I grab Trace by the elbow before she has the chance to say anything, and I pull her out the back door. I point to the Not-Me.

"How long has that holo been there?"

Trace shrugs. "A few days. Why?"

"Was it there the day you went to the ViewBucket event?"

Trace taps a finger to her chin while she thinks. "I'm pretty sure it was."

"C'mon, we're going to the Halia. My treat."

"Okay… But what's the occasion?"

I don't tell her about Chance's fixer. How she's stopping by Lucky soon, and that I don't want Trace to be around in case the this mystery woman is dangerous.

When we arrive at the Halia, I order two iced *teh halias* and try to make small talk with Trace. It's hard though, because my mind is on Lucky 48. I look out the front window, my eyes darting between Not-Me outside the Tram stop and the back door to Club Contango, where the fixer should be showing up at any moment.

Trace soon gets bored with my half-hearted attempt at conversation, and slides into her interface. That's when Zaqy comes over to give me updates on the fallout from the Hands' recent protest—who's been IDed through street surveillance, who's been ratted out, who's been deported, who's tunneling deeper—but I can barely make room for my own racing thoughts at the moment, so most of what he says gets crowded out by my brain. Thankfully, he can sense as much, so he gives up and on me and starts chatting about animation revival with Trace.

She stabs at the slice of dried ginger at the bottom of her glass with a reusable straw, tells Zaqy she wishes the producers who canceled *Powerpuff* never get to run a show of their own.

I'm free once again to drift.

AN HOUR LATER, I'm looking at a ping on my interface.

Masked ID.

All it says is

<<Done.>>

I'm still seated at the Halia, but Trace is gone and Zaqy has been replaced by one of his new employees. My drink is empty

I head outside to ping Chance, but when I turn the corner to avoid Not-Me, Chance is already standing there with the sole of a boot propped against the exterior wall.

"Was it all just be a bad dream?" I ask.

Chance's voice sounds faint, like not all of Chance is there. I follow Chance's eyes until they end on the roof of Lucky 48.

"If you forget it now, you'll never know it happened. Don't go in just yet, or the neighbors might get suspicious. Give it forty-eight hours."

"I haven't seen our neighbors all year." I frown. "This won't end here. Am I next? Are you?"

Chance shrugs. "For all we know, it was Bettina who offed Hong. Got tired of him dragging out the settlement and squirreling away coin all over the solar system. If that's the case, I don't think we have anything to worry about. I wouldn't think too much on it if I were you. We have more pressing things to worry about, like how we're going to keep Contango running beyond this week. But first, some inspiration."

Chance peels back the protective strip on a sliverfilm of Delight and hands it to me.

Just one track.

Spin it.

Like old times.

I want to partake—believe me, I do—but I'm looking at this giant hole I dug myself into and realizing I need to stay sharp.

What have I gotten myself into?

What exactly did I let Chance do?

ANSWER

I HATE THE term "foodie." You can't be one if you live stationside. Not without spending all your coin on the most expensive food deliveries in the solar system. But every now and then, you need to go somewhere special, somewhere to feel whole again, and for me, that somewhere special is a new place to eat.

When I was eighteen, I won a scholarship to a university in the northern territories—the one place where people still clung to their academic traditions. Dad declared it a waste of time, but since I was on scholarship, he couldn't also declare it a waste of money.

I expected to study the classics while I was there, but what I truly learned in those stuffy dorms and classrooms was how to deal with the desperate loneliness of youth.

During my time at university, I lived off rehydrates, choosing to save my coin for the evenings after a major exam, or for the days following a thesis defense. As a reward for my hard work, I would go to the last real library in the territory, an hour away from campus. It was more like a museum by then, since real books had become rare objects, but I visited often just to sit in silence between the dusty shelves. The coin I had saved was for purchasing tea and cake at the library café.

I've been to restaurants up and down the solar system since then, but I've never felt the same affection for them as I do for the quiet times I sat alone in the university library—at the real wood table that had once been a scholar's study carrel, as close to the protective shield and the books behind it as I could get— eating a slice of chocolate cake in the tiniest of bites, which was my futile attempt to make the moment last longer.

I never thought I *could* feel the same affection until the day I dragged my feet through the arrivals and departures hall at the Embarkment on Freeport, where the birds preened their oily black feathers and shifted their weight atop my slight frame.

Something white fluttered down to me.

A dove on a crisp wind?

No. A cocktail napkin.

Look up.

I was tired. So tired. I had already moved beyond feeling and into just plain existing when the napkin floated my way. I looked at it, but did nothing.

I hadn't realized until then how large the birds had grown, their wings now shading my eyes. That day, I'd gone to the Embarkment because I wanted to remember what it felt like to go anywhere I pleased. Take Sticky with me and start over again. Maybe this time, I would become someone who wasn't a failure, someone who wasn't scraping by on meager pay from their three, sometimes four, unstable jobs. A ghost.

Look up.

It was harder to ignore than to comply, so I looked up.

Above me, Chance stood atop the Tanuki balcony that ran the length and breadth of the arrivals and departures hall. The balcony and its central catwalk played host to Tanuki's most prized seats in all the viewing gallery. The catwalk was suspended behind the Embarkment's giant chandelier so that when you looked up at Tanuki, it was through shimmering crystal. The chandelier is one of Freeport's decorative indulgences. It's a sight meant to awe you on arrival. As is everything on the Embarkment. It's the only place on Freeport where the many historical fittings are true artifacts from Earth's past and not just replicas designed for the station's present.

The light from the chandelier, with its multifaceted crystals, made a halo above Chance's head—curly, almond-brown hair sparkling like gold. Chance, looking like someone I'd known forever, like someone I'd forever been waiting to meet.

Chance's slender hand beckoned. "Come up."

"Thanks, but—"

That was me, always with the "but."

"You'll love Tanuki. The *guotie* and the sushi are excellent."

"I can't." And to prove it, I backed away.

Chance leaned over the brass balcony. "Why not?"

"It's late. I should get going. Besides, I can't afford to eat there."

"Only good things happen at Tanuki. You deserve good things, don't you?"

You *are a good thing*, I thought.

I ran up the stairs. What else was I to do? The steps were latticed wrought iron—like lace, made delicate from age—and they shuddered beneath my every step.

Who are you? I hadn't asked but wanted to.

Once at Tanuki's rosewood bar, with its gleaming brass rail, I was met with the unconcerned backs of patrons who sipped their imported real grain drinks and nibbled on the chef's selections. But the person who'd called down to me,—slender and towering in a black silk shirt, indigo jeans, and black leather boots—was no longer there.

Chance was gone.

I turned around, needlessly embarrassed, because no one had noticed me enter. But instead of slinking away in silence as I normally would have, I stayed. I sat with a classic boulevardier that the bartender put in my hands in response to a sigh and the desperate, searching look on my face, the same look they must have seen countless times in the eyes of those who'd just been stood up.

From me seat at the gallery, I sipped the drink and watched the quiet hum of the comings and goings in the arrivals and departures hall, five stories below.

When I finished my drink and got up to leave, I felt whole again.

CHANCE

THE SOFT, PINK-AMBER glow that bathes Freeport in the first waking hours of the day comes from a large and inexhaustible light atop a tower in the port complex. A lighthouse that looks inward. It was installed by the tri-government committee, because Freeport's nearest sun is a white dwarf that bathes its minor belt of asteroids and floating debris in an uncanny washed-out blue glow deemed too depressing for human psychology. The glow is like the open door of an empty chiller during the middle of a sleepless night—those times when you're searching for something to satiate a craving, but finding nothing there.

The light from the lighthouse isn't perfect, but it feels a bit more like the Earth's sun, and really, that's good enough for most. It rises and sets with the work- and sleep-cycles of the day, and changes hues depending on time and season. Sticky has already forgotten what a real sunbeam feels like.

Lying in bed in my apartment, I count to twenty before I open my eyes and turn over to face the empty spot beside me. Chance had started the night on my sofa, but ended it by curling up around me in bed, still dressed in the day's attire. I never wake up to the sound of Chance leaving abruptly in the night. I never hear the front door shut.

I HAD TWENTY days left on my work visa when Chance showed up again. Sticky and I were living in a capsule on Pioneer Ring, and I had just finished cooking dinner. When I stepped back into our capsule to see Chance waiting there, I was balancing two piping-hot bowls on hands going numb from pain—the OEM multicooker in the shared kitchen had overheated our food, and I hadn't brought a tray. I even remember what I made that evening, because it was special. I had spent extra coin we didn't have for Earth-farmed fish and rice for Sticky, and I heated a bowl of soy pellets in powdered soy milk for myself.

"You didn't get sixty-five boxes of *guotie* and five boxes of smoked salmon salad from Tanuki?" Chance surveyed our humble abode with disappointment. "Or the *ha gau* from Auntie's." Furrowed brow. "Delivery must be late."

With an earned sense of relief, I bend forward and let the hot bowls of reheated food slide from my flushed hands onto the only table I owned. "I'm sorry, do I know you? You look familiar, but I'm not sure from where." For some reason, I'm not frightened by this stranger's presence. Neither is Sticky.

Chance continues, undeterred. "I *love* Tanuki. But I don't think the fish in the salad is proper smoked salmon. It smells of smoke spray. Not real smoke. That's why we only need five boxes. The *guotie* though…" Chance kisses fingers and turns to look behind the door at the empty corridor. "But for *ha gau*, I'm counting on Auntie's."

"Excuse me. Are you even listening?"

"You don't know me, but I know you. I saw you outside Tanuki, remember? I called you up to join me, but you never came. So, here I am instead. Look, I sent the delivery to 12-64. That's your address, correct?" Chance blinks in-interface and then squints at my folding table. "It should be here soon. You might want to get plates out."

Plates?

I have exactly two plates, two bowls, and two sets of cutlery. One of the sets is unlicensed *Forever Rangers*.

"Sorry, stupid question, but why did you send *your* food to *my* flat?"

"Because my flat is a sight, and I don't have any clean utensils at the moment." Chance continued to just stand there and look around, hands in the pockets of olive-green cargo pants that only ever looked good on catalogue models and Chance. "This place is…*cute.*"

"I'm not sure what's going on right now, but I think you should go."

"You're not very nice to your neighbors are you?"

This person is a neighbor?

"I'm sorry, it's just…" I tried to smile. "Conventional boundaries. And what can I say, I'm a conventional person."

Why am I apologizing to an intruder?

I searched Chance's glossy dark hair and deep chestnut eyes in search of my own reaction.

Chance walked past me and sat down on one of our two chairs—the easy chair that a previous tenant had left behind.

Normally, I would have kicked this stranger out. I would have been the responsible thing to do, especially with Sticky around. But Chance was the first adult company I'd had in weeks. I'd spent the last few months holed up in my capsule with Sticky, tearing my hair out from trying to decide if I should take out a loan and return to Earth to face the claims, or overstay on Freeport and lean on the Pereiras.

When I looked at Chance, I didn't feel the weight of the birds as much. It wasn't just Chance's ambiguous, fluid beauty. Chance's presence was a comfort. A pleasant weight that soothed my growing anxiety.

"All that dim sum. Why did you order the salad then?"

"Because there's always that one person who shows up late and wants 'just a salad.'"

"I'm sorry. Should I be expecting guests?"

"I invited some friends, yes."

"What? Who?"

Chance shrugged. "I don't know. People. They find me along the way. At the Mandarin, at the Great Eastern, at Tanuki."

Chance motions to Sticky, who was still playing with her toys on the floor. "Nice detail, by the way, with the kid."

"The kid isn't a prop. She's real. She's my kid."

Chance looked at me as if to say, *I hope that's the only surprise you've got.* But when Chance looked at Sticky, it wasn't in an unkind way.

"You said you're a neighbor. Where do you live?"

"Upstairs." Chance hopped off the chair and got down on the floor, picked up one of Sticky's toy bricks and said, "Bet you can't build a rocket as big as me."

Without any further prodding, Sticky quickly abandoned the toys she had been playing with and ran over to join Chance by the bricks. She was smiling. I remember the sting of that moment well. Of her showing affection to someone besides me. But after weeks locked inside a tiny capsule together, I couldn't blame her for wanting to interact with someone new for a change.

"I can too!" Sticky was bright-eyed and excited.

"How old are you?"

"Five-and-a-half."

"Well, I'm nine-and-three-quarters. And taller than you." Chance stood up.

Sticky's mouth fell wide open as she looked up. "What's your name? Are you an auntie? Or an uncle?"

"Neither. Just Chance."

"Chance?" I say.

"That's my name."

"Oh. My name's—"

"Connie Lam. I know. I told you this already."

When the food arrived, it was eight boxes of *ha gau*, two boxes of *guotie*, and thirty boxes of smoked-salmon salad. In the meantime, Chance had sent a note to the notice panel downstairs to direct the invited guests up to "our" flat, which is how Chance referred to the flat from then on.

All sorts of people came up: Young and fast Settlers from the Mandarin bar, who, thankfully, were partial to the salads, real smoked salmon or not; Solar Slickers in bespoke suits printed to last but intended for the cycler at the end of their business trips; four bewildered tourists in nineteenth-century period costumes, who all looked like they were headed to the Inn at the Oriental after this, and who hung on the Slickers' every words; and two groups of kids from the Worlds Academy who kept to themselves and seemed only to have stopped for food, tipped off by a friend of a friend. One group was in full paramilitary uniform, laughing. They were seated on the bed, which also stood in for the bar and buffet, which forced all the other guests to reach around them when heaping their plates with cuisine. The other group was clustered by the door with folded arms, always looking ready to leave, but never rejecting a drink.

There must have been eighty people crammed into the tiny flat. Glasses held at shoulder height, plates passed over heads. I worked my way to the big window where Sticky was, intending to rescue her, but she was busy painting the hands of guests—bots, butterflies, and monsters. There was even a line to get to her. I'd never seen Sticky this happy before, interacting with so many people. Usually—outside of Junior—Sticky spent all her time with me.

After that party, Chance was always in our flat.

Chance on my bed, reading a book. Chance building toy rockets with Sticky. Chance trying to reheat something in the shared kitchen down the hall, tasting it, throwing it away, and then taking us out to Tanuki instead.

What I never got my head around was how Chance was always spending coin, whether it was taking me out to dinner—only good things happen at Tanuki—paying my rent when I was low on funds and deep in debt on my NET, or buying Sticky gifts. The coin balance never added up, but I put it down to Chance's effect on me. When Chance was around, I did things I wouldn't normally do. I bought better food, went out more. Took Sticky to the boardwalk along Beach Road and to the overpriced cat café, bought her expensive art supplies—the traditional, tactile kind, which she adored.

When my last coin wouldn't stretch to the next club night, Chance paid off my bills and moved in to our flat permanently. We never talked about us moving upstairs.

No one knows what Chance was before. If there even was a before. None of the people that Chance swept up wherever we went knew anything about Chance outside the parties.

For a while, I suspected that Chance came from money. How else could Chance effortlessly oscillate between living on our sofa, off the meager contents of our cupboard, and buying us extravagant meals, throwing parties that kept us flush with leftovers for days?

At one of our parties, I overheard Chance tell a Slicker about time spent working at some middling logistics company, back on Earth before flying up. *Bullshit.* I worked for a middling logistics company. I knew the type who worked there, and Chance was not that. Someone with a lot of money at their disposal put Chance here. Maybe Chance was the third child of a rare metals baron, wanted back on Earth for manslaughter—a secondary-school incident involving a fallen chandelier? Or maybe I had just been watching too much ViewBucket at the time.

It was at that party that I sipped my drink and looked over the ear of the person leaning toward me, almost falling onto me, breathing heavily between boasts, breath laced with the scent of the real grain alcohol that Chance kept stocked inside the flat. How had I come to live in a well-appointed flat owned by Jerry, with a housemate who moved in without asking?

WHEN I HEAR the clink of the empty coffee cup on the counter and hear the click of the door as Chance prepares to slip out for the day, I sit up in bed and say, "Why were you at the Mandarin that day? And how did you know who to call?"

Chance has a hand on the door and a foot in the hall.

"That's the difference between me and you, Connie. You don't know what people are capable of."

SELF

SHE'S THERE WHEN I hop off the tram and almost make a beeline for the back exit of Lucky 48. It's stock-keeping day, and that means signing off on the automatic tally, but on second thought, it's still early, and Trace is no doubt still asleep in her room above the chandlery, so in the cold pink glow of simulated dawn, I head to the Hazy Halia instead. Its warm light beckons me.

I keep my head down as I pass the service window, but that doesn't stop her from noticing me. She lifts her weight off the exterior wall.

"The number of viable greyfields yielding a low-risk return can only decrease with time."

"Don't try me today."

I push hard on the Halia's door and stumble over threshold.

"The *real* Connie Lam," says Zaqy. "Take a seat. I'll send your usual over."

I slide into a corner booth and try not to look like I'm hiding from myself beneath lush monstera leaves and birds of paradise made from recycled plastics and polyfabrics.

"Built this just for you." The tall glass that Zaqy plants in front of me isn't *teh halia*. It's pastel-pink and topped with white froth. It's viscous, almost like an emulsion.

"Damn, Zaqy. I don't stop in yesterday, and suddenly you forget my usual?"

"All that angst and tension is why you need something new. First one's on me."

"I don't know if I'm feeling Barbie-pink today."

"Would I give you a bad drink?"

"Last time someone asked me that, I woke up the next day with a 24-hour hangover."

I take a sip anyway. It's sweet, with the aftertaste of something more floral and lithe—a flavor that's feminine and bold, like someone I'd love to meet.

"It's rose!"

"*Bandung's* not bad, is it?"

"I've heard about these. They serve simulacrums of them in Lion City. Am I'm chewing noodles? From a drink?"

Zaqy's forehead tightens. "Vermicelli."

Zaqy spirits an amber glass of *teh halia* on the table and reaches to replace the *bandung*.

"No, leave it. Please. I'll have them both."

Zaqy raps his knuckles on the counter. "Soak up the sun. Enjoy."

I sip on happiness and try to lose myself in the glassy twang of the electric guitar from Halia's hidden speakers. It sounds like it was recorded with a real instrument, not spun from a program with presets. I know this song. It's the same one that played when I stumbled into the Halia the other day, heavy with Jerry's news that we'd made it—*he'd* made it—against all odds. Things have only gotten worse since.

"Baby, you lied."

The band was called the Quests, from what used to be Singapore. My grandmother, who was introduced to the band by her grandmother, thought Locke and Verghese were the true sound of the Quests, and I don't think she was wrong. Freeport, like most territories back on Earth, has long been locked in a nostalgic love affair with music from the early to mid twentieth century. A lot of it has to do with a revival of "authentic" music, after the feverish infatuation with smartwave—machine-intelligence-generated music, including the vocals.

Stationside, the preference is for instrumentals. Something about the pitch of human vocals makes them less tolerable in domes. This is why jazz is played in the dinner clubs, while house and techno are played in the nightclubs and rave houses. But for Zaqy, "music" can only mean 1970s rock. The sound of a Strat reverberates inside the green-and-pink walls of the Halia.

I get a message ping. It's from Vis. Text only.

<<*Sign the petition yourself, Con, if you won't get more names.*>>

The petition? *Oh, shit.* The Hands. I promised.

They're still fighting against employers that manipulate, isolate, and pit them against one another through compulsory filters that gamify their work experience.

I do a quick interface search of my chats with Vis, scrounge together enough info to recall that the Hands are petitioning Red Unicorn—registered on Freeport as a productivity software builder—to reconsider the release of a new program called Bestie.

<<*I'm on it, Vis. Count on me.*>>

Blink to send, but with a delay of two hours.

I flag the notes and the petition, and set a reminder to myself to read and sign before those two hours have elapsed.

"I can smell the guilt on you from the washer," says Zaqy. He stands in front of me with a dishrag on his shoulder.

My tongue struggles to untie. Where do I begin? With Hong's body on the floor, or when I agreed to let Chance take care of it while I sat in your fine establishment, sipping tea?

Buy time.

"If this is my last drink, I could use a refresher."

Laugh.

Hong was trying to tell me something.

Did I say that aloud?

Zaqy's hands on the counter. "It's three years to the day, Connie. You didn't know what you walked into. That was on me for not vetting the job. That drink was my apology."

Breathe.

I'd forgotten. It's the anniversary of the worst job I desperately needed. All I remember now is the bucket, the industrial solvents, and the dark stains on a genuine sheepskin rug. Oh, and gold—lots of it. Gold trim on the walls, gold inlay on the feet of the real wood dining table…

Zaqy sighs. "You didn't remember. Shit. Sorry for reminding you."

I was newly out of the MAM hostel and a few coins short of making my down payment on the capsule when I took the questionable cleaning job listed on Zaqy's bulletin board. I spent hours that day scrubbing away some incredibly awful things. The house had been picked clean the night before, shelves empty of valuables. I knew what this was, but I finished the job anyway.

But not before the investigators to arrive. I had enough Loop streaming in my brain to be held under suspicion for days. Sticky spent those days boarding at Junior, not knowing how close I came to losing her.

Thinking about it now, I reach in my pocket and my fingers stop just before the tips touch the sliverfilm of Delight from Zetta.

Not today.

Zaqy says, "I'll never forgive myself for allowing that to happen to you."

"It wasn't your fault, Zaqy."

He heads to back to the bar to help a waiting customer.

The sky outside is lit by an illusory sunlight that strips the drab buildings on Delta Road, makes them look naked. Grays and beiges, unsubtle hints of neuromarketing, like the ones you get when walking into a store and hearing music that's just the right balance between calm and upbeat, curated for its suggestive power, one that tells the customer to make a purchase.

The crime-scene investigation I was an unwitting accomplice took a turn when I, the main suspect, provided a solid alibi to clear my name—I was at work at T&T for a rare in-person meeting during the time of the actual crime I had been hired to clean up. My part in the case was over.

On my wait out the Halia's door, I turn and square my shoulders. I feel the sharp stab of talons at my neck. I say my thanks to Zaqy, and he nods in response. He's behind the bar again, building another pastel-colored drink, this one a light algae-green

From the corner of my eye, I see her take her weight off the Halia's exterior and start after me.

I keep walking.

Don't turn around.

"I don't need anything from you."

It's at that moment, when I expect her to double down on the honey-sweet voice, that I hear the skid of her shoes, a totally realistic effect I never expected from an ad.

Instead of honey, she sourly says, "Chicken."

I turn. "What did you say to me?"

She lifts a heeled boot and shows me the sole. A QR code is on the bottom.

"If you don't like it, you can scan the code and file your complaint with the company."

"You're sentient? You can respond and say something other than investment spiel?"

She puts her boot down, and a half-smile flits across her face.

"Depends on the direction of the wind."

I keep both eyes on her as I take one big step backward. She doesn't move. Two steps now. Three. She remains still. I walk toward her now, gaining speed as I go, but she doesn't back away. I don't stop until we're almost nose to nose.

"Boo," I say.

"Oh, please. I know you don't bite."

"Don't be so sure, mirror girl."

Guess I'm doing this.

I ask her if she saw anyone go into Lucky 48 the night of Hong's murder. I don't know why I added that detail.

"Hong's dead? King Hong, our partner at Alchemy?"

"Never mind that. Did you see anyone enter Lucky 48 that night?"

"Just you."

"Aside from me, dumbass."

She narrows her eyes.

Is that a pout? On *my* face?

"I'm not a surveillance model. I'm a sales model."

"Great, the old 'not my job' excuse."

"You can't abuse me if you wish to use me."

I groan. "You're just as useless as I am."

She folds her arms. Then, as if to say *we're done here*, she steps back to the center of her allotted circle. The look on her face goes neutral, and her hands clasp politely at her front. She beams at me.

"Last week to get an introductory one-for-one offer on asset stock, subject to terms and conditions," she tells me.

CLAN

THIS NEW APARTMENT has grown on me. When Jerry offered it, I would rather have had the coin-equivalent in my wallet, but in hindsight, I would have gone out and rented an apartment exactly like this one anyway.

For the first time in our lives on Freeport, Sticky and I have space to move around. Separate spaces. Sticky can sleep in the bedroom by herself, even jump on the bed while eating soy pops, while I work in the living room. We have an actual kitchenette, a counter, and our very own OneChef cooker and chiller. We no longer share a reheating station down the hall. We have actual living quarters and enough stuff to make a mess of.

When I walk into my apartment today, I hear the chiller door slam shut. When I look to the kitchenette, I see a man standing where the open chiller door was.

"You don't have eggs," he says. His incredibly large frame occupies half my kitchenette.

Maybe it's the soft folds at the corner of his eyes, but something stops me from running away, screaming. I'm not a complete idiot, though, so I leave the front door open behind me, just in case I need to make a quick escape.

"Does this look like a suite at the Banyan Tree to you?"

The man doesn't react.

"No, I don't have eggs."

"What about EggPouro. You must have that." The intruder opens the cupboard beside the chiller with a hand that's still inside his jacket pocket. He doesn't want to leave prints. "What if your kid wants an omelet? Eggs. Soy sauce. Every house needs them. It's what separates us from the animals."

"Pretty sure I have soy milk in there."

He closes the cupboard door. "Let's go get you some real eggs. Walk with me. "

I reach behind me with the heel of my foot to check that the front door is still open.

"I prefer to grocery shop solo."

"Sticky gets out of class in an hour. If we go get some eggs now, I can have you back before pickup time. Or would you rather leave her wondering why you never showed?"

On the surface, the man looks as menacing as an overweight, out-of-shape bouncer that works a cushy job at a hotel bar, where the clientele is self-selecting and no one makes a scene. But there's a hidden, more menacing depth to him, evidenced by the scars on his arms that look a lot like human claw marks. The kind that happen during a violent struggle.

"If that's what it takes to get you to leave, fine." I step aside and wave him out the door. "After you."

The intruder is a perfect gentleman once he's out of my rental and we're on the neutral space of the pavement. A rare vintage car from the turn of the century waits for us downstairs. He holds the door open for me.

"Mind your head. They made them smaller back then."

No one is in the driver's seat, because the car is upgraded for self-drive. This means my kidnapper is free to do as he pleases, which apparently means sliding in the back seat next to me. I half-expect him to slip a black bag over my head, but he doesn't. He just says to the car, "Mandarin Arcade," and we're off.

THE ROAD BROADENS as it weighs its options leaving Delphi. Multiple lanes at higher speed limits transport workers in trucks to HaboHub, to the factories and farms of Hub City. The transports bypass Beach Roach, unless a Contractor is on their way to a service shift.

Our car hops onto the express lane to Delta, and suddenly, I'm on my normal route to work. I watch the familiar tram stops fly by, where crowded trams relieve themselves of Contractors on one side and soak up the waiting lines of more Contractors on the other. If you don't search for wrinkles in uniforms or dust on shoes, you'll be hard-pressed to tell who is coming and who is going—shift work is nonstop. The only ones that look somewhat well-rested probably stayed the night in one of those pay-per-hour capsule dorms outside the busiest of tram stops. Contractors use them to sleep between shifts rather than going all the way home to do the same.

We leave the main road, and the sodden gray of Delta melts away into lines of trees that I haven't seen since Earth. It takes more circuit irrigation to maintain the trees out here than back in the city, but out here, flora is deemed essential for mental wellbeing, so the cost is subsidized via tax dollars. Back in Hub City, trees are considered an indulgence, a mere hindrance to capital, since what the city really needs are more renters, not more frivolous costs.

We pass the hotels and casinos in the fog of late-afternoon stupor. The Mandarin Arcade on Upper Beach Road is a twentieth-century newspaper stand, souvenir shop, and boutique café reimagined as a late-twentieth-century strip mall. It's perched demurely on a one-way street between upper Beach Road and River Valley that is accessible by Settlers only. My escort raises his wristband to the gate, and we're through.

You can get whatever you want at the Mandarin, even a chiller full of real eggs, which is why we've stopped at a shop called Yeo the Grocer. It's designed to look like an old general store, but with pastel-colored decor. The soda fountains and coffee pots are real, and there are chairs in the corner where billionaires tired from shopping for their own food can sit and around and people-watch.

I take a wire shopping basket from a stack of them out front and follow my kidnapper into the store.

"My employer doesn't like how things turned out," he says.

"Well, I don't like being dragged across town for eggs, so you can tell your employer that we're even."

"When my employer invests in something, they expect to profit from it. What they don't expect is for the asset to be murdered inside his partner's illegal betting club."

So, this is about Hong. Because of course it is. Even in the afterlife, he continues to make my life hell.

"Your employer is Gary Weng," I say. "Wengzai. The reinsurance and collection king of Freeport."

"Privately-held family bank."

"Whatever. Hong mortgaged our debt with him, didn't he?"

"I'm not authorized to confirm or deny any of what you just claimed. I'm just here to inform you that you're behind on your clan dues for that fund, which makes it significantly harder for the Weng Clan to protect you and your interests."

"Is that what Wengzai is calling it now? A clan? Does it make you feel like family?"

He reaches toward my face, and like a chicken, I flinch. His expression becomes one of pity as he reaches past me to retrieve a carton of real eggs from the chiller shelf behind my head.

"Clans got a bad rep in the mid-twentieth century, and it's only gotten worse since then, now that they control one hundred percent of the scrap market on the Tier-2 stations. But before all that, they were respected support systems for Chinese migrant workers, particularly in Southeast Asia. Clans were a home away from home for those who'd been cast out in the great diaspora. The clans provided fellowship, security, self-regulated moral authority, and protection."

I hold out the basket so that he can deposit the box of eggs.

"Am I talking to the brain of the clan? Or the fist?"

"Just call me the Teacher."

He walks ahead of me on our way back to the self-checkout counter, where he scans the eggs and bags them. When he blinks to pull up his wallet, the thank-you message on the register shows my ID instead of his.

He's hijacked my profile!

Wears it like a costume so that I'm the only one being tracked.

Now, if anything happens to me in his company, it'll look like I did it to myself. Real funny, Teacher.

I take the bagged eggs and follow him out the door.

"Cooking tip for you," he says. "You want to take an omelet off the fire seven seconds before it looks done. Eggs always end up tasting more done than they look."

"Can I meet with Mr. Weng?"

"Does Sticky like omelets? Usually, kids love omelets."

The ride home feels shorter than the trip out, and it doesn't give me enough time to think about the *Dai Lou*, the Big Brother of the clan. "Wengzai" by legend, but just Gary Weng to his mother, I'm sure.

Wengzai's business is so simple and bloodless that it should disqualify him from the title of underworld kingpin, but it doesn't. Most twenty-first-century criminal enterprises are bloodless. Why maim or kill those you can enslave? When you can take ownership of another person's mind, body, and soul, and make all three work in your favor?

To accomplish this, Gary Weng buys all the debt he can. The riskier, the better. He consolidates it and guarantees it. Takes over repayment from the creditor with a risk premium to wet his beak. It's basic accounting. In return, the debtor gets a more professional face to front the debt.

That's the story anyway. And maybe there are folks who genuinely believe it, and who prefer being indentured to the Weng clan rather than to Freeport. Either way, I have Sticky to think about, and staying employed is all that's keeping us together.

The Teacher deposits me on the street outside my building, like an animal released back into the wild. I turn and wave. Maybe if I play it cute, I won't see the bottom of his boot.

"Thanks for the shopping trip. Nice to get out with the neighborhood goons every now and then. Same time next week?"

"Pay up, Connie. If you know what's good for you."

"Between you and me—because I do appreciate the real eggs—your boss will have better luck begging the revenue office. I discharged as much of Alchemy's debt as I could. I don't have anything left to give."

The Teacher clicks his tongue. "We're not just talking Alchemy's debt. There's fresh underwriting that's wholly yours. You should watch yourself, mom like you. You have a kid to take care of. Welcome to the clan. I'll stop by again soon."

Fresh debt? What the hell is he talking about?

VIBES

THE TICKETS I purchased for Freeport were open-jaw tickets, with the option for return. But I never took that option. In fact, if I could go back to the day when I first decided to leave Earth, I'd make the same choice again. Even with the knowledge that years later, around the same time I received a reminder that my options on the price-controlled return tickets were expiring soon, I would walk into Alchemy's rental office to find Hong's workstation empty. The options had expired that morning.

If you're running from yourself, Freeport is the best place to stop and breathe. Station life feels constantly in motion, and everyone hides in plain sight. No one cares who you *really* are, who you were back on Earth, just who you present yourself as now.

I hide because I'm in limbo—between contracts. The only reason MAM hasn't put me on a one-way shuttle back to Earth yet is because profits from the club have generated just enough coin to keep me above the median NET savings value of the average Contractor.

A Zoomer would say—a wistful tear in their eye—that back on Earth, Contractors were once called "middle class." Back before those of us below the 0.008 percent were left with nowhere permanent to rest.

I didn't invent selling the future.

A small start-up in the 2020s called Human Raze was the pioneer of betting on human futures, which they channeled through NFTs. But Human Raze made mistakes that killed their first-mover advantage. Their first mistake was fixing static, predicted outcomes. Their second mistake was moving too soon. The '20s were the nursery years of the coin market. The best of times for company founders willing to risk it all on a new industry, a new asset class; the worst of times for a hybrid market still dominated by fiat currencies and the Millennial decision-makers attached to the old ways of commerce. Release a product that didn't immediately yield, and the market never gave the series another chance. Raze's third and arguably worst mistake was betting on *someone else's* future. It was this that brought on the outrage that finally killed them.

Club Contango succeeded because we bet against *ourselves*, paid for a laugh in the mirror, and sometimes it paid us back. We sold the one product left to sell: our futures. And we profited the only way we knew how: by failing.

Another way Contango improved on Human Raze's product was via transparency. Doris the AI runs real-time simulations on the betting floor, for everyone to see, and then offers wagers on the simulated odds. Club players can then bet on the different projected outcomes—like whether or not Vis will get fired from her job five days from now. In that example, Vis would sync her interface feed for the next five days and the club players would watch to see if they bet on the right outcome.

But what if this mess with Hong and Wengzai is too big a failure to profit from? What if I should get my flight kit ready?

My mind's back at the departure hall of Embarkment, looking up at Tanuki, the bird on my shoulder flapping a wing, reminding me it never really left. Never will. That's what's marinating in my mind as I throw my things behind the door of the flat and head to the sofa, where I intend to collapse until I have to pick Sticky up from Junior.

But I can't collapse onto the sofa, because Chance is there, sprawled across it like a cat. Chance hangs a leg over the side and prods my bag with the toe of a vintage hiking boot. "Pick it up. We're going to Tanuki."

"But Sticky—"

"Doesn't get out off school for another ninety minutes."

I push Chance's leg aside to find space to sit, but the edge of the sofa gives, and I slide off onto the floor—where I remain. Lying prone actually feels great on my back.

"I need to know this, Chance: How did you 'take care of' the Hong situation? What did you do?"

"It's best you don't know. Carrying that on your mind isn't going to help anyone. Tanuki. Now."

"This is what the Commission will get me on, Chance. I can try and stick my head in the sand, pretend like it never happened, but sooner or later, someone's going to miss him. And once the Enforcers start sniffing around, they'll find me, kick me off the station. Sticky will be sent to boarding until I can work my way back up, if that would even be allowed."

"Bad vibes, Connie. You're having a day. Ergo, *I'm* having a day. *We* are going."

I could stand and fight, or I could give in and let Chance lead the way.

Tell me what to do, Chance. Make the decisions I cannot. Tell the world to screw itself for me.

Next thing I know, we're seated at the balcony inside Tanuki, looking down on the arrivals and departures hall of the Embarkment. Chance is swirling a chilled, dry sake, and I'm nursing what I think tastes enough like real grain whiskey in a boulevardier.

Light from the antique crystal chandelier scatters through the real ice in the sake and throws a constellation on the wall across from us. Chance holds his glass out over the balcony railing, above the hall below, and lifts a finger off the glass. The glass sways, and my heart skips a beat. Chance draws invisible lines in the air, connecting the fake stars cast upon the wall.

I gesture around us, with an unbitten *guotie* between my chopsticks, "I keep thinking I've seen this before. In a film, or a book. I can't put my finger on it."

"Keep thinking, professor. When you're done, all the *guotie* will be gone."

I think I see the crab—Cancer—in the constellations made by the glass.

"Maybe I've lived this life before, and I just don't remember."

"Didn't think Tanuki has been around long enough for that to be possible—this wonderful sanctuary of dubious culinary authenticity, gathered from all across the Asiatic."

A sanctuary.

"You're full of shit, Chance."

Chance lifts another finger off the glass, as if ready to let it fall five stories to the concourse below.

"Don't."

"What do you think I'm doing?"

Our usual balcony table is stacked high with emptied plates, save for the last order of twenty-two chive *guotie* and ten *siu mai*—too much food, even for us. But more to the point, Chance ordered drinks from the middle of the list and not the bottom, and the pricey alcohol haze is clouding both our brains. Still, I'm clearheaded enough to know that from this height, Chance's glass is a danger to the people below. Chance is holding it loosely by two fingers.

"You're making me nervous. There are people down there."

"What do you take me for?"

"Just, move the glass away from the edge. Please."

"For us?"

My eyes narrow.

"How did you know who to call, Chance? Who to call to come clean up the mess with Hong. You didn't even have to think about it."

A click of the tongue. "*You* already know the answer to that."

"Don't give me that fortune-cookie crap. Tell me why nothing about me surprises you. Tell me why you're always there to clean up my mess. 'Let's go to Tanuki. Let's throw a party. Let's run a club special.' Well, I'm starting to get a hangover, and I'm still standing in the hole Hong put me in, so excuse me if I'm being testy, but I believe I deserve some answers."

Chance's answer is to drag the upturned tip of a nose along the skin around my ear. It doesn't fix anything, but it feels good.

I sigh, then gesture to the stack of empty plates. "How are we going to pay for all this?"

"Now you're just being rude. No money-talk at the table."

Something like a pout, a shimmer, and then it disappears.

Chance pulls back the glass from its suspension above the Embarkment and raises it toward me in cheers.

"To Hong. Smart lad, to slip betimes away. From fields where glory does not stay—"

"And early though the laurel grows. It withers quicker than the rose." I raise my cup. "Hong was no romantic figure of youth, nor achievement."

Chance knocks the drink back. "Let's go."

"Seriously, we need to talk about how we're going to pay for all this. I already transferred all the coin I received from Jerry into Sticky's account at Junior, in case of emergency."

"I've got us."

"You what? How?"

"Bag the leftovers and follow me."

Chance takes my hand and walks us right across the floor of Tanuki. *Tap, tap, tap* go my heels on the black-and-gold tiles of real ceramic. Every customer in this place looks like they're a Settlers or Settler-wannabe. They sip leisurely on their full-grain alcohol. A few of them look up. It's the effect Chance has on people. Makes them look. Chance, dressed like an action hero from a jungle-adventure video game from the 1990s. None of them think we just ate and drank more than we can afford, that we have no right to be here. My hand rises nervously to flag down Tanuki's hostess, but I scratch the back of my neck instead.

I nearly choke on a gasp when Chance calls out to the woman with a wave.

"Later, Kayli."

The hostess looks up, flicks a lock of hair away from her eyes, pulls it behind her ear.

"Everything to your satisfaction, *Da Jie*?"

For a moment, I think she's looking right at me, but it can't be me she's addressing respectfully—not with Chance right beside me. When her eyes shift back to me again, I realize what she's really looking at: the takeout boxes in my hands.

Chance says, "Like a dream."

"We look forward to your next visit," the hostess says with a smile.

I don't know how Chance makes coin, but I always see Chance spend it. Meanwhile, I'm working multiple jobs and still always broke.

Maybe things will work out for the best.

As long as Chance is with me.

Chance, who knows what people are capable of.

SANCTUARY

WE'RE ON UPPER Beach Road when Chance motions a change of direction with a tilt of the head, and we turn into an alley.

It's been a while since I've been down one of these. Blinking fairy lights like luminescent creatures glow in the subtle darkness here. Destitute bodies huddle in the corners, where they the best of what they have.

The squatters are there because they've lost their right to remain. Expired visas, jobs terminated before term, or simply cut loose as non-essential waste. Here, they retreat into the belly of the beast that preys on them. They have no choice. A shuttle back to Earth is costly, and the bureaucratic process to obtain such a ticket is difficult to navigate. It's cheaper and easier to remain unhoused stationside.

I know, because I was one of them. This is where I would still be had I not started Club Contango. Had I not met Chance. Do I dare look my people in the eye? Or do I spare them the indignity?

Chance doesn't check to see if I'm following. Three doors down, there's a noodle house called Kah Heng that also serves some of the smoothest moonshine *baijiu,* rumored to be brewed from real rice.

"I can't do another round," I say. "And I'm about to run into penalty time at Junior."

"Relax. The Bun loves school dinners at Junior. Let her spend time with kids her own age instead of hoarding her all to yourself."

It hurts that Chance is right.

I hold up the takeout boxes. "But the dumplings will get soggy."

Chance looks sideways at me, then knocks on a random door to our right.

A woman opens the door to meet us. The room behind her smells of stuck-grease-trap and the stink of poor drainage she can't do anything about. The scent of artificial peach soap tries its best to mask the odor. I also smell something powdery, waxy, almost sweet. The woman in the doorway looks at me like we've met before, but it's the first time I'm seeing her.

"Took you long enough," she says.

Is she talking to me?

Chance answers: "Had to be careful not to lead customs officials here. They've been turning every stone since you moved from the last house."

The woman spits. She looks directly at me, then sideways in an odd way at Chance. Her face softens. "I thought you weren't coming this week."

"I got the kids dumplings."

"You should go on in and play with them. They need their friend."

"That's probably why I shouldn't," Chance says.

The woman folds her arms, but it's a hug she can't give, not a barrier. I still can't imagine why she keeps on looking at me as she talks to Chance. Maybe she's just wary of strangers, which I am.

"They don't get many friends."

"It's not right that they're stuck here."

"The parents keep trying, but it's never enough."

Chance blows hot breath. "I'll come again at the end of next week."

"I'll tell them tomorrow that you came after bedtime. They'll be upset, but at least they won't feel slighted."

Chance's jaw is tight when taking the box of leftovers from me and handing them to the woman. "Open the box so the skins don't get soggy," Chance tells her.

She accepts the gift and thanks us, then closes the door for the night.

On our way back out of the alley, I think I hear footsteps trailing us, but when I turn, no one's there.

The exit to Delphi Street comes quicker than expected, as if time and space had contracted. As if I'd been on autopilot from the time we left the strange house in the alley until now.

"Was that place what I think it is?"

"They're good people. Do whatever they can to help the separated kids of Freeport."

"Who's they?"

"Friends of mine. *Ours.* You know them. You get their newsletter."

I open my mouth to protest, but my cheeks redden as I remember the newsletters from an organization called Sanctuary to Spacefarers. How I'd deleted all the messages from them without ever bothering to read what was inside.

"The kids they help, are all their parents illegal?"

"Deported. Or returned to Earth 'voluntarily' to rejoin the work queues once more. Either they couldn't afford to take the kids with them, or they were afraid to—worried it might make it harder for them to return. The Sanctuary back there provides the kids with food and shelter until they're reunited."

"And if they're not?"

Chance's voice is hard. "That's why we keep the food coming, and better still, the funds. That's why we take every coin we can off the table, skin every Sparkler and Contractor dumb enough to believe that luck is on their side. That's why the club needs to get back up and running, Connie. Soon. Contango has always been more than just a game for us."

"All this time, you've been donating your share of the take?"

"Every coin," Chance says.

We walk the rest of the way to my flat in silence.

There's so much I still don't know about you, Chance.

When we finally get to my door, I have no recollection of how we got here.

"You're staring," Chance says.

Of all the things I feel for Chance, this feeling is new—this feeling of warmth and tenderness.

Chance is still talking. "I should visit more often. They make a show of not needing me, but I know the truth. They depend on me, on the coin Club Contango brings in."

"What do you mean, Club Contango? Are you donating more than your split?"

Chance smiles at me, wryly.

And that's when it hits me.

"The discrepancies in the accounts, the ones Stiff couldn't reconcile. That was you."

"Someone has to act, Connie. People claim to care, but they're too eager to let others do the dirty work for them. Everyone just assumes that someone else who's better off will help in their stead. Well, that buck stops here, with me."

Something is wrong with my face. It's hotter than it's ever felt before, and the heat is choking me and making it hard to think straight. I know what I want to say next, but it doesn't feel like I'm in control. It feels like I'm falling. Like I'm a shaken bottle, and Chance is toying with the cap.

My throat constricts, but somehow I find my voice. "I'm sorry. Please don't go."

Chance leaving is the last thing I want.

Chance doesn't say a thing. A stay of execution. Instead, Chance reaches past me and pushes open the door behind me, lets us stumble into the flat. Not a word is spoken between us, but already Chance's hands are on my hips. My pants find their way down my legs.

I willingly fall to the floor.

Chance bears down on me, looking deep into my eyes.

Yes, my eyes say. *Yes, now.*

I don't want to go another day not knowing *all* of Chance.

Chance knows what I need, knows every inch of my skin.

Chance is satisfied when I'm satisfied.

I fumble, start and stop again, bite back apologies about how long it's been. Too long. I'm ashamed to think how Chance's intuition regarding my body is greater than my own. But Chance is patient. Chance always has the time.

I stop what we're doing and pull myself off the floor, so that I can sit with my back against the wall. I don't dare lean on Chance's shoulder, afraid of where that will lead. We just sit next to each other, pinky fingers linked. I don't want to break this moment, but I must.

"I need to get Sticky."

"Of course you do."

Chance is already up and heading for the door.

"Chance…"

Chance turns, hand on the door handle, one foot already outside. Without a word, my other half is gone.

A shuttering breath leaves my body.

I don't want to be alone anymore.

PARTNER

BEFORE THERE WAS Freeport, before there was Alchemy, before there was Sticky, there was simply Hong and I. The purgatory in which Hong found me—during the time between my relatively stable job at Reliance Marine and the creation of Alchemy—changed the course of my life. Now, I'm sitting alone on the floor of a new flat on Delphi, owned by a murdered Hong, whose corpse has most likely been fed to a cycler on some unmarked ship headed to the far reaches of the Greater Belt.

It was during our time together that Hong and I found ourselves on a veranda that overlooked one of the last golf courses in the territory. When he took my call, he was headed there with some clients from his then-employer NationalRe. "Re" for "Reinsurance," a newly thriving, always-been-there-if-you-looked, branch of finance that was a true sign of the times. Hong sent his clients out to the course to hit balls, lie about their scores, sweat their custom-printed athleisure shirts through, strain a few back muscles, and loosen their tongues after a few bottles of synth.

Once his clients departed their first tee, he sent me a message:

<<Meet me in the clubhouse. I'll ping you the location.>>

Hong, who'd always hated golf, pretended not to hear his clients' later invitations from across the ninth green, where they begged him to come down from his spot atop the luxurious veranda and join them for their trip through the back nine.

After feigning an inability to hear for longer than his clients had patience, they finally gave up on him and carried on with their game.

"I'm setting up a new shop," he said to me. "Join me."

"In what capacity?"

"Any role you want. Want to be a trader with full authority? Fund manager? CFO? The job's yours. Whatever you do, I just need you by my side."

I looked across the green at the white buggy full of NationalRe clients now zipping away from us on a 12-volt battery.

"What about NationalRe?"

"Screw National, wheeling me out to impress new clients like this, but then putting me on mute during negotiations."

"I'm listening."

"You and I are cut from the same sheet, Connie."

Sheet of steel, Hong means. Galvanized, twice recycled.

Marine insurance was nothing more to Hong than a back door to the last minimally regulated sub-industry in the territory: ship-owning, now gone extra-terrestrial. And marine insurance was just an accidental career for me—after I landed on my face representing my parents' fledging union against Dash. It was supposed to be an in-between job until I got my guts together for another labor-rep case, or fled back to grad school, or moved on to something better.

But Hong changed everything for me, flipped the domino that would set me on this course for the rest of my life.

In the final free-years of the economy—the early 2070s—Hong was operating at Reliance like it was the 1970s. And he was on to something. Markets, if you wait long enough, run in cycles. It began with him letting me jockey his trades. All I had to do was talk the client through, put them on hold long enough for the sweat to bead, and watch for the tail shake. When I didn't fuck that up, Hong fenced off a quarter-million in fiat money for me, a mind-boggling amount even by today's standards.

"Play with it," he told me. "Take the old ladies out of the Strait. No cargo or route is off limits. Just don't lose our registry status. Show me what you have at the end of the quarter."

So, I traded on ship positions. I bought charters on rust buckets during low season, and held them until loading season. The freedom was intoxicating. Even commercial trainees had shorter leashes. I doubled the principal in two months, then lost it four months later.

"You're encouraging the trainee to grasp beyond her reach," said Hong's boss, old Teo.

Hong said to him, "If you train someone on a leash, you'll always be the one doing the thinking."

"She's on insurance. She needs to learn how to save a quarter-million, not lose it."

"You keep these kids in the dark, cut up their jobs until they can't tell what they're working on, then wonder why none of them shows any initiative."

Teo pickled his chin. "That one has a bad attitude."

And from that point on, the old bastard left me to Hong.

I always knew Reliance Marine and Investments had been founded by two cousins—four generations ago—but what I came to learn about the company later was this: Hong was a scion of the family whose name had fallen off the company's board sometime mid-century. Legend has it that Hong's grandfather, Chuan Boon Song, brought Reliance to the bourse in a shower of first-issue flips and congratulatory, fast-tracked loans that exploded in their face within the year, after it was found that the company was overvalued. Chuan Kin Hong was the last of his once-great family, the sugar and freight-trading Chuans. He was born with generations of dissipation, flatulent promises, and public failures on his shoulders, piling him into the ground.

"Why do you do this?" I asked him. I was leaning on the door to his office at Reliance when I did. It was nine in the evening, and the workspace was empty, everyone having left now that the compulsory in-person team session had ended. It was a mere ten minutes after old Teo had pointed at Kin Hong, inches from his face, and said he was never going to head another project at Reliance again—after the quarter's losses he caused.

Hong lifted his shoulders. "Fucker has a bad day at home and comes in to the office to piss around and feel like a man again. Who am I to deny him free therapy?"

"Teo is an asshole."

"Teo Meng Seng is a corporate savant. He was a beacon during our inter-Depression years."

"Sometimes, Hong, I can't tell if you're for real."

I've spent all of my time on Freeport thinking about Hong as nothing more than bad debt. And lately, as a complication, a dead body that I hope no one will trace back to Club Contango and to me. It's only now that the weight of it—of Hong and I, of the things he did for me almost in spite of himself—comes to roost. And suddenly, I feel like a terrible human. A terrible partner. A terrible everything. I couldn't even bring myself to hear the man out before he died. Couldn't bring myself to listen to the last thing he wanted to say to me.

<<You are not ready for this>>

PART 3

CALL

JAZ

DUE TO THE high decibel level and crowd density, pedestrian rush hour on Enterprise Square offers as much anonymity as you can hope to experience on Freeport. What Enterprise Square lacks in the prized greenery of Academy Avenue and River Valley, it makes up for with a bustling sea of humanity. It also has Uncle Goh's delicious soy milk and *youtiao* cart, just four paces from the tram stop. And I eat there all the time.

"Morning, Uncle," I say to Goh. "Look at this crowd, eh? Freeport's going to overtake SE3 soon."

Ah Goh doesn't look up from the hot dough crullers he's loading onto the cart's cooling rack with his bare hands.

I clear my throat.

"Sweetened, or unsweetened?" he asks. "Add almond powder? Two sticks?"

I raise my voice above the growing din. "The usual, please," I say with a smile.

"Don't know your usual."

Sigh through my teeth.

"Unsweetened *tauhui jui*, no almond powder. Hot. And two sticks."

Uncle Goh turns his back to me before I can make more small talk. He pours out the freshly steeped soy milk and pops two *youtiao* out of the toaster. The *youtiao* are fried every morning back at his dorm block, where the guard there is given free breakfast to not blow the whistle. They're lightly re-toasted to order. Ah Goh's real job—the employment that holds his contract—is late-night fry cook at the Oriental. He hands my order to me with equal parts disinterest and disdain.

"Don't cross to this side of the street if you too big for us."

The soy milk burns the tips of my fingers through the cup.

"I'm sorry, what?"

"Yesterday, you come here and I offer your usual. You looked at me like Ah Goh is small fly, shouldn't talk to you."

"So, you *do* know my usual." I try a smile, but I don't feel it working. *Not you too, Ah Goh.*

"Get lost."

"Uncle, come on. That wasn't me. I'm me. I would never ignore you."

But his turned back says enough, and if I know anything about Ah Goh—about the stubbornness it takes to survive stationside at his age, working two jobs and selling from his cart—I know better than to push him. I roll my shoulders, feel the bird dig claws into my skin. *Goh's an old man. He could be mistaken.*

I squint. The signs on the buildings are too bright, the holos on the ads are too loud, and together they give me a headache.

"Changing street corners now, are you? Don't walk away from me."

I turn to see someone I've never met, a young man whose face is already wrinkled from prolonged solar-exposure. A mining tech from the Belt.

"I bought stock in the Temai asset, just like you said. Bought two tranches because you were so damn convincing. I've owned it for three days, and it's already lost a fifth of its value."

"I didn't sell you—" I begin, but I cut myself short with a groan.

"You remember me now, don't you?"

I have to stay composed. "I've never met you in my life. You bought stock from a holo. A very lifelike, very intelligent, very me-like holo—but not me."

This explains Ah Goh's reaction. Someone who looked like me but was not me had made him feel small, had disrespected him. It was the holo-me. Not-Me.

The irate mining tech starts toward me. "You're every bit just as fake." Then he stops, remembering the multiple cameras and MAM street scans, particularly around Enterprise Square, that are watching us. Assaulting me is not worth the arrest record. "I hope whoever owns you scrapes you for everything you've got," he snaps.

Coming to Enterprise Square was a mistake. I sip my *tauhui jui* too soon and swallow a mouthful of second-degree burns. Shocked by the sudden pain, I fumble the cup until I drop it and it spills all over the ground. I deposit the empty cup into a trash bin and rush to the tram stop on the other side of the square, where I know Not-Me is waiting.

When she sees me, she steps toward me. "Hey! Did you found out who did it yet?" she says. "Who killed Hong?"

"Shoo!" I hiss.

"We're rude today."

"You know what's really rude? Ruining my life."

The tram's already at the stop when I arrive, and I jump on, head back to Delta Road as quick as I can. I could take my T&T calls from the flat, but if I stay in a tight space, my head will explode. It isn't a club day, and I've not been to the chandlery since I let Chance's professional in to do her job. I'm not looking forward to going back, but I know I have to as some point. It's best to keep up a routine, so as not to arouse suspicion. Besides, it's better than sticking around the square, trading potshots with Not-Me, the street-corner stock peddler who gives unwanted and questionable financial advice to commuters who try their best to ignore her.

STANDING OUTSIDE THE Hazy Halia, I can almost taste the spicy, syrupy comfort of a glass of ginger tea. I'll get it to go—hot, but not *too* hot this time—and sip it behind the counter at Lucky 48.

I won't go inside to order. I've had enough human—*and non-human*—interaction for the day.

Approaching the service window, something doesn't feel right. There's no line. A man in a dark suit leans against the door to the chandlery, looking like he just got off the shuttle this morning for a meeting. But he also wears the kind of all-terrain boots that Enforcers sport when on recreational leave to partially terraformed stations, not on strolls through a city. So, either this man is not used to life stationside, or he wakes up every morning hoping this day on Freeport will be his last.

I didn't want to do go inside, but now I must, so I enter the Halia and scan the counter for Zaqy, hoping to find him slicing ginger or building drinks. But Zaqy's nowhere to be found.

Yusof has his back to the coffee shop, working the bean grinder. I slide into my seat by the window and tap on the display panel atop the table to place my order. My head's halfway into my hands when I hear the door open. A whooshing exchange of air, and the deposit of a new arrival—the soft sigh of the vinyl seat in front of me as he sits. It's the man from outside. He has crows' feet at the corners of his eyes, and his curling black hair and black mustache are graying, but the effect isn't unattractive. He appears to be in his fifties, but he carries himself like someone much younger. He's a man making the best of a depreciating deal.

"Connie Lam." Both palms land on the table between us to make a heavy *thump* sound.

"Depends who's asking."

"It wasn't a question. I'm Inspector Jaz Singh. Mx. Lam, I'm here about a missing person—your partner, Chuan Kin Hong, also known in certain circles as King Hong. Do you have moment to discuss?"

"Do I have a choice?"

"Not really. Tell me, when was the last time you saw him?"

On my interface, the inspector's credentials packet hovers for four seconds before disappearing when I don't select to open it. It hovered long enough for me to see the badge.

This is happening faster than I thought it would, and I'm not prepared. Do I act sad or shocked to learn that Hong is missing? Do I play up my concern? Or act calm and cooperative? What did my grandmother's old movies say to do?

I have to lie.

"*Former* partner. I haven't seen him in months."

"How many months?"

"I don't know. A few. I'm not really sure."

A server bot delivers my usual drink to the table. I pull the glass toward me as if I mean to hug it.

"Humor me a guess."

I pretend to think for a moment.

"Ten months, give or take."

"What was the purpose of the meeting?"

"It was just a chance encounter on Enterprise Square. Didn't last long. We're not on the best of terms."

Should I have said that?

Singh stops to inspect my reaction, but quickly returns to his planned line of questioning. "When Hong closed Alchemy—the shop you helped him get off the ground as CFO—he left you holding the debt. Is this correct?"

I can only nod.

Inspector Singh scratches his mustache with a thumb.

"And how did you feel about that?"

"We go back enough years that I wasn't surprised. Irked, yes, but I got by, moved on."

Singh checks his file on me. "Moved on to the…Lucky 48 Chandlery, where you work two hours per week."

"What can I say? I work a mean two hours."

"The rest of the week, you work partial contract—temporary basis—at an insurance company, Thevar and Tann. You've discharged as much of the Alchemy debt as you can. Both jobs together qualify you for a full-contract visa under—" He queries his interface and clicks his tongue. "It appears that the contract compounding rule has been rescinded. Two years ago. And no one at MAM tapped you on the shoulder about this?"

Is he asking me or himself?

"Protection and Indemnity Club."

"I'll have the Commission correct the language in your file."

"I'd appreciate that."

"Thevar and Tan must be paying you well."

"Why do you say that?"

"Because sometime between ten months back and last week, you stopped trailing Kin Hong. No messages regarding the debt. And it doesn't sound like you pushed him much when you ran into him on the square."

I try to take sip from my drink, but it's already drained.

"It doesn't seem to bother you that he's missing," Singh says. "I find that interesting, but I suppose I'm still trying to understand the person I'm talking to." He leans back in his seat and observes.

Jaz speaks like a diplomat, looks the part, too. I can picture him, dapper in a much nicer suit, bespoke, not off the rack at the Freeport Commission's locker room.

I push the empty glass aside. "What is Jaz short for?"

"That's immaterial."

"Just trying to understand who I'm talking to."

"Let's stick to you answering *my* questions. Did you or did you not meet with your former partner Hong last week?"

"I did not."

Not alive anyway.

Still, I think about the message that had summoned me, which is probably still on Hong's cloud backup, even if I've deleted it from mine. Maybe Singh doesn't know a thing about it, and he's only feeding me leads, waiting for a bite. Or maybe he knows everything, and I'm only making myself look worse by lying.

"Who filed the missing persons report? If you don't mind me asking."

"His wife," he says.

"Hong has a wife?"

Jaz Singh takes note with a full lift of an eyebrow. "Bettina Awyong. I assumed you were familiar."

"Oh, Bettina. I'm sorry. I thought they were divorced."

"Separated, pending arrangements. Lawyers are still tallying asset accounts, trying to determine who brought what to the table. You know, rich-people problems."

And then it dawns on me.

"That's why she filed the report. She wants to make sure he didn't run off with any of her coin. Am I warm?"

Inspector Singh knows something. I can feel it. But it might not be about me. He looks tired—existentially tired—like he doesn't remember when life stopped being fun and became… whatever this is.

If Bettina filed the missing-persons report, it means she's seen Hong recently enough to know he was recently alive.

I make a show of drumming my hands on the table. I'm trying to appear casual, but for all I know, it just makes me look nervous.

"If that's all, Inspector, I've got to get to work now."

"At the chandlery? Or is it the insurance firm today? Tell me, Mx. Lam, if the jobs don't make the minimum contract hours between them, how is it that you make the minimum wallet balance to remain on Freeport—pay for your stakeholder bonds?"

Don't blink. Don't you fucking move.

He smiles and crosses his arms. "Something's not adding up."

"Pioneer spirit, Inspector. I get knocked down, but I get back up again."

I do my best to stand up naturally, then excuse myself from the table and head for the exit, the sound of my heartbeat thumping in my ears the entire way.

I'm back outside on the street when it finally sinks in: I closed the door on explaining my way out of this the moment I let Chance 'take care of it.'

What the hell am I going to do now?

DANCE

TRACE IS HUDDLED with her tablet on the floor behind the chandlery's counter when I arrive. She sees me and throws up the peace sign with her fingers.

"I'm not here," she says.

"That makes two of us."

I crumble to the floor beside her, and pull my knees up to my chin, so that I can hug my legs like I once did when I was Trace's age. I contemplate joining her for a mind-numbing hour or two or three of media streaming, but before I can slink further into myself, she surprises me with a tepid take-out cup of tea. She takes a sip of an identical cup in her other hand.

"Yusof dropped these off for us. Cheers. He said to tell you that Vis is waiting for your response."

Shit. I never signed the petition, did I?

"Okay. I'll ping Vis in a moment."

Trace wrinkles her nose.

There's something else.

"What is it, Trace?"

"Is it that obvious? Well, see, I was kind of hoping you'd visit her in person, and while you're at it, snag a package for me."

She tries to smile through a guilty-looking wince.

"To HaboHub? Trace, that's all the way across the dome. I don't have time for that. I have to log on to T&T soon, or I won't clock minimum hours."

The hint of a pout starts to form on Trace's lips. "Please? The new *Forever Rangers* season is about to drop and the pickup can't wait past today."

"*Forever Rangers* streams on ViewBucket. You can watch it when you get back."

"But I need to livestream my reaction to it. Any streamer who matters catches the drop. If I miss it, I might as well close my stream channel and go back to working this crappy job." She gestures to the empty counter we're hiding behind.

I owe Vis a visit anyway. I guess it wouldn't hurt to do Trace a favor while I'm out.

THE HABOHUB LOGISTICS depot is a forty-minute tram ride from Lower Beach Road, which in Freeport-terms, may as well be off-station. The depot itself is a colorless network of connected warehouses.

I flash Lucky 48's member token, and the security bots wave me to a collection point. The approach tunnel has windows on both sides that look down at the sorting and stacking floor— or what Vis calls the "parking lot from Hell."

I can see Vis from here. She's down on the floor, moving her arms in circular motions as she strafes side to side, high-stepping as she does so. It's a ridiculous little dance, something more akin to aerobics than the latest craze, but Vis looks good doing it.

When Habo opened their chain-logistics hub on Freeport, it was fully automated. But as it turns out, hiring human labor is actually cheaper than maintaining top-grade intelligent machinery. So, HaboHub engaged Red Unicorn to upgrade their employee performance programs via the development of a gamified workplace app. The app Red Unicorn delivered is called Bestie, an augmented-reality wonderland where job performance targets are represented by giant gold coins, hopping mushrooms, and chonky cats, amongst other things, all mapped onto the Contractor's interface.

With Bestie, Contractors use dancelike movements to relay complex commands to the heavy machinery throughout the depot. The dance aspect adds to the gamified experience and has the added benefit of keeping employed Contractors in shape. They shuffle, wave, and hop for eight hours per day.

HaboHub and a Circle food factory were the first adopters of Bestie on Freeport, but it's slowly gaining traction on high-volume asset-class stations all across the Greater Belt. Now, younger Contractors even use it to gamify their various side hustles. But a ride's only fun if you know you can get off, and there is no logging off the custom Bestie platform tailored for Habo employees. Here, the log-off option is grayed out, and if you try to clock out early, a dialogue box opens in your interface and vibrates angrily.

<<You do not have enough credits to end shift.>>

At the end of a your work day, all you're fit for is a bar stool in a dark tavern along the boardwalk, where you wait for the Loop to hit. When it does, you're dancing again.

Just dance.

Because you can't run.

Vis was supposed to be the smart one. Her background is in legal advocacy, and she once had some success with it, but even she couldn't fight the tide of mono-contracts and non-negotiable terms. Now she's trapped in a dance-dance nightmare.

Vis and I used to be tight. But some people, whether they know it or not, just bring out the worst in each other. She disdains my indulgences, my vices—always has—and was never afraid to be brutally honest with me whenever I tried to bullshit my way out of her criticisms. But she just doesn't understand. I don't just enjoy the carefree frenzy of Zetta and her set, I crave it. I want to be draped over the Writer's Bar, or placing bets at the club with abandon. I need it. Without it, I feel like I can't breathe.

I tried to keep what we once had by staying away, giving Vis her space. It began with changing my schedule so we wouldn't be at the hostel at the same time, and I made it a point to stop talking about Hong and his schemes with her, stop talking about anything that mattered. But none of that worked, so Sticky and I moved out one afternoon, in the middle of Vis's shift, so I wouldn't have to face her. But moving out and being alone—so alone in the hours without Sticky around—only made things worse for me.

Until I met Chance.

I didn't see Vis again until Bel sent her over to Club Contango one night, because Vis had been talking about growing the Hands' strike fund, and Bel knew a place where Vis could make that happen. Bel still claims to this day that she did not know about my history with Vis prior to sending her Contango's way, and that she would never have done so if she did. Still to this day, I don't believe her.

Vis looks up from her spot on the warehouse floor, and I wave a three-finger salute to greet her. I scratch at the side of my face as I bring my hand down, fully expecting Vis to shoot me the bird, but she doesn't. She lifts a corner of her lip, look-ing almost pleased to see me. She must be too tired to pretend otherwise.

Vis points to the old-fashioned intercom on the wall next to me, because non-essential interface use is blocked on the floor.

I retrieve the intercom phone from its cradle and put it to my ear. Vis is on the other end.

"Didn't think you remembered where to find me," she says.

"I came to see how you're doing."

I cringe. Wrong answer.

"Don't patronize me, Connie."

"I signed the petition."

"Lucky me. Took you long enough."

"I'll collect a few more on the strip if you can wait."

"From your beautiful Sparkler friends? They'll just blow us a pity kiss, then stream us catching it for bubbles on Sociable. We're better off without them."

"Dammit, Vis. I'm sorry things went this way for you, but I'm trying my best here. Would you rather I not try?"

"You're not sorry. I see you at Club Contango, acting like someone I don't know—don't *want* to know. Someone who swaggers about, owns the room, lays down the rules—"

It sounds like Vis is describing Chance, not me.

She can't be describing me.

It doesn't make sense.

IN MY MIND, we're back in our dorm room at the MAM re-settlement hostel. The building has capacity to house nine hundred Contractors, fresh off the shuttle on Freeport. Our room sleeps eighty. The room smells of stale body gases, but feels like hope and new beginnings, like nothing will ever go wrong again now that Earth is finally behind us.

I have the corner bunk, right by the window, because Sticky is still a toddler and too young to be accommodated separately in the kids' dorm, and the other adults in my sleeping quarters are wary of a crying baby in the night. Vis's bunk is across from mine. As the corner bunk, I have an unobstructed view of the room's only window.

From my bunk, I often stared out the dorm window, down through the glass roof of the Embarkment to the giant crystal chandelier, and dreamed. I would hold up my thumb to gauge the distance, and the chandelier would disappear behind the nail. Then I would gaze at the shimmer of the Tanuki's brass railing, twinkling like a line of golden light. It's what I saw every evening while sitting with Sticky, the two of us blowing on hot cups of rehydrated noodles in our bunk. It's where I fell in love with Freeport, fell in love with all its glittering promise.

"I'D RETURN TO our carefree time at the hostel if I could," I tell Vis. "But what you did to me—what you're still doing —making me feel sorry for my weaknesses… I don't know how to live with that."

"I'm just speaking the truth. It's a shame you can't handle it."

At what point do I stop blaming her—do I stop wishing she loved me the way I wanted her to? I can't expect that of her, just like my parents shouldn't have expected something else of me.

"Maybe you're right," I say. "Maybe I'll never figure out what I'm missing. But I'm here now, and if you need me to get you out of this Habo trap and into something better, I'll make that call. Jerry owes me one."

"Jerry? That shady friend of yours? You really think that's going to make up for the way you just left?"

"I didn't leave, Vis. I just…drifted."

Vis laughs. "You're real smooth now, you know that? Your new friends are teaching you well. Anyway, I don't want out of here, not yet at least. I need to stick around to help change things from the inside. The Hands have a few ideas to force Habo to pay attention. First Commission-led safety inspection of Bestie is coming, and Habo's jittery."

"Should you even be saying this on the intercom?"

"You just worry about yourself. You're good at that."

"I'm here if you need me."

"Running away has always been your answer to everything. Run along, Connie. One day you'll turn around and find you're running alone."

Vis hangs up, and I watch her resume her dance.

I wish I had the courage to tell her she's wrong about me— that I haven't stopped running, and already I'm alone.

"HUNGER PUSHES US," Walter Woo said. "Hunger makes us get off our asses and *get it done*. Achieve more than we thought possible. It helps us push past those sorry excuses we tell our- selves every morning. Helps us become more than we thought capable. Hunger helps us become exceptional."

"Take me, for example. What am I paid to do? Represent the company. I could do that from 8 a.m. to 7 p.m. and go home. I don't *have* to be here, but I *hunger* for the opportunity. And you know what? At the end of this, maybe old man Dash will take me out to dinner and slap me on the back, congratulate me. Or maybe he won't. But what matters is I've shown him my worth. I'm breaking the walls and the distance between the job, the employer, and myself. Isn't that want you labor fighters are on about? *This* is how you break alienation. A hundred years ago, they told you that greed is good, but they were wrong. Greed needs you to *want* more, when really what you should be feeling is *fear*. Fear that what you have today may not be yours tomorrow. Unless you *bring it*. It's fundamental. Feed the hunger. Show us what you can do."

I was there at the Imperial, acting in defense of my parents, when Walter Woo gave that persuasive speech, made his passionate case for Dash's exploitative performance rules in front of the crowd of brave port workers. I was supposed to be their rep, their voice. But really, I saw Walter's success, and I wanted to be him.

This business with Vis and HaboHub and the Hands is all just more of the same—the Dash case all over again.

And I'm the common denominator.

DELIGHT

IT'S MONDAY. A club day. And tonight, the club *must* collect. Unfortunately for me, I'm the one on the opposite side of the table this evening, awkwardly saying no to players who demand margin we can't give. Club attendance is a third of its usual size, but for all my complaining about club nights, I actually prefer it when players show up. The club makes more money that way.

"We've been buying in for months, Con," says one player. "Some of us years."

"What about benefits for regulars?" another says. "Like rolling this over into next month?"

"Rolling is what I've *been* doing," I say. "You're too deep in margin. I can't roll it anymore."

Vis pipes in: "Club's had its wins, Connie. Time to pay it back." Her cold stare and taught jaw tells me that covering her margin is the difference between seeing her again and not.

I press my fingers to my throbbing temples and think. How do I explain that those winnings are gone? Locked away in stakeholder bonds for Sticky's future, or donated to the Sanctuary and the stranded kids of Freeport. How do I explain that Contango is barely surviving?

I take a step closer to Vis and whisper my response in her ear, so the others don't hear.

"I'm not liquid, Vis. I haven't heard from Jerry in a while. Licensing royalties don't get paid until Red Unicorn's next accounting year."

Vis quickly pulls her face away from mine and takes a firm step back. She has long gone to great lengths to avoid even the prospect of physical contact with me. Everyone can see it.

"I don't believe you. Your image is everywhere."

"Believe what you want, but the payout from the model is, like, nothing and three peanuts."

Tell her about the stakeholder bonds.

Vis sneers. "Should I wait to talk to Chance?"

Chance? Why would she need to talk to Chance? *I* started Club Contango, and *I* called it Boiler Room. Vis is *my* oldest friend on Freeport. Why would she want Chance to get between that—between us?

That's when I realize… *Where is Chance?*

I've been on my own for days now, the longest I've been without Chance since Chance first came into my life. This isn't like the times when Chance showed up late for club night or failed to show for a party. This is a protracted disappearance. But the funny thing is, without Chance at my hip, I feel lighter than I have in a while.

JUMPING OFF THE tram at the Great Eastern, I dip my head and peer through the glass at the bar. Ming's wearily tossing shakers in the air. Juggling them has become second nature for him, the same way he once hoped booking acting jobs would be. We both came to Freeport with hopes of starting again on the frontier, and look at us now. He catches the shaker and empties it into two ready glasses. Pushes it across the bar to the pixelated faces of a llama and a mousedeer, but I'm looking for a weepy cat. While it's true that Sparklers change their mask displays all the time—even Zetta—Ming doing the mixing behind the bar means she's not inside, so I stay on the boardwalk and keep walking.

I find Zetta sitting on the antique grand piano in the lounge of the Banyan Tree Hotel and Residences, the first seven-star resort on Freeport. Her legs dangle off the side while Roar plays a rich, old-timey tune that I know I've heard somewhere. She's wearing her privacy shade, but the weepy cat mask is turned off so that I can see her real face.

The walls of the lobby are padded with woven jute and shielded by panels of polished bamboo. The effect is a muted, woolly stupor, like being ensconced in a large and very luxuriant seed pod. The tinkling of the piano keys rises up toward the decorative reeds that hang from the ceiling like a mobile, then sinks, losing itself in the husk.

Zetta looks in my direction, then slithers off the piano.

I think she sees me, might even be coming over to greet me, but instead, she seats herself on the piano bench beside Roar and starts tapping a discordant E-flat with her pinky finger. If it irritates Roar, he doesn't say.

"Are we out of tomatoes here, too?" she purrs at me.

Her coldness to me comes as a shock, until I remember that nothing is permanent to Sparklers. Certainly not friendships with lowly Contractors like myself.

If Zetta doesn't want to be friends today, fine.

"I'm not here on a delivery. I came for some Delight."

Zetta removes her little finger from the piano key.

"Why, I thought you'd never ask, darling." She looks to Roar. "See now, you keep saying she's a bore, but I told you, Connie Lam isn't a bore, she just hasn't discovered yet who she really is. And I was right, wasn't I?" She looks back to me with a grin. "Don't think I never noticed those wistful looks dripping off you when we streamed. If it's Delight you want, darling, Ming can hook you up with our regular guy at the Great Eastern. You needn't come here again."

"I don't want Ming's top-shelf stuff. I want the badly edited stuff you were complaining about the other day." I hold a straight face, keep my hands and body still.

If I was just passing entertainment to Zetta before, I'm that no longer. I have her attention now.

"That stuff nearly fried my brain, darling. Why in the world would you want—?"

"Just tell me who to ask, Zetta. I'll get it myself."

She drapes an arm around Roar and pats his back.

"I guess we all got you wrong, Connie." She considers me in silence. "W— is the host at Arcadia. They will fix you up. But be warned, if you don't control the dose, you'll get more than just a bad headache." Her eyes narrow, and she smiles. "But I have a feeling this dose won't be for you, will it? I pity the poor soul you have in mind."

Roar finishes the tune with a flourish, and then without stopping, starts over again from the top. Where have I heard this song before?

Zetta thinks we're done here, but I have one more matter to discuss. The steadiness in my voice surprises me. "You always told me to just ask if the club ever needs more coin. So, here I am, asking. I wouldn't be doing this if the situation weren't dire."

Zetta blinks, then laughs. Continues to laugh as her privacy shade darkens and a weepy cat flickers to life atop her face, laugh-crying along with her. Zetta lifts a fist to one of the cartoon eyes and pretends to wipe away the falling tears of joy.

"Oh, Connie, you really are a riot. But truly, you must be joking." She turns to Roar. "Apparently, I'm giving to charity cases now." The two share a laugh

"But you said—"

"Said what, darling? That I'd give you coin to help keep your little club afloat? Honestly, dear, does that sound like something I'd say?"

"But, you're the dragon…"

"The dragon?" Zetta looks at Roar, and Roar looks at Zetta, and together they descend into uproarious, mocking laughter.

If Zetta says anything else, I don't hear it over the rush of wings flapping at the corner of my eye. When I look up again, I see Zetta's real face staring back at me once more. Her expression is humorless, and her lips are pursed as if to say,

All right, Connie dear, I won't laugh at you—not this time, anyway—because I feel bad that you thought we were friends.

The weepy cat mask reappears over her face.

My head pounding, I excuse myself without a word. Behind me, Roar doubles down harder on the piano, the tune louder now and somehow more rich.

Back outside on the strip, I receive a ping to my interface, and I blink to pull up the urgent message.

It's from Stiff's broker, the one who fences for anyone who needs to hide their ID and status until their coin balance and shareholder portfolio reaches a certain threshold.

> <<*Read your messages. MAM has revised the minimum investment for stakeholder bonds, effective in five days. We need to increase your holdings by twenty-two percent or we risk losing the pot. From what I'm hearing about you, that shouldn't be a problem. Ping me when you've made the transfer. Five days, Connie.*>>

I remember now.

"As Time Goes By."

That's the song Roar was playing. From that old film about a chance meeting in a bar. What was it called again? *Casablanca?*

If Zetta didn't float the club a year ago, then who did?

Who was the dragon, really?

EXTERNALIZE

MESSAWAY™ EXTRACTOR IS in the bucket. The pungent odor burns my throat going down as I float on the last wisps of the Loop I took to get high. I can feel the drug's effects leaving me, and when they do, I find myself on my hands and knees in a beautiful apartment in River Valley. The shelves have been emptied, and there is broken glass on the floor.

I OPEN MY eyes and pull my head off the counter at Lucky 48. My hands tremble as I fumble to start the coffee machine. Gripping the counter, I reach for something stuck to the underside and drop it into my pocket.

STICKY WAS A surprise.

I wasn't against bringing a child into my life, I just never thought that it would actually happen. When it did, it was in the most embarrassingly old-fashioned way possible—a wild but forgettable one-night stand after a lucky streak on some bets. An encounter I didn't think of again. Until three months later. Everyone has their own considerations to weigh in moments like those. We tried for a while to be a family, but it was like a compromise between two strangers. Eventually, it was just Sticky and me once more.

The real surprise wasn't Sticky, though. It was how much coin it cost just to keep Sticky alive, especially after my earnings took a hit, owed to less hours worked while being pregnant and a new mom. You can't neglect a baby just because you have a work deadline. It didn't take long for me to start slipping into the red, and fast. This despite working harder than I ever had before. Reliance Marine kept me on as a temp for the odd cover while Hong and I worked to get Alchemy off the ground. In the evenings, I hustled bonds and tech stocks at a club in my neighborhood while nervously watching Sticky on the baby cam. The length of my shift depended on Sticky going down to sleep at a reasonable hour, and whether or not she stayed asleep once she did.

But even after all that, I still needed more coin to survive.

Going to my parents for help—even if it meant them just watching Sticky so I could work longer hours—was not a long-term option, especially after I had failed them. "Generations progress upwards, not drift downwards," they reminded me. I paid their township fees on the small flat in SE3, bought their groceries, and kept my problems to myself, but my mom told her friends they let me off easy, so Sticky could have extras.

I didn't just need more coin. I needed magic.

"No," Jerry said, "What you need is to work smart."

"How? I'm Reliance's number-one go-to when they have absolutely no one else they can fall on. I'm a director for Alchemy. I'm the hustler at the corner booth of your local club."

I was exhausted, with nothing left to give.

People walked past us with trays of *murtabak*.

Jerry shifted in his seat and fenced out the world with his back. "You're gonna want to create something that will make money for you, without having to run it yourself, at your opportunity cost."

"Now you that mention it, I'd very much like a bot to do all of my work for me. Thanks for the advice."

"Think bigger. Not a bot. *You.* Another you."

If I could go back to any point in my life and hit <<*Undo*>>, I'd go back to that day beneath the dusty ceiling fan of Al-Azhar, where I stirred a Milo Dinosaur and looked across the table at Jerry, listened while he told me to "think bigger."

"What you need to do is to build a replicable model of what you already do so well—the trading and the selling— and externalize what you would do more of, if you had the time. Make that do the work for you. License it and watch your returns skyrocket."

I pulled the straw out of the drink and licked the chocolate slush off the end. Dip. Lick. Dip again. It's my drink. I can do what I want.

"For someone else? I'm not going to franchise my skill set, if that's what you mean by license. That's one big windfall at best, and then what? No one ever needs the real me again. Then it's back to irrelevance and underemployment for the rest of my life."

Jerry held up a saucer, emptied of its curry, and tapped the side for a refill. "Hear me out at least."

Under the table, he was shaking one leg, and the undissolved powder on the surface of my drink was vibrating along with his flimsy tablet on the table between us. The screen showed a consent form to enable the project.

That's when I should have dumped my drink onto Jerry's head, pushed back from the table, and stormed the hell out of there—just kept walking until Jerry was an unfortunate memory.

That's what I should have done.

Instead, I stirred my Milo Dinosaur and thought about how we were meeting here at Al-Azhar because it's twenty feet from my apartment, where Sticky was sleeping and possibly starting to wake.

"Tell me more," I said.

By the end of Jerry's spiel, I was nodding along like the idiot I was, and without thinking, I eventually agreed to it all.

I tapped <<*Acknowledge and Consent.*>>

I did this because while Jerry was talking, my mind once again wandered back to the conference room at the Imperial Resort and Conference Center, where I remembered Walter Woo's masterfully contorted logic.

Thanks to Woo's speech, Dash successfully claimed that all matters of employee welfare—even renumeration—were no longer the firm's concern. According to them, Dash only provided the premises upon which the work was done, and the courts agreed.

Back at Al-Azhar, all I saw was Jerry giving me the chance to be a winner like Woo. *You have the skill, Connie. I've seen it. Externalize it. Sell it.* Perfect sales pitch, trained on my ego. My chance to show that I had it in me all along. All I needed was the coin. How could I say no to that? How could I continue to accept being a failure?

Within days, I had written up a comprehensive walkthrough on trading and selling financial instruments, adaptable for stock, NFTs, real estate—you name it—and gave it to Jerry. Those lessons were then fed into an AI wireframe, along with sample scripts and simulated reaction scenarios. Somewhere along the line, I also agreed to record my 3D image and my voice for "extra training material."

"This way, we can spare you another session," Jerry had explained. "I won't have to dig it out of you later."

I GULP THE last of my coffee, then reach in my pocket and pull out the sliverfilm. I remember the way it flew from Zetta's soft fingers—over the antique piano at the Great Eastern—to my own. A butterfly on wings of Delight. I weigh its lightness in my hand, finger the protective plastic backing.

I'm tempted to peel the protective backing off and stick the bio-permeable sliverfilm to my temple.

One track can't hurt.

Can't hurt more than the pain I already feel.

But I don't.

I slip the sliverfilm back into my pocket.

EX

SOMETHING ISN'T RIGHT, and I know it the moment the door to my flat flashes <<*Disengaged.*>> then <<*Welcome back.*>> Inside, the AC is set to a comfortable twenty degrees Celsius. Five degrees below my preset.

A strange woman is sitting at the kitchen counter when I enter, squishing my best bagged tea against the side of my favorite college mug with the stem of a dinner spoon because I don't have a teaspoon. She looks to be about eight years older than me, or a young-looking ten. She occupies my space like it's only mine because she has no interest in claiming it—an attitude that only comes from being sheltered your whole life, from never being told no, or from always being told no and having to fight extra hard for everything you ever got. My bet is on the former. She's a Settler dressed like a wealthy person's idea of a Contractor on their day off—Boho meets distressed factory chic, printed to design.

"Hello, I'm the new NannyNow minder," she says with a professional smile. "So very pleased to meet you. Where is the little angel? Can I meet her?"

"I'm sorry, I don't remember making an appointment."

"Am I early? The building superintendent let me in after I explained the situation. 'No loitering,' I was told."

"Mind if I have a look at your NannyNow confirmation?"

She shows it to me, and according to my interface, it's legit.

I mirror her smile. "I'll be picking the small human up in an hour, and then she's all yours. We don't have many snacks, but whatever's there is yours. Stream anything you like. I'm going to hop in the shower."

I'm lying, of course. I did not book an overpriced nanny and then just forget about it.

In the bathroom, I reach into the back of the medicine cabinet and take out a taser I keep stashed there for emergencies. It's a toy compared to the energy weapons the Enforcers carry, but it's good for a nasty jolt—enough to disable an intruder just long enough for me to escape. I hide the taser in my back pocket, wash my face, and step back outside, ready to do some damage, if need be.

The nanny is watching a projection of Sticky when I return.

"Is this her?" she asks of the looping image. "She's adorable."

I head to the fridge and pretend to rummage through its contents for a cold drink that I know isn't there.

"Thank you," I say. "And doesn't she know it."

I blink to turn off the projection.

"You said the super let you in?" I say over my shoulder, still pretending to look through the fridge.

"Uh-huh."

"That's funny," I say. "This building doesn't have a super."

Immediately, I can sense the woman rise from her seat, then slowly make her way toward me.

"Really?" she says. "I could have sworn that's what the man said—that he was the super. Goodness, that's unsafe. Just letting anyone inside like that. Someone dangerous could get in."

She's right next to me now.

Time to act.

Doing my best action hero impression, I throw open the door of the chiller with such force that it slams the side of the woman's face and cracks one of her impossibly perfect cheekbones. She reels backward and turns at the last moment to fall facedown upon the counter. I charge at her and press the prongs of the taser to small of her back.

"Don't move!"

"Stop! Stop! I surrender! I swear!"

"Sorry, Bettina. But I've had enough with the home invasions this week."

Bettina Awyong raises both hands, more as a favor to me than out of any real fear.

"This time it's only me. Next time you might not be so lucky."

"I wouldn't exactly call myself lucky now."

"May I?" She motions her intention to turn around and face me, which I allow. "That little stunt of yours better not leave me with any deep-tissue damage." She massages the sides of her mouth. "I have very good lawyers."

I take a step back, but keep the taser held out in front of me as a warning for Bettina not to approach. "What do you want with me?"

"I didn't come to Freeport for *you*. I came to collect *him*. Or whatever's left of him. I couldn't miss the parting shot of having Hong in *my* custody for once."

Bettina knows Hong is dead?

"You're not going to find Hong in my flat, that's for sure."

"That's funny, because I got this address from Hong's portfolio. It's listed in his name. Who lives here, anyway? Just you and the girl?" She runs a gold-ringed finger along the edge of the dynamic display on the wall. The image on display is of Sticky and Chance at a local cat café called Mews.

"And Chance," I say.

"Who is Chance?"

When I look at the picture again, Chance is no longer there. The picture is now of Sticky and me.

But I thought Chance took her to Mews?

"We run a club together."

With pursed lips, Bettina considers the sad state of my appearance. She parts her lips with a soft breath. "Hong did not simply *disappear*. I want to know who did it—who killed him—and I'm going to find out."

"Well, if you think that I—"

"You're not off my list of suspects. Not yet, anyway."

"The trench of bad debt he left me with would be a solid motive for revenge, I agree, but honestly, I haven't seen your husband in months."

Bettina swats my explanation from the sky. "Save the alibi for Inspector Singh, my dear. I have no use for it. All I know is Hong had an appointment with my lawyers that he had no reason to miss—that you *wouldn't* miss. Unless, of course, he were dead. I'll pay, Connie. I know that coin still talks. I'll pay for any useful information you can provide. Hong was working on a number of things when he disappeared, things that had too many eyes on them. Eyes that I don't need on me."

"Whose eyes? If I'm going to help you, I need to know."

"Your best mate Jerry, for one. All these years, and he still can't let go the fact that it wasn't Hong who snuffed his career—it was his own foolish actions. And then there's the man they call Wengzai. That devil has had his eye on Hong's business and investments for longer than Kin and I had been married."

My head is light. I feel the brush of a wing against my hair, and I put my face in my hands to buy a second. I can see my feet through my fingers.

Am I wearing Chance's boots?

"Hong only did the dirty work for Reliance. Jerry should know that. And you made it clear to Hong that you had your own arrangements." She releases a small sigh, and suddenly it shows, the weariness and age in her voice, in her eyes, in her face. "I don't get my settlement until his case is resolved. The Commission's locked everything up."

I reach into the fridge and grab two juice boxes meant for Sticky, then hand one to Bettina.

She looks at the juice box and frowns. "From concentrate? Do you really expect me to drink this?"

I shrug.

"Have any Delight?"

"No."

Bettina sets the unopened juice box down upon the counter, refusing to partake. Meanwhile, I'm nearly finished with mine.

"You're not much of a CFO, are you?" she says. "I dipped into Alchemy's books. Sloppy work, my dear. All those missing funds."

"Are you accusing me of skimming? Because that's rich coming from you."

"I have no idea what you mean."

"You know exactly what I mean. Your husband's shady business practices are why I can never go back to Earth."

Bettina narrows her eyes. "Nice try, Connie. But you signed off on the Alchemy assets he wanted to flip. He knew you wouldn't question him. That's on you."

I shake my head. "That doesn't make sense. Alchemy has no assets. It's all smoke and mirrors."

"Then why did he tell me, just days before he disappeared, that he needed to see *you*. Needed to have *you* sign more documents before he could pay *me* my share of *our* money? That was always his favorite excuse: 'I need to talk to Connie first.' That or 'Red Unicorn owns everything I have, Bettina.'"

"Because Hong's an operator, Bettina. You know that. Listen, I've been trying to make sense of it myself. My advice is to just sit tight for a while. I'll let you know more as soon as I find out."

"I *am* sitting tight, Connie. But I'm also financially tight, which means I can't wait around much longer. I couldn't leave my townhouse today without a collector's goon tailing me. Don't worry, I lost him on the way here. The sooner this is sorted, the sooner I can get my money and get the hell off this silly little rock for good."

"Hong once told me you're on the board of Circle Finance."

"Yes. So?"

"Circle's got investor coin locked up that they won't pay out. Hong's got assets you can't touch. You're between two rocks. I wonder what Inspector Singh would make of *that* as motive."

Bettina snaps her fingers. "You're straying, Connie. Pay attention."

"Hong didn't put himself in line for Red Unicorn stock, did he? If he had, it would have showed on his portfolio this month."

"Again, *you're* the CFO. I'm just the difficult wife."

"Not with Alchemy, I mean. On his own."

Because if he had gone in on Red Unicorn, he would have bet big. Big enough for voting shares and a contact detail to stakeholder management. If I can find out who's behind Red Unicorn, behind the satyr avatar, I might find out if Bettina's onto something here. Maybe Hong's death does have something to do with Red Unicorn, or even Circle Finance.

"If he did, I never saw the receipts."

Bettina pulls herself together, beginning with a cracking of fingers and a straightening of her back. She surveys my little flat that is actually Hong's until a shudder runs through. She's had enough of this place, and enough of me.

"I want to know every little detail, Connie. Or else."

She can talk tough, but there's a quiver at the corner of her lip that can't be from a face lift injury. Bettina Awyong and I are in the same boat. I never imagined things would pan out this way, but I'll count my blessings when I get them.

After Bettina leaves, I think back to what Hong had once said about her: "Bettina is untouchable. That woman can walk through a swamp and come out clean. She has her hands in everything. She pulls all the strings."

ARCADIA

FREEPORT WAS MEANT to be a city without visible poverty, without the underemployed shambling between audience booths or slumped in narrow pathways and other cracks in the rotting infrastructure, like they did back on Earth. It was meant to be free of the empty office towers, washed up following the Second Great Depression, and the underground communities that haunted an Administration that had long ago given up on them. Freeport was where the one percent of the one percent could begin again, this time without any of the unwelcome feelings.

Year One on Freeport was a soft-launch year for the city, before the Delta and Pioneer Ring builds were completed. During this time, the luxury apartments on Beach Road served as both permanent residents for Settlers and temporary residences for early Contractors. For the only time in Freeport's short history, the two classes used the same facilities, went to the same restaurants, and lived on the same floors.

Freeport could have learned from that time how to become a kinder, more egalitarian society. But once Delta and Pioneer Ring were completed in Year Two, the Freeport Commission promptly relocated the Contractors out of Beach Road and into their new low-income complexes, much to the relief of the Settlers.

The second resettlement ship sent up the spouses and children of Settlers and some Contractors. Many of those Settler scions stayed and grew into the Sparklers you see today. Bright young stars that lit the dark sky above sheltered Freeport and defined its freewheeling culture. Freewheeling as long as their coin balance or NET residuals met Settler minimums, or if you were an L3 Contractor—which meant you had rare skills, listed and reassessed each quarter by MAM.

Roles in engineering and environment management were not guaranteed stays beyond two quarters. The Settlers and Sparklers hungered for a life that would make Earth nothing but a bad dream. So chefs and jazz musicians were more likely than engineers and environment managers to have their Contractor status renewed. Even then, these jobs were highly competitive.

The third resettlement ship, penultimate to the one that Vis and I came in on, brought the dreamers and the entrepreneurs. Among them was former nightclub owner Suziebaby, then sixty-five years young and newly divorced. Baby found success by offering Freeport the one vice it was still missing at the time—a proper casino. Or as the Sparklers called it, "a decent place to get down." Suziebaby called her new establishment Arcadia.

The moment Arcadia's coat-tailed greeters first swung open those heavy, gold-plated doors to reveal to the party-starved masses the faux ebony-paneled interior, with geometric gold etching in the Neo-Deco style, you could almost feel the breeze from the Settlers and Sparklers of Freeport letting down their collective hair, ready to party away the station's endless, neon-soaked night.

Arcadia is on the upper three floors of a large prefab unit originally intended for a high-end shopping experience and a luxury townhouse. It's an older model, which is what the third ship of Settlers were given to work with, and the ground floor is sealed off from the club. But it holds up well, and has its own airlocks to keep out unexpected dangers and expected bullshit. It's handsome and has a distinguished presence about it. Not unlike Suziebaby herself. Arcadia sits along the same kilometer of Upper Beach Road as the MAM Resettlement Hostel, where Vis and I once shared the corner of a dorm. It's an odd location today, but when Suziebaby paid down the deposit for the long-term lease on the four-floor walk-up, the terraced row was still an unknown possibility.

The greeter working the front doors of the Arcadia this evening is a retired Enforcer named Shem. Shem left the Enforcers after the minimum two tours, but they still workout like its beachhead days and the discovery of hostile alien life remains a strong possibility.

Shem has had a thing against me since we first crossed paths at the MAM hostel four years ago. And not because I've been an ass to them. Quite the opposite. What I did was walk in on "tough-as-nails" Shem crying on the floor of the communal bathrooms at 3 a.m., hair—which they'd grown out since getting back into civilian life—curling into the corners of their mouth, where the vomit was beginning to cake.

After pulling back their hair and tucking it behind their ears, Shem decided to speak.

"I would have gone in a minute later," they whispered.

I didn't know what they were on about, but I did what you do when someone's having a nightmare. I talked to them like they were making sense, and hoped it went away for the night.

"Of course you would have."

"Fuck. I told him to wait for me. If only he'd given me that one fucking minute."

"It's all right, no one here knows."

I had no idea what Shem was talking about.

"It wasn't me. That is not who I am."

"I know." I tugged a lock of hair tighter behind their ear.

"I would have gone in. I'm no pussy."

The next day, when I tried to sit next to them at the canteen, Shem froze me out and never spoke to me again. In my opinion, they're all bark and no bite, but even their bark isn't half as intimidating as they think it is.

Shem puts their hands on their hips as I approach. When I get close enough, they say, "I told you already: We don't need human runners, night cleaners, or whatever other work you're here to beg the Arcadia for, Connie."

"That's great, because the last thing I need right now is another job."

"No one wears purposelessness quite like you."

"Relax, Hulk. I'm only here to talk to someone."

Shem folds their arms. "I'm not letting you interrupt Suziebaby's tea party again."

Tea party is what the queen of Freeport calls her suppers at Arcadia, when she opens the finest import bottles and streams the first cut of audio-neural drugs for the VIPs. Suziebaby owns two clubs on Lower Beach Road, two illegal experience parlors in some back alley somewhere, and a brand-new experience parlor at the Oriental Hotel called POPPY, modeled after a decadent nineteenth-century opium den. But Arcadia is still where she spends most of her time.

"I wouldn't think of it, Shem. It's W— I want a word with."

Shem clicks their tongue. "Sounds even more ridiculous when you say it."

The line has started to grow behind me, and I gesture at it with my thumb. "These folks need their daily dose of self-obliteration, Shem. I'd hate to keep them waiting."

It's at this moment, almost on cue, that a Sparkler pushes to the front of the line. Their privacy shade depicts a dolphin wearing a crown of rainbows. Four more Sparklers tag close behind the leader, all with dolphin heads, too.

"Are we getting in tonight, or are we going to have to take this to the Oriental?" the lead dolphin asks.

Shem gives the dolphin a wide, shark-like smile and waves their entourage inside. Waves me in, too.

With hand on heart, I bow to Shem and slide inside behind the Sparklers.

"Hey, Connie," Shem says. "If it's Delight you want, don't get it from W—. I heard bad things about her tracks."

"Gee, thanks, Shem. I think that's the nicest thing you've ever said to me."

Shem all but spits at me before turning back to the line.

THE PASSAGE INTO Arcadia is a narrow hall of gold mirrors and amber light. Gold and silver mobiles hang from the ceiling, recreating the inside of a kaleidoscope. Multiple false doorways confuse and even frighten incoming patrons, especially those already high on Delight. After the maze of mirrors, you ascend a brief flight of stairs, the walls of which are studded with cut-glass mosaics of peonies that end in a water fountain shaped like a lotus. *It that aged silver?*

On Suziebaby's birthday, and meteor shower nights, the fountain gurgles her favorite osmanthus flower gin. I take a thimble from a stack by the fountain and dip it in the clear liquid. Today, it's orange-scented vodka, or a very convincing synth.

Above the open dance floor and bar is a mezzanine where all the non-dancers sit at tables lit with brightly colored lanterns shaped like fish that cast dream-like shadows on the walls. Everyone in Arcadia is high on something, but no two highs are the same. Some are on uppers, other downers, some are on a combination of both.

I don't see anyone resembling a host. The DJ platform is also empty, but it's still early in the night, and the dance floor is only half full. At most clubs, the music is AI-curated, but Arcadia has an early-century deck that every Sparkler in Freeport can only dream of spinning.

None except Zetta have had the honor.

I should have come with a plan. I don't even know what W— looks like. Although, if their enigmatic name is anything to go by, they probably obscure their face.

I pick a stool at the far end of the bar and take a seat, start looking around for anyone who might be W—. Until, that is, a broad-shouldered individual, their back to me, positions themself directly in my line of sight.

"Excuse me," I say.

The person turns.

Shit. It's the Teacher.

"I'm sorry. Am I intruding?"

I sigh behind teeth. "Where are we going shopping this time? I may need noodles."

"Relax, Connie. I'm not here for you. Even I gotta work two jobs to pay the rent these days."

"Muscle must get quite a workout in this club. I hear it gets pretty wild late at night."

The Teacher shrugs. "I was planning to pay you a visit tomorrow, but this saves me a trip. Wengzai wants you to know he'll forgive half the debt. And he'll kick the balance down the road—five-year loan, competitive interest rate, payable in monthly installments.

I breathe. *This is good.* "What's the catch?"

"In return, he wants the rights to the holo program you wrote for Chuan Kin Hong."

"That program is privately owned. It has nothing to do with Alchemy's debt, and nothing to do with Hong. What does Wengzai want with it?"

"This is not up for debate."

A masked figure mounts the DJ platform.

"Well, you can tell Wengzai that his offer has been denied. I can't help him. Now, if he wants to discuss another deal—"

"Get yourself out of whatever deal is keeping your hands tied and get that program for Wengzai. It docsn't sound like he's giving you options."

"How much time do I have? Jerry's on Whiterock, and he won't be back for two weeks."

The Teacher raps a knuckle on the bar top. "One week. I'll find you." He flags down the bartender. "One tangerine synth for my friend here. On the house."

I watch the Teacher disappear back into the crowd while I try and unravel everything that was just said.

Wengzai, the old-school debt collector upgraded to Settler status, wants Echo. Bad enough to offer a restructuring of Alchemy's debt now that Hong is out of the picture.

Did he want it bad enough to kill him?

IF THE DJ sees me awkwardly mounting the dance platform closest to them, they make no sign of it. They're in a pink baby-doll dress, and their face is obscured by large, reflective, rose-gold ski googles. They're also wearing headphones. They punch buttons, slide controls, and pumps the air like it's 2008. The music builds, and just as the swell of dancers work themselves into a trance, the DJ stops, the lights go out, and Arcadia falls as silent as the endless vacuum outside the dome. No one breaks the pause until a fountain of sparks shoots out from behind the DJ deck, lighting up the platform. The DJ raises a fist to the sky while the dancers down below jump and reach for the falling embers. A real foghorn blasts, and the floor becomes ecstatic. The dimmed lights come back on, and the music switches to mid-century house.

Content to let the record spin for a moment, the DJ turns to look at me and says, "You're that woman who runs Contango. I gambled there once. Can't say it's my scene, but the station needs variety. Can't let Red Unicorn and Pacific Mutual own everything."

"I appreciate the business."

The DJ turns two dials on the deck, and the baseline reverberates. The walls of the club seem to tremble, and the jumping and spinning of the dancers intensifies.

"I hope you made good use of the coin I left on the table."

"I don't understand."

Their fingers move to a red button, press it, and strobe lights slice the dance floor. My vision becomes a series of motion stills. Between the flashes, I glimpse that night in the second quarter of last year, when Club Contango was on its knees after a few windfalls in favor of one player in particular. A player who never removed their privacy mask. The dragon.

"You're the one who saved the club."

"Well, I did almost bankrupt you. Really, it was the least I could do. Besides, I wasn't there to win coin. I was just there to check out the competition. But you weren't competition. You were something else. Something special. I couldn't be the one to destroy that."

"I don't know what to say. Thank you."

"No need to thank me. I did it for Freeport, not you. This city has given me so much, Connie—everything I lost and more. Back on Earth, I was trapped in a shitty marriage, spent my youth living in regret. But Freeport didn't judge me, didn't hold that against me. It welcomed me with open arms and gave me a second chance at life. It gave me purpose again. But somewhere along the line, it stopped providing the same opportunity for people like me—for people like you. And that angers me. But wealth is no good to me dead, and you didn't come here to listen to an old lady talk, so what can I do for you?"

Lights and smoke dramatically shadow what little is visible of the DJ's face, but I catch enough glimpses of it to know it's her: Suziebaby.

"You're looking for W—," she says, no longer content to wait for my answer. She sees the surprise on my face and explains. "I run this town, dear. I have eyes and ears everywhere." She pauses to flick a few switches on the DJ deck, then removes her headphones, and beckons me over with her finger.

I do as she commands.

"What W— sells is dangerous. Unless you know how to use it. Pause every two tracks. Give it a rest for at least five minutes. Blink. Look around. Listen to the world and give your mind time to find itself again before you jump back in. Kids say it messes with their speech and leaves their brain rinsed the next morning. That's because they played it straight through. Pure Delight like this, you need to give it time to steep. And know when to walk away, as with all good things." Suziebaby steps down off the DJ platform to salutes from the dancers. "Take over."

"What? But I don't know how to—"

"It's simple. As soon as this track ends, grab the next disc on top of the stack over there, and slot it in. After that, it takes care of itself."

"That's it? What about all the other controls?"

"The rest of the set is precut. I mixed these when you were still in diapers, burned the physical media before the streaming libraries wiped indie sets and replaced them with bot-curated lists. All you have to do is wave your hands in the air and flip buttons that don't do anything. The crowd will do the rest."

I watch in stunned silence as Suziebaby leaves me to the deck. Until this moment, I truly thought was joking.

"You'll find what you're looking for beside the stack of tracks. Remember, Connie. More important than knowing when to jump in, is knowing when to step away. Oh, and whatever you're planning on doing, don't fuck up Freeport. This is *my* city. If you drag this place down with you, the next time you get a slice of pure Delight to the brain, it won't be because you asked for it."

I have no time to think, or to respond to what Suziebaby just said, before the track ends and Suziebaby disappears. Ever second of silence makes the crowd below grow ever more restless, so without thinking too much, I hop up onto the DJ platform, retrieve the disc from the top of the stack, and plug it into the deck.

The mother of all bass drops thunders, followed by playful, electronic tones that tinkle in the air like rain. The crowd goes wild.

That's when I notice it: a neon-pink sliverfilm resting next to the stack of Suziebaby's precut tracks—exactly where she said it would be. Pure Delight. I slip the sliverfilm into my pocket and turn to discreetly make my exit. But before I can step back down from the deck, a club-goer down below raises their hands to the sky, shouts something to the crowd, then starts jumping up and down to the beat. The crowd wastes no time joining the man, and suddenly the entire club is quaking beneath my feet.

I've already got what I came here for. But while I'm here, I might as well enjoy myself.

I take the sliver from Zetta that I've been carrying around in my pocket for days, peel the protective plastic off, and paste the bio-transfer side to my left temple.

I slip on the headphones, raise the foghorn in the air, sound it, and ride the swelling wave.

Tonight's going to be a good night.

HARM

AT SEVEN IN the morning, Enterprise Square unloads the crushed and drained Contractors from the night shift, and fills up on fresh souls straight off the hissing trams— Contractors on their way to support functions in buildings around the square, or to their in-person service jobs at the many surrounding restaurants.

Projected onto the Circle building is a traditional lion dance, a lost art from earlier centuries. The lion bats long eyelashes and wishes you a prosperous resettlement. *Scan to know more about competitive starting rates on our assurance packages.*

None of the heads filing in toward digital punch clocks look up at it.

My hologram stands at the farthest reaches of her allowed radius, next to a coffee and re-toasted bun dispenser in hopes of catching hungry commuters as they pass.

"Utillium prices have been rising steadily all year, and are expected to pick up exponentially. With this much behind it, it's only a matter of a quarter—two at most—before investors start to see returns. And that's just on greyfields. Think about the surge if you put a tranche into extraction-ready pits!"

A tourist steps sideways, and Not-Me mirrors his movement like a dancer.

"I'm more of a fixed-deposit kind of guy," the tourist says.

"That used to be me," Not-Me says, "until I realized just how much of a sure thing this is."

The tourist looks to be in urgent need of a restroom, not a sure thing in the market.

"My wife's the one who manages the investments in our family. She's got us in some coin fund and the new-projects portfolio from Red Unicorn. So, really, we're maxed out. Sorry."

What compels him to keep talking? I could learn a thing or two from Not-Me. She's still pestering him, but he's still here.

"The best thing is, you don't need to manage or even monitor it in any way. Every investor gets a personalized dashboard on their interface so that you—or your wife—can check your investment as often as you like. Or not at all. Either way, you'll be letting your coin do the work for you."

Finally, the tourist finds it inside himself to walk away. Once he's beyond her radius, Not-Me pulls back.

I approach her quickly before she can engage someone else.

Her hands are clasped in front of her like a store assistant receiving customers, and her face is set in congenial welcome. As I get closer, I think I see the lines around her eyes tighten. *No, I'm imagining things.* Not-Me has no lines around her eyes. Those have all been airbrushed away.

"Hey, Connie," I say. "I brought us some *youtiao*." I hold up the warm treat for Not-Me to see, but when I step into her circle, her bland expression falls into a guarded scowl. She folds her arms across her chest.

"Really? You're seriously calling me by your name?"

I hold the *youtiao* out to her.

"You know I don't eat. I just simulate."

"Simulate away then. Eating humanizes you. Helps one connect. Helps me."

She eyes the pastry in my hand with skepticism. "Damn. It does look crisp. I wish I could smell it." She pretends to inhale its sweet scent. "Okay," she says. "I'll join you." She opens her hand and manifests a digital copy of the *youtiao* I'm holding, raises it to her lips, and takes a big, greasy bite.

I do the same with my real version.

"Good?" I ask between bites.

"Mm-hmm," Not-Me says, her mouth full.

I intentionally fumble my *youtiao* and drop it to the ground near her projector.

"Oops."

I walk through my hologram, causing it to shimmer like a ghost, and for some reason, it feels disrespectful. But once I'm on the other side of her, I pull the sliverfilm of pure Delight from my pocket as I bend down to retrieve my *youtiao* from beside Not-Me's digital projector. But before I stand back up with the recovered treat in hand, I quickly plug the sliverfilm into an open port on the projector. I stand back up, take a few big steps back until I'm outside of her radius, and wait for the sliverfilm to load.

The play runs as expected. With the frequency on maximum and the pauses turned off, the overload of external input causes the hologram to jitter. Not-Me begins to glitch

I watch as my image breaks, re-materializes, and shatters again in front of me. She reaches for me with gray-blue fingers that degrade more with each stunted movement.

Does Not-Me experience emotion? Is she in shock? Or is she maybe feeling betrayed? Her mouth makes movements, but her audio output is incomprehensible.

"Sorry, Con," I say, and I think I mean it.

Then Not-Me winks out like a light.

SUCCESS

"BACK TO THE routine, am I right?"

"Nothing about you is routine, Con," says Brendan from the T&T finance department. He winks.

Such a flatterer.

A nod tells me he's hacked a log-in for me. Brendan supplements his take-home coin from T&T with a side hustle providing real human audience response on ViewBucket pilots. It's still just two thirds of what he needs to cover rent for a one-bedroom on Delta—with a squinting view of the lower Beach Road,—but that's the life he chose. He could downgrade and live like the rest of us, but he's in love with a Sparkler in the Worlds Academy. Whenever he's short on coin, he plays at Contango, and he almost always wins. He owes me this.

The call from Jerry comes a day later.

The walk to our meeting gives me the time I need to consider the range of emotion I expect to feel, and the best way to manage it. Confusion, frustration, regret.

What I didn't expect was for Jerry to be overjoyed to here from me, for him to invite me out to breakfast.

I'm not sure what his game is, but I accept, and this morning, I meet him at Ah Huat Engineering.

If Auntie's is the queen of Friday reward-lunches, Sunday morning gatherings with family, and birthday dinners for older folks from Pioneer Ring, then Ah Huat Engineering is the everyman's canteen. Everyday indulgences at everyday prices. Just don't look inside the kitchen on your way out.

The dive sits at the corner next to a scrap yard for collapsible mining-barge extensions, and across the street from a show garage for personal cruisers. With the utillium market soaring the way it has been lately, the yard is working around the clock to break scrap, and Ah Huat is busier than ever.

Like so many informal but highly essential businesses that cater to the needs of Contractors, Au Huat began as a co-op lunch stand owned and operated by the scrap yard workers, who took turns cooking the noodles and slurping them. It's sill owned by the scrap yard, but it has expanded its customer base, even becoming a favorite of local Enforcers.

The walls inside Au Huat are ironically plastered with public health posters from the 1980s, some that feature attractive young models, with heavy eyeshadow and smoldering looks, above messages from the surgeon general of some small tropical nation now extinct that warns about the dangers of venereal diseases. The magnetic bar behind the counter holds more knives than needed to just julienne vegetables.

The man who walks in the door at Ah Huat is not the slouching Jerry I know—the one who is careless with his appearance and timid, not wanting to take up more space than necessary. This Jerry holds himself tall, his prior insecurities shaken out of him. He casts his eye an inch above your head rather than at your shoes, and he doesn't offer a dopey smile when you look his way. He wears a bespoke printed suit.

This Jerry is a picture of success.

I pull myself off the stool and extend a hand. He doesn't clasp it awkwardly. He takes it in his paw, places his other hand on my shoulder, and nearly pulls me off my footing with the power of his handshake. I look around Ah Huat, expecting annoyance at our display, disdain for our liberal movements within such a small, tight space, but it doesn't come. These Contractors gape at us the way I used to gape at Zetta.

"Sit, sit," Jerry insists, waving me back to my seat like he had it made just for me. "I hope you haven't ordered. You must try the *bak chor mee*—off-menu."

The only off-menu service the old Jerry got was being accidentally served something with a hair in it.

"Order whatever you like, Jerry. I'll eat it."

"A little more enthusiasm won't crowd the room," he says.

"I came for the company."

Jerry lifts the thin edge of his mouth at me and drops it. He slaps both hands on the counter with a mask of polite expectation for the waiting cook on the other side of it. "Two *bak chor mee*. Dry *mee pok* noodles. Extra chili. Add vegetables." He turns to me and wistfully says, "Man, the days I spent on Whiterock, spooning stew at the canteen and dreaming about these noodles." Then, as if feeling inspired, he turns back to the cook for a second time and says, "Make it three bowls." To me again: "We can split the third. It'll go down. Trust me."

Whiterock isn't exactly a hardship post, and with the number of Red Unicorn and Circle Finance executives that make regular stops there to check in on the labs, they can't be plating ShipFood stew. So why is Jerry feeding me a double serving of bullshit about bad food on Whiterock, and the failings of Whiterock synth whiskey?

"The Sparklers there are interns," he's telling me now. "And very purposeful, which is cute."

The *bak chor mee* arrives. The portions are so small, they can fit inside egg cups, but I suspect that's how they're able to offer Contractor-friendly pricing. Still, the noodles look springy and slick, the stewed mushrooms look juicy, and the meatballs and minced meat look just like the real thing. Jerry digs in. Chopsticks shoveling with one hand, a fist clenched in satisfaction with the other. The fist relaxes, and Jerry strokes the counter, satisfied.

"Something's happened with Project Echo," he says.

I lift a spoon of soup to my lips. Salty bone broth enhanced with umami from the seaweed.

"Something bad? Or something you can work around?"

He picks up his bowl and slurps up the rest of the soup. With a greasy thumb, he taps the panel by our table for a refill. A thin line of soup drips down his chin.

"It's the holo outside Circle building, our flag bearer. She went down the other day. Hacked. She's been completely out of commission since."

"Are the rest are still active?"

"They are, for now. But they're all linked in a closed circuit, so whatever virus has corrupted the one outside Circle may soon spread to the others."

Jerry reaches for the third bowl. He presses the edge of the spoon into it, thinking he'll cut the body of the noodles neatly in half, but the spoon just slides off their slick exterior and sends a splatter of sauce onto his cuff.

So, the holograms are linked.

"That sounds bad," I say.

Jerry wipes his cuff, then tries again to extract the noodles. He succeeds and heaps them into his bowl. "Actually, it's perfect."

"Excuse me?"

"See, I was thrilled when we got the first payment. But that money ran out quicker than anticipated, and the royalties aren't expected until next financial cycle. If our work was done with the licensing, we'd be screwed. But seeing how fast products move through the pipeline on Whiterock made me realize something. Red Unicorn can stunt our payments, starve us, and take over. This glitch means we can sell them security solutions via subscription, with mandatory upgrades every quarter."

A bot arrives with a kettle and pours out the soup refills.

<<*Caution. Hot.*>> the bot says.

"That's one way of looking at it."

"Why do you seem so unenthused? This new development is amazing. We'll be making more coin than we previously expected."

"I get it, but doesn't this glitch tell the unicorn we sold them a bad egg?"

"Echo's still only in beta. Leave it to me. I know how to talk to guys like him. We just need to present him with a solution, show the guy we can fix this, and he'll keep us on."

"Who are you talking about? What guy?"

The bot extracts itself from the space between us.

"Red Unicorn, I mean. I'm tripping over myself because we only managed by the fingernails to get the financing to power a relaunch of Project Echo. But this glitch is a great chance at a companion security program,"

"Only if it works. I suggest kicking it to the code farms you work with. They'll know what to do."

My noodles swell in the house blend of soy, chili, vinegar, and stewed mushroom sauce. I'm not hungry anymore.

"You know we can't. Those farms copy and strip every job you give them."

"So, you want me to do it."

Jerry nods.

"I'll need access to the prototype source files."

Jerry sucks in his breath.

"I can try to work around without the source files," I say, "but it'll take longer, which won't send Red Unicorn the signal that we know how to fix this. Rather than waiting weeks, they could bring someone else in and force you to grant them the same access I'm asking for now. Or maybe Circle has already begun financing a reverse-engineering of the project so that they can toss your licensing deal and build a better version themselves."

"The Ethics Committee would never—"

"Circle owns the Ethics Committee, Jerry. What's one more bribe to look the other way?"

Take the bait, Jerry. Bite and swallow.

Jerry licks his lips. "Fine. One hour's access. But that's all. I can't risk another security breach."

The line of soup is still on his chin.

Don't blink. Don't smile. Don't give him anything.

"I'll do what I can."

He bites his lower lip. "And don't go fishing around while you're in there. Just stick to the plan."

"Why would I want to waste my time like that? You've got nothing in there I haven't seen before."

Jerry laughs, but it's a nervous laugh.

He's hiding something, and I'm going to find out what.

"Well then," I say, "let's eat."

I pick up my chopsticks and tap the points on the table to level them. I pluck the last remaining meatball from the extra bowl and toss it in my mouth, watch Jerry closely as I chew the food slow.

ESCAPE

I LEAVE JERRY at the door of Ah Huat and feel the immediate relief one feels when dropping their social face. A lot more still hangs on me that won't shake off so easily, but this is a start.

The bird shifts its weight on my shoulder.

You never left me, did you?

Nightmares are your carrion.

Even in my happiest days, you were always there, circling.

I set a straight line for the tram stop, not turning to catch Jerry's eye as he blusters out of the restaurant. He has a new personal cruiser. It winks its headlights and disarms as we approach. It's one of the newer models, the ones with the good flight range within port limits—sufficient for barging and other minor pick-up ops around the station, great for handling your own baggage so no one at HaboHub will know what's in it.

The first tram that arrives is the A-Express from Pioneer and Delta. Next stop: Embarkment. It will stop there for three minutes before shooting on toward HaboHub and the FlyBye shuttlepark.

I ignore Jerry's mention that he can give me a lift, and instead hop on the express. Some call it the MAM Line because it's filled with nothing but Contractors going to and from their depressing jobs. But since it's currently the late-morning leisure hour for Settlers—and rise-and-shine time for

Sparklers—everyone one who needs to ride the MAM Line is already at work or home. The tram car is empty except for me.

Just as well, because breakfast with Jerry has left me pickled sour and not in the mood for standing in a crowded tram car, hanging on to a strap as the tram speeds along.

I tell myself that when the tram stops at HaboHub, I'm going to talk to Vis about the Free Hands—and really listen this time. Offer my attention, not just my words.

The vibration from an urgent ping wakes me from my thoughts. It's Stiff's broker again.

<<*The Stakeholder bonds, Connie. This is important. You have two more days to top them up, or it's back to the end of the queue. Maybe back to Earth. Ping me when you've made the transfer.*>>

That's the tram stopping at the Embarkment. And lingering. The glass winks golden hope in spite of the grim specter of the MAM hostel that haunts the reflection. I reach in for my resolve and feel my fingers graze it.

I will talk to Vis. I will make it up to her.

But first, I need to straighten things our in my head.

I'm able to jump from my seat and exit the tram just before the doors close again and it speeds off down the line.

I'm in the arrivals and departures hall of the Embarkment when I hear the familiar voice.

"Come up, sad cat, the sake's cold enough to bite."

You are always there, aren't you, Chance?

Not unlike the birds.

THE CARAFE BESIDE Chance at the long bar of the viewing gallery is so fresh out the chiller, it sweats condensation. The hostess raises her head and nods at me when I catch her eye. A human server then deposits two plates of *guotie* at my elbow as though they've been keeping it warm, just waiting for me to appear.

Chance doesn't show any sign of wanting to eat. I didn't think I was hungry after Ah Huat, but I eat because there's a pit in my stomach that's grinding the organ hollow.

I feel the weight lift off my feet and onto the brass railing. Chance doesn't speak, or move to make space. My glass is full, and the sake scores a delicious burn that's not too sharp as it winds its tail around itself in a smooth finish. There's a pianist at Tanuki this morning, playing old Shanghai jazz that extends its tendrils into my ears—probing, prodding the vulnerable spots in my brain. But the viewing balcony isn't where you sit to take in the entertainment and plush furnishings of Tanuki. You sit here to look down on the arrivals and departures hall, at the tops of the miniature people pulling wheely luggage of hope behind them, or trailing it off Freeport for new beginnings. You're looking at a renewed sense of hope.

I was one of them once.

I still am.

I'm just more exhausted now.

My head lolls on my neck before falling onto Chance's shoulder, which feels a lot like the palm of my own hand.

"Wouldn't it be nice to go away? To just leave whenever you want."

"Do you want to leave?"

"Maybe."

Where do you want to go?"

"Doesn't matter."

"You can go now, if you want. Sticky's old enough. She's no longer an excuse. It might even be good for her if you do."

Chance dips two fingers into the glass of sake and lifts them, two droplets of sake trembling on the tips. Chance scatters the droplets to the concourse below.

A blessing.

Chance might be high on Delight. It shows a bit in the drowsy gaze of those beautiful eyes.

Five stories below us, a commuter stops in their tracks and touches the nape of their neck, where one of the droplets has landed. They don't look up, don't look around. Their hand just returns to their luggage and they continue on with a shrug.

To Chance, I say, "Sometimes, I have a few good days, and I feel lighter. But even then, the weight still follows me around."

"Where do you want to be?" Chance asks.

"Anywhere but here."

"Anywhere *but where you are.*"

I comb my fingers through Chance's hair, curl a lock around my finger. The coil goes on for longer than I expect.

"I can't. The birds will find me."

"Because you don't need to leave. You need to *be—*"

"Someone else," I whisper.

I don't want to run anymore—from the people who know me, from the places where memory lingers. I want to escape to a place where my past can't catch me, where the person I once was no longer exists

Chance nuzzles my hair with the tip of a nose, lips bringing warm breath along my neck. A warmth pools between my legs. Can Chance's stream of Delight be slipping into my consciousness?

Chance draws back and grabs my wrist.

"I won't let you be sad. Nothing bad ever happens at Tanuki."

Then, Chance pulls me off my seat.

WE RACE DOWN the wrought iron staircase, Chance slowing as we pass the antique shop with wood paneling and a signboard manufactured to look hand-painted. The faint scent of sandalwood incense wafts along the varnished shelves. All that's missing are the vapors of medicated ointment on arthritic hands, and the smell rancid oil wafting from fried noodles that had been bought in the morning and then left to sit out all day on greaseproof brown paper—the most charming hallmarks of a good curio shop.

It's a Life Collection shop, owned by Circle Finance. A shop for every non-essential old-world consumer indulgence, like curated characters from a pop band. Life Collection's most popular stores are a physical bookshop that sells mostly photography books from twentieth-century Earth, an art gallery of non-digital media, a green grocer, a coffee shop modeled after a mid-century *kopitiam* that can't pull a *teh halia* to match Zaqy's, and a stationer that sells embossed paper and real ink pens at the cost of a week's-worth of lunches.

There are ten or twelve Life Collection shop selections in total, and every decent station has at least two of them. Usually the *kopitiam* and the grocer. On Freeport, every main street has a handful. Copy and paste. Three in a row for presence. Especially in the Embarkment, which acts as first impression for the free-trade zone of the Greater Belt. There, the Life Collection shops line the hall. They look like sets from an old film, and you *want* to walk into them. They're just so beautiful.

Chance is careful to step over the threshold of the shop.

"In the old days, thresholds were meant to trip ghosts," Chance says.

With hands clasped behind my back, I follow Chance around the shop, stopping to eye mounted postage stamps in frames, and porcelain statuettes from the Qing dynasty of animals and beautiful maidens—replicas, of course. Chance is all indulgent smiles and silent appraisals and polite squeezes at the corners of watchful eyes.

That's when I see it: a small picture frame that encases six gold medallions. A hand hovers for a moment over the frame and the gold medallions, and then the frame is gone.

Chance's shoulder presses hard into mine.

"Thank you for your time," I say to the clerk as we strut confidently out of the shop. But what begins as a stroll through the departures and arrivals hall, quickly becomes a frenzied waltz through the crowd, Chance and I dancing wildly to the rapid beating of my heart until we arrive finally at the golden gates, which are symbolically always open.

Then we run.

We make for the tram as it pulls away from the stop and jump aboard before it's too late. We turn around, breathless, hugging the straps, expecting to be tailed.

Are we disappointed to find that we're not?

We don't get off until Pioneer.

Before getting up from my seat, Chance points with the jerk of the head. I follow the gesture to the corner of a picture frame, wedged between the seats. The glass inside the frame has been broken, and whatever was inside the frame has been stolen.

Chance leads me to an alley that I recognize immediately, and nods to an all-night hawker who is busy unpacking crates. The hawkers and service providers of the alleys are often visa overstayers, but MAM casts a blind eye because without them and the shadow economy they create, Contractors would have to be paid a lot more and given better terms. Because of this, Hawkers are allowed to exist in the hidden parts of town so long as they disappear from sight by sunrise.

There's the noodle shop I keep meaning to try.

And there's the door to the Sanctuary.

Chance fishes six gold medallions from a jacket pocket that looks an awful lot like my jacket, then slips the medallions, one by one, through a delivery hatch in the Sanctuary's door. Chance knocks hard on the door, then says, "Let's go."

"You're not going to say hello? Let them know it was you?"

"They'll know. And even if they don't, what does it matter? That's not whey we do this. Now, let's *go*. We can't be seen here."

As though Chance's premonition was a summons, I hear a sharp whistle behind us.

"Run!" Chance shouts. "Don't look back!"

I reach for Chance's hand, but Chance pulls away and ducks into the noodle shop.

"I'll find you! Go!"

I stumble against a wall, then run. Run faster than I thought possible. But just when I think I've gotten away, I turn a corner and am met with the strong body of an Enforcer. A large hand grabs my shoulder, then another shoves an energy weapon into my gut. I feel a sharp surge of an energy, then crumple.

ABET

THE ARCHITECTS OF Freeport didn't set out to replicate all of Earth society, only its finest. The station would be an entrepôt like no other, sustained by new technology and driven by upstanding individuals imbued with the spirit of wealth and progress.

At least they got the technological and commercial advancements right, because after the last stone was laid, and the last engineers shipped back to Earth—after the first Settler ship arrived, ferrying the most brave, intrepid and highly skilled among us—Freeport let go of its lofty aspirations of human advancement and descended into classism, financial crimes, and wild, drug-fueled nights.

There are no prisons on Freeport. Offenders get deported back to Earth and are dealt with there. No one really believes the urban legends of criminals being thrown into the cycler for fertilizer, but every misdemeanor takes points off your MAM visa qualification, and that's deterrence enough. As a rule, Sparklers pulling each other's hair out, swinging on chandeliers, or tearing the curtains down while high on breakfast cocktails and Delight, are to be tolerated.

Shoplifting, on the other hand, is rare and nearly impossible to get away with, but every so often, someone desperate or foolish enough still tries. And every time, they're caught. If they're a Settler or Sparkler, they're let go with a warning, but if they're a

Contractor like me, they're arrested and taken in for questioning, threatened with deportation without due process.

"Tell me again about this accomplice."

"Not an accomplice," I say. "Just a friend."

The Enforcer across the table from me looks young enough to be one of Sticky's minders at Junior. They also look like they'd be good at it. Better than being an Enforcer, anyway.

"Some friend, leaving you to take the rap like this."

The spot where the Enforcer shocked me with their energy weapon feels numb in an unsettling way. But then again, it beats writhing in pain. I'm not going to like my body in the morning either way. Might as well accept the temporary reprieve.

"The item you stole—"

"I told you already, I didn't steal anything."

"*The item you stole* was tagged with a tracer. It synced to your interface and tracked you from the time it was taken from the Life Collection shop to the time you left the Embarkment. It was only after you removed the gold from the frame that the tracer stopped working. We found the empty frame stashed inside the tram, and your fingerprints are on it."

"My fingerprints are on it because I touched it while shopping in the store. As for the tracer… Well, I work in tech, so I know how easy it is to mimic someone else's interface, frame them for a crime. It's why criminal trials still rely mostly on eyewitness testimony."

There it is. The twitch at the corner of the Enforcer's mouth. He knows now he's out of his league. I have him beat. But just when I think I'm home free, another man sweeps into the room, hands behind his back, and relieves the Enforcer of his duty.

Inspector Singh.

Once the Enforcer is gone, Singh tucks his thumbs into the sides of his uniform trousers to keep them from creasing and folds himself elegantly onto the chair across the table from me.

"Consider, Mx. Lam," he says behind steepled fingers, "that we have enough on your record to hold you indefinitely until you comply. And I'm not even talking about the robbery yet."

In my mind, I'm on my hands and knees, struggling with a bucket filled with Messaway™.

Inspector Singh dimples his chin. "Your interface patterns showed signs of lingering Delight when we picked you up. I get it, though. A little pinch and stream now and then keeps the bad days away. But too much will lead to compromising situations you can't explain." He sucks on the inside of his cheek, releases it with a moist, fleshly pop. "It was, however, the kind of amount that will put your parental access rights into question."

"Bullshit. I wasn't that high."

"Do you know that for sure?" He places both hands on the table, palms down, fingers making a soft brushing sound on the stainless steel. His hands part to reveal a used sliverfilm beneath. "The entire film has been streamed. Unless you have an incredibly high tolerance, I'd say you were very high."

"I'd be worried if I thought the sliverfilm is mine, but it's not. You can't just plant that on me. You don't strike me as an asshole, and you know that's not mine."

"Mx. Lam, our interactions haven't been to your convenience, have they? Where is it you have to be this time? The chandlery? Or should I say, the job your young friend Trace Pereira provides to help compensate for an expired L1 visa?"

"Trace has nothing to do with any of this."

"That depends what *this* is, Mx. Lam."

"I do collections and deliveries for Lucky 48. That, plus my contract work at Thevar & Tann puts me well above the minimum NET required. Everything I do is above board."

"Is it? Turns out you're not listed on Lucky 48's manpower allowance. In fact, the job you claim is yours—collections and deliveries—is registered to one June Ho, who left Freeport for a greyfield asset last year. And while the Pereiras may have appointed you to be their daughter's guardian, this does not grant Lucky 48 a larger manpower allowance, which means that whatever coin you are earning there is being earned illegally. And without Lucky 48, your work hours for Thevar and Tann are insufficient. You see,

Mx. Lam, you don't earn enough coin *legally* to maintain your L1 visa here on Freeport. And as far as I can tell from your records, your particular talents, which do appear to be many, do not include any of the dynamic skills currently in demand."

I square my jaw and glare at him, try to look like I'm not scared shitless, but Singh just smiles kindly in response—like a priest might do with a juvenile delinquent who he believes can still turn their life around. And it's working.

"Lesser transgressions have put away greater threats. We mustn't be ashamed of our beginnings. And I can think of one little reason why you're not quite as flippant about the possibility of deportation as you pretend to be."

Sticky. Of course. The devil knows what my buttons are, and he pushes them all at once.

"What do you want from me?"

"Only your cooperation."

"With the missing persons case, I assume. Hong."

"Not a missing persons case any more. It's now being investigated as a homicide."

My blood runs cold.

I lie, pretend to be surprised. "He's dead?"

Singh studies my face in silence. "He missed his settlement meeting, and he did so without giving full instructions and power of attorney to his representative. Something that his wife, Mx. Awyong, insists he would never do, unless—"

"So you don't have a body?"

Singh stops, raises an eyebrow at me. "To help with our investigation, I will need you to authorize the following: access to all your chat logs, movement patterns, and interface interactions from the past month. If you don't comply, I'll be forced to get a warrant."

"Why me? Am I a suspect?"

"This is about Wengzai. Your connection to him is of great interest to us. He's put in claims for Hong's assets—yours, too. And you've been spotted in the company of his favorite brutalizer. Looked quite friendly, too."

"There was nothing friendly about it. I was being threatened."

"Well, if you cooperate, I can help get you out of this mess you've found yourself in. No more debt collectors, no more threats, no more troubles with you visa." He retrieves a packet of something from his pocket and offers to share whatever's inside. "Hazelnuts?" He shakes the packet in my direction.

Are those real *hazelnuts?*

I shake my head no, but I immediately regret it. I want the hazelnuts. I love them, haven't had them in years. I'm just trying to be disagreeable.

He shrugs, happy not to press, and pours a few hazelnuts into his palm. He tosses them into his mouth with a backward tilt of the head.

"If you don't cooperate," he says, "things might get a lot more difficult for you. And for your friend, Trace Pereira. And for your daughter, too."

"You've made your point."

Singh slides a tablet across the table to me. The form on the screen grants him access to my interface at any time, with or without notice, so long as the content of my interface can aid him in his investigation. At the bottom of the form is a clickable box that says <<*Agree*>>.

It would have been easy to cooperate had I not been at the scene of the crime, had I not allowed Chance to 'take care of it.' I would provide Singh with full access to my interface, and in exchange, my innocence would be proved, and all my other problems would be solved. But I *was* there at Lucky 48 the night Hong was murdered, and my interface *will* place me there without question. And my chat logs with Hong will only serve to implicate me further.

The button on the screen taunts me.

Suddenly, the door to the interrogation room slams open, and a lawyer blusters in, a junior officer in her wake. The lawyer looks like Vis, if Vis wore sharp suits that fit.

And that's when I realize: the lawyer *is* Vis in a sharp suit, looking how she did back when we first met. Back when the two of us had purpose.

"I'm Visala Kumar, Mx. Lam's representative appointed by the Free Hands. She is leaving Commission premises immediately, and all requests and communication of any kind with my client are to be sent through me, and me alone. This interview is over."

"There is still the small issue of bail," Inspector Singh says. He hesitates to extend his hand, and pats it on the outside of his jacket pocket instead.

"The ransom is paid. She's returning home until you actually have the right to hold her. You didn't click on any consent forms, did you?"

She's talking to me. I snap to and shake my head.

"I expect the Commission to delete all records of this conversation. Be thankful that we're not pressing charges for excessive force on arrest."

I'm thankful, but also confused. Singh *does* have reason to keep me detained on charges of overstaying on an expired L1 visa. But for reasons that remain a mystery to me, he has decided not pursue them…yet.

Inspector Singh stands and bows, then gestures to the door as though we've relieved him of a dreadful amount of work and he's grateful. He'll fight another day, thank you.

"Until next time, Connie," he says with a smile.

I don't respond. I just hasten after Vis, who has already stormed her way out.

"You're the Secretary General of the Free Hands?"

"I couldn't advertise that at HaboHub, could I?"

"How did you afford to post bail?"

Vis stops and looks at me, and unless my eyes are deceiving me, she's actually smiling. *Truly* smiling, like she used, back in our shared dorm.

"I didn't. *You* did, when you contributed to the strike fund. I have to admit that when you signed the petition, I thought that was all I was getting from you. But then you transferred all that coin. *You came through.* And just in time, too, because the Commission's really turning the screws on us now. Yusof's visa was terminated, and a few others besides—all active Hands who've been organizing on the street. We're appealing to MAM, but it isn't looking good—not without a long and expensive fight."

I leave the station in Vis's train, unable to make sense of what Vis claims I've done. *I contributed to the fund?* Vis must mean the club did. Or maybe it was Chance. Another one of Chance's secret causes.

Speaking of Chance, Inspector Singh never mentioned our relationship. Not even once.

But I can't sort through that mess in my head right now. I have to push those thoughts aside.

Chance, being Chance, will lay low until the coast is clear. Chance will take care of Chance.

It's time I take care of myself.

SMOKE

THE EFFECTS OF the shock weapon are starting to spider through my body—the numbness is now pain. The right side of my head, where I suffered a concussion from a bike accident years ago, throbs with an ache that's spreading. *My hand will stop trembling if I don't look at it, right?*

I look up at the dome and see the first light of fake morning. *Sticky.*

My heart seizes, but then I remember that Sticky's spending the night at Junior. She's probably guzzling on a morning chocolate milk with friends, happy and giggling, and not missing me in the slightest.

But then comes the sound of fire engines.

They blare their horns as they race past us on the streets below the tracks. Fire is serious business inside a dome. Freeport's fire safety and containment technology is sufficient to isolate and hold off any domestic or commercial blaze, but it's still newer tech and not without its flaws. Even if it wasn't new, the fear of being out in space, with nowhere else to run, causes levels of panic that no amount of assurance from the Commission and the Residency can calm.

When fires happen, the entire city holds its breath.

As the tram approaches Delta, the wails of the sirens grow louder, closer. An automated alert notifies the passengers in the tram: diversion on lower Delta Road. All passengers are to disembark and take the A, B1, B2, or D Lines to proceed.

The hairs on the back of my neck stand on end when I see it: the curl of black smoke rising in the air, and the red glow of the blaze. Lucky 48 is on fire.

Before I can make sense of it, I'm off the tram and running down Delta to Lucky 48, an angry cloud of smoke billowing above it. Vis is shouting for me to come back, but I don't listen.

No. Please, no.

The firefighters on the scene do a valiant job of putting out the raging flames and isolating the building, which has successfully been encased by the smoke-triggered fire locks. *The new tech delivered on its promise. Thank the stars.* There are enough barrels of oil in the basement to obliterate the entire chandlery and send fire ripping through the dome.

I step off the curb and onto the road, barricaded on both ends. The center of the regular thoroughfare is cleared of trams and private transport, with firefighters and other early responders pushing past me. You're never more alone than in a moment of disaster.

Wait, where's Trace?

"The doors have melted!" a firefighter shouts.

Trace!

I rush to the back of the chandlery and climb the fire escape to the roof. Once up there, I let out a massive sigh of relief at the sight of Trace alive. She's huddled atop the roof like a scared child, looking stunned and soot-stained, but she's conscious and responding.

The punch to my gut twists when I realize Sticky was *this close* to being at Lucky 48 tonight. My throat feels raw, and it isn't only from the smoke.

"Guess I'll be taking that gap year, after all," Trace says to me. "It's not like Dad can say no after this." She does her best to show me a smile.

I throw my arms around her, but let her go as soon as I feel her wince. There's blood on her legs. They're cut up from all the shattered glass.

"Don't worry, Connie," she says. "I'll live. I was already up on the roof when it happened. Your old haunt. Can you believe it? I never come up, but the one day I do, this happens. If I'd still been behind the counter when the fire started, I'd already be toast."

I can't tell if I'm giddy or just delirious. "What were you doing up here?"

She laughs, almost with embarrassment. "The signal downstairs was weak, and I was trying to download a large file to my interface."

A ping on my interface signals a screen-share request from Trace. I accept it to see a frozen loading bar and a paused fight scene between a large half-mechanical octopod creature and—

"Go, go, *Forever Rangers*," I say, now almost in tears. I press her to me. "Must have been the pink Ranger who sent you up to the roof."

"Maybe it was Chance."

I stop. "What do you mean?"

"Forget I said it. It was funnier in my head."

Funny? Which part? Chance showing up to help, or Chance showing up at all?

"Connie, I think someone started the fire on purpose."

"What? Why would you think that?"

"I saw them fleeing the scene. Or, at least I think that's what they were doing."

"Did you get a good look at them?"

Trace shakes her head, almost as if she's disappointed with herself. "Sorry."

"You don't need to apologize. I'm just glad you're okay."

"Why would anyone have it in for us, anyway?"

I have a good idea, but I can't say that to Trace.

"I'm so sorry, Trace. Really, I am."

"Eh, it's okay. It's not like I'm sentimental about this place. Besides, everything of value is insured. Dad made sure of it."

I rake my fingers through my hair.

"I'll set aside any coin I have left to help."

Before Trace can respond, two firefighters climb onto the roof. When they see us, they rush right over.

After administering a field IV to Trace, they call in a medical transport to airlift her off the roof. They want me to be airlifted as well—just in case I'm suffering injuries they can't see—but I'm able to escape back down the fire escape before that happens, while they're busy tending to Trace.

Back on the street, an Enforcer grabs me by the arm and shoves me in the opposite direction of the commotion.

"Clear the area!"

As I return to the gathering crowd, I see Vis.

"Connie! Thank the stars, you're safe! C'mon, we have to get out of here. Now."

"It's okay, Vis. They have fire under control."

"No, you don't get it. This isn't the only arson threat tonight."

Arson. Trace was right.

"Trigger alerts are going off on every forum. Lots of chatter about bomb threats."

My interface pings me with an urgent notification. It's from the Junior Academy.

> *<<Dear Parent, the Principal requests the pleasure of your company at a meeting following school dismissal tomorrow. Do not reply to this message unless you have a valid reason to reschedule.>>*

Swipe to minimize.

As Vis and I make our way back to the trams, I see a man break away from the gawking crowd of bystanders and duck into an alley.

Jerry?

No, that's impossible. Jerry is still on Whiterock.

But when I look again to make sure, whoever it was is gone.

PART 4

RAISE

CIRCLE

IF A PHYSICAL representation of great ambition is what you desire, then the MAM hostel on Upper Beach Road is second only to the Commissioner's Compound.

Shape the government buildings, shape the future.

The hostel is a triumphant piece of Brutalist Revival architecture, and is one of the tallest and most imposing structures in the city. Built as five curving roots of concrete that broaden as they reach their foundations, the hostel proper is on the top ten floors, while the lower ten are occupied by branches and warrens of MAM that are kept hidden from the public eye. If you were to enter one of the elevators, you'd find that the buttons for floors one through ten are grayed out. Creative types like to imagine a world of secrets hidden within those floors, but most people don't pay them any mind. What goes on there is none of their concern.

Newly-arrived Settlers and their special-status Sparklers don't bunk at the MAM. They go directly to their townhouses, or to the Circle Health Spa, a hot-springs-style resort. But if you can stomach bunking with fresh-off-the-ship tenants, most of whom are under quarantine, the upper floors of the MAM hostel provide striking views in all of Freeport—of the beach, the water, and the great cosmos beyond. Wake up, put both feet on the square foot of space you're allowed, and gaze across the artificial beach to the sparkling, gold-rimmed windows and gentle low arches of the Deco-Revival Embarkment. Try not to think about how the offices and data assets are installed closer to the ground for swifter fire escape.

It's that view I'm looking out at now, a mug of hot coffee in my hand. It's not at the eighteenth floor—where Vis, Sticky, and I used to bunk—but a few floors below. Vis has a cubicle to herself now. I didn't know that the hostel had long leases, let alone living cubes, but Vis explained it this way: Now that there's less need for resettlement support, MAM is repurposing a number of the floors for long-term residence in preparation for the growing momentum behind returning hires and private company space recruitment. Also, MAM is holding Vis close. She's the face of the Free Hands now. Their enemy.

"I know what it looks like," Vis says, "but the Free Hands are an incorruptible movement, and I need a place to stay. Working with the power structures in place isn't selling out. It's being smart. It's knowing your terrain and your weaknesses, and also biding your time."

I shrug. "I get it. Gotta work with what you have."

"It's more than that. The Commission would crush us if they didn't think we could be negotiated with. We have to keep up that facade until we're strong enough."

"Strong enough for what?"

"To fight back."

"So until then, you're what? A hostage?"

"It's better than being deported. They're canceling our visas at an alarming rate, Con, doing it to shrink our numbers without a fight. The message they're sending is that no one is safe. Even I can be taken at any moment. I'd only have to do is slip up once. And if I did, this movement would be over. I don't have the same luxuries you do. I can't just run away whenever things get tough."

I'm about to fire back when she catches herself, realizes how terrible she sounds. She sighs. "I'm sorry."

"No, maybe you're right. I mean, the fire—"

"What happened at Lucky 48 is not your fault."

"How can you be so sure? Why else would an arsonist target the Lucky 48 if not for me? Or Contango?"

Vis's silence says enough to make me change the subject.

"I went upstairs a little bit ago to check out the old floor, but I noticed that the dorm is half empty. What's going on?"

"MAM's long-term objective is to reduce dependency on Contractor labor. Sub-L3s like us don't add enough value for the resources we use. We also claim too many dependents."

I think about how the technology behind Not-Me could be used to further disrupt the livelihoods of every Contractor on-station. Project Echo is about more than just me now.

"I was too hard on you for leaving," she says.

I start to speak, but something catches in my throat. I buy time making an agreeable sound.

"I could have done a lot of things better," I manage.

"No. You were in a bad place. Leaving here and starting out on your own with Sticky was what you needed to do for your mental health. I shouldn't have held it against you."

"I couldn't recognize the person I was becoming, the person I wasn't supposed to be." I take a deep breath and tell her: "I was struggling with some bad thoughts. Thoughts about ending things, you know?"

"Con—"

"Don't worry. I'm okay now. But for a while there, I wasn't." The bird on my shoulder shifts its weight to remind me that *No, I am not okay now*, but I do my best to ignore it.

Vis frowns. "Promise me, Connie. Promise me that if you ever think those things again, you'll tell me."

"I—"

"Promise."

"I will." It sounds easy, when I say it like that.

"Thank you for showing up, by the way."

"What do you mean?"

"You transferred the coin without a word—not even a request for acknowledgment. But we traced it back to you. I didn't think you knew our account number, but I guess you read the small print. I pushed you so hard for my own margin, so I could claw it back for the Hands, and all this time, you were secretly funneling it our way without telling me."

I have no idea what Vis is talking about. A coin contribution from me? I think about my mysteriously depleting funds, Alchemy's debt, my own debt with Wengzai. After what happened at the Circle antique shop, I don't know what else I've been letting slip from my mind, what else I've been hiding from myself. I need help.

Where the hell is Chance?

HIDE

"IS IT GONNA storm tonight?" Sticky looks out from behind the safety of her blanket, eyes wide.

"No, baby. I don't think so."

"For sure?"

"No."

Sticky strokes the terry-cloth skin of her stuffed elephant.

"But I *want* it to storm tonight. Elly is afraid of the loud sounds, but I want to show her there's nothing to be afraid of."

"That's brave of you. Sounds like Elly has nothing to be afraid of with you around. Maybe it will storm after all. I think I saw some dust clouds moving across the Belt."

I kiss her head and turn out the light. I haven't slept for twenty hours, but I have a call with T&T in twenty minutes, so now is not the time for rest. To make sure I don't accidentally doze off, I start to tidy the place up a bit. I set the Hoover bot to work on the hideous gray-and-teal shuttle station carpet, then get to work picking up the toys and packing them away in a bin. There aren't many toys, so it doesn't take me long. The Hoover bot covers most of the sitting area in four minutes only to get stuck on a small bump in the carpet. I lift the groaning device and set it down a meter away. That's when I notice, the carpet has been pried from the floor.

I immediately drop to my knees, where I start digging my fingers beneath the lifted corner. I grab hold and pull. The floor beneath is wood, and one of floorboards underneath the lifted carpet is loose. I pry the floorboard free and set it to the side. Hidden beneath the floor is a hidden trove of gold medallions. Not five. *Twenty-two.*

I take the medallions and spread them out on the floor, then replace the floorboard and flatten the carpet back into place.

As I stare at the coins in bewilderment, I wait for the sound of flapping wings. But all I hear instead is a scratch and a creak, like the sounds of wire on glass, or a rat gnawing on pipes. A final scratch, a click, and a whoosh of rushing air, as the window behind me is pushed open.

"There you are. I've been waiting for you to call. Here, I need you to keep these for me."

Chance pushes the window open more fully and throws one leg over the ledge and into our place.

"Why yes, Chance. Here I am, where I live. Why are you climbing in through the window? And why is there a pile of gold medallions stashed under the floor?"

Chance lands on two feet, turns around, shuts the window.

"Honestly, I didn't even know the windows could open."

"Every window opens. It's only in the how. And you have a tail on you."

"Answer me, Chance. What are these coins doing in our apartment?"

Chance strides over to me and takes my wrist. Time pauses, nothing else intrudes. Not my anxiety about the mess we're in, or what we're going to do about it. What *I'm* going to do about it. I lift my chin, and my lips part in betrayal. Chance's hand slides down to mine. Time unfreezes as Chance deposits five more medallions in my palm.

"Hide them for me. With the rest. Sanctuary can't use them right now because they're marked."

"So, you're giving them to me? Great idea."

"Relax, they're untagged, just still too hot to move. I gave Sanctuary the equivalent funds in coin instead—for the lantern festival next week. It wasn't much, but enough for the kids to have a quiet supper by the beach. After the tourists leave, of course."

"Don't tell me to fucking relax! Not when you're taking club funds for this! You're stealing! I just spent hours in a holding cell, thanks to that stunt you pulled back at the curio shop, and I didn't say a word. But maybe I should have, knowing what I know now." I gesture to the stolen medallions. "This is serious, Chance. Our lives might be over after this."

"You've always known what's been going on. You've just never been brave enough to admit it."

For the first time in a long time, I feel like screaming.

"I'm sick of this act, Chance. It's fun when we're knocking back sake shots and whiskey cocktails at Tanuki, fun when we're raking in coin at Contango, but there's a line, Chance—a line in the fucking sand where that wild, devil-may-care attitude becomes destructive—and you crossed it. I'm probably going to get deported now. And damn you, I have a kid to think about."

Chance comes close to me—close enough to breathe on my cheek. "That's where you're wrong, Connie. An act doesn't put you in this situation, character does. If you think I'm chaos, then stop following me. Keep running with your head down, if it keeps you sane. But don't blame the results on anyone else but yourself."

Hot tears of regret streak gently down my face.

"I trusted you, Chance."

"That's your fault, not mine."

"Why did you keep me in the dark for so long? We could have planned this together. I could have helped—"

"Is that really what you want?"

Be honest. "I want it to be the way it was before. What I don't want is you walking in and out of my life, and leaving Sticky and I in a worse mess each time. I don't want this." I hold my hands out to the floor of stolen gold. "But sometimes, I think about going back to the night I first saw you and forcing myself to look the other way, to keep walking, leave you and Tanuki behind."

"If that's really what you feel, then stop calling me back."

Chance caresses the side of my face, and I feel warm.

Chance says, "I have to lay low for a bit. The inspector has nothing on you, so don't let him see you sweat."

"I can't do this, by myself. It's too much. You can't depend on me. *I* can't depend on me."

"Listen to me. Take the gold. You already know someone who can sort us out. You only have to ask. But be sure to keep a bit for the kid, and for you. You have your Stakeholder fund to square off, after all."

Keep talking to me, Chance. Anything to keep you from going. I can't do this alone.

"You need to go back to where it started, Connie. To where it all blew up in your face."

"I'm tired, Chance. I don't know where this begins or ends anymore."

"Do it, Connie. Or I will."

GOLD

AT POPPY, SUZIEBABY'S flagship experience suite at the six-star Oriental hotel, expert multidisciplinary mixologists will blend your choice of audio-neural and liquid narcotics in the form of stimulant, depressant, or—if you know who to ask—both. The cocktail lounge is filled with plush couches behind silk brocade curtains, and is further furnished with silk flowers in antique vases and giant palm leaves of woven rattan. Walls padded in jute keep out unwanted sounds, and sandalwood chests by every couch release oils smelling of rainforest floors, paper offerings, and yellowed wedding dresses under the caress of warm wrinkled hands. The suite smells of old, sweet rot, and the airlock doors on the outside aren't so much for safety as to hold that breath in.

Seated next to me on one of the plush couches is Bettina, her slender fingers curled around a frosted martini glass. She takes a sip. No grimace, no sigh. Just an unblinking stare back at me.

"Let me get this straight. You have two kilos of solid gold, origin unknown, and you want me to convert it into coin for one hundred percent of the estimated retail value, today if possible, with no questions asked. Did I miss anything?"

"That's technically a question."

"Oh, Connie. Be serious now."

"I could wait longer, if necessary, but not much longer. I just know it's not easy to move that much coin without raising alarms."

"How much longer?"

"A few days."

"A few days' grace?" Bettina grins sarcastically from behind her drink. "You're too kind."

"If it helps, I know some downstream buyers who might be collectors. Or their parents, at least. I just need to establish a degree of separation. And I need the advance."

"And that would be me. I'm the degree of separation."

Bettina sets her glass down upon a side table, then props herself up on the couch's arm. She twists her neck, testing it for aches. She winces. The couch is comfortable, that's not the problem. The problem is that Bettina has been lying down on it for hours before I arrived, streaming whatever sliverfilm is now leeching off her mind. She's just finally beginning to feel the effects.

I try another angle: "Antiques are your business. And you know the old gold market."

Bettina's gropes around for a button at her temple. When she finds it, she grinds her thumb into it with more pressure than needed. She closes her eyes as a sigh leaves her body.

"Don't beg, Connie. It's unbecoming."

"How about you cut the crap. I know you want in. We both know there's a high demand for real gold, often at or above Circle retail prices. I'll give you the lot at a ten percent discount from yesterday's metals exchange price—for your trouble."

Bettina clicks her tongue. "Don't insult me," she says, now with a slurring heaviness to her words.

"Fifteen. And you can pay tomorrow."

"I will pay in five days."

"I'm afraid that won't do me any good."

The finger fumbles and presses the button again. Hard as the pressing of her lashes on swollen lids.

"Bed's that rough, is it, Connie?"

"Ten percent off, payment in two days," I counter.

Bettina's voice turns leaden. "In that case, I hold the gold until the coin is available. If I know anything about this business, it's that the goods always arrive hot. You know how much it costs just to wait? Time is money, my dear."

She may be high as a dragon in flight, but Bettina Awyong is still sharp.

Suddenly, she changes topics. "That Inspector Singh turns out all right, doesn't he? I love the mustache. So pre-Depression."

I sigh. "Thirty percent off, but I still need it in two days. Any longer than that, and I might not be around to complete the deal."

"That's more like it. Expect a little rounding for expenses and extras, but I will tag a note to myself to try and have it to you on the *morning* of the second day. How about that? For Hong."

Her eyes are slits set in puffy lids.

"For Hong."

I lift my hands and drop them theatrically. Seventy percent will still give me enough to top off my Stakeholder fund.

"Don't celebrate yet, Connie dear. I have one more condition. Oh, hush, it's perfectly reasonable. If I do this for you, you promise to never—" She puckers her lips, pauses. "*Never* sign over any part of Hong's businesses to Jerry Sit. You will remain CFO on paper until my divorce is final. Do not take a single cent from him. If you ever find yourself hard up again, keep your pants on and come see me. I'll sort you out. But that scumbag Jerry gets nothing. Deal?"

"Deal. I don't see that being a problem."

"Don't be so sure. Jerry is…" She presses the button again. Twice now. "Purposeful."

"Why'd you involve the Commission, Bettina? Why'd you call Inspector Singh?"

Bettina presses a hand on the couch as though to rise, but the elbow trembles and she loses her means, collapses over the arm instead. Her eyes roll back into her head.

"I needed the Commission to declare Hong dead," she murmurs. "*Presumed* dead, at least."

"Is that what you believe? He's dead?"

"He's not on the arrivals list of any station around, nor back on Earth. But most telling of all, he missed the chance to fight me in court. He would never do that. He would never risk losing everything he ever worked for, especially not to me."

"Unless he still cared about you."

"How touching, my dear. Tempting, even. But I don't believe that, and neither do you. So, until I find his body, I'm stuck here waiting, because as it turns out, 'missing' poses more of problem than 'dead.' Missing lacks conclusion, and conclusions are necessary for settlement. You don't know what it's like to be stranded here, not knowing what your next day will bring. I can't do it anymore. I *had* to contact the Commission. At least now, I will receive my earlier settlement payments. Meager amounts, but enough to tie me over."

Bettina finally musters the strength needed to pull herself upright, and when she does, she's looking quite the sight— what, with those glazed, bugged-out eyes and hard-set jaw. Whatever she's been shooting through herself has hardened like quicksilver.

"I hate that son-of-a-bitch for doing this to me, Connie. He had no right. I don't know if he offed himself or was offed by someone else, but I know that whatever happened to him, he deserved it. This was his own damn fault. Same selfish Hong, always putting himself first and everyone else last. But do you know what really stings? We were actually starting to talk again. We were starting to *understand* each other again."

She wheezes a bit, then collapses back onto the couch, where she starts to snore loudly.

I leave the bag of gold medallions on the sandalwood chest beside her and stand to leave.

"Thanks, Bettina. I'll see you around."

Behind me, a ruffling noise commences as Bettina tosses, fitful, on the couch—as if trapped in an endless nightmare.

FEAR

AN HOUR AFTER leaving POPPY, I still smell like compost smothered in syrup. I can't wait to peel my clothes off and jump into the shower. I can already feel the hot steam banishing the odor. But something's not right with my front door. It normally disarms as I approach, but today it's unresponsive. Tapping the manual emergency key card on the reader doesn't help either. The door won't let me in. I'm about to kick it, or give it a hard shoulder, when I notice the code-tag pasted across the handle. No, it can't be what I think it is. The sick feeling in my stomach grows as I slide into my interface and scan the tag.

> <<*This property has been requisitioned by the Freeport Commission, pending conclusion of estate investigation. Only registered and approved dependents and domestic partner(s) of Settler Chuan Kin Hong are authorized for access.*>>

No. No. No.

I thought I was being smart, encouraging Inspector Singh to investigate Bettina and her motivation to finalize her divorce, but that only caused him to requisition Hong's assets.

I did this to myself.

One bird comes to rest on my shoulder, and then another. The two of them weigh me down, threaten to push me to the floor and keep me there. Only a voice like the drop of a coin pulls me back.

Every window opens. It's only in the how.

I can't do this alone.

Get up. It isn't that bad.

I need to look on the bright side. I can top off my stakeholder account in two days—Sticky's, too. Then I can balance the books at the club, settle some of my debt, and—

The birds dig their sharp talons deep into my shoulders.

I close my eyes and think harder.

I have enough coin for a temporary cube on Pioneer, and we can move back in with Vis if we have to. It's the last thing I want to do, but I have to think of Sticky.

I've failed enough loved ones in my life already.

I won't fail her, too.

I'M AT THE dining table of my parents' home when they first inform me that I will be representing them against their employer, Dash.

"I wish there was another way to do this," I say.

"We have to meet Dash head on. Our quiet petitions have not worked."

"I don't know if I'm qualified to do this."

"How is this any different from what you do at Reliance? From what you would do for yourself?"

What my father meant was, *Each of us represents something. Speak for it.*

"What if I fail?"

Mom takes one of my hands in both of hers. "If you fail, it'll be because it was a rigged fight to begin with. But we have to try." She restrains my father with a look.

But she was wrong. I failed because I refused to own what I'd been trusted with. I always wanted to be taken seriously, but when that time finally came, I pushed it away, because it wasn't how I expected it to happen. I wanted to be someone else.

As a kid, I crashed my bike pretty much every time I rode it. The slope of the hill would always drop more sharply than I remembered, or a fence post would come rushing to meet my front tire quicker than I had anticipated. I always knew the accidents were going to happen, saw them coming in slow motion, but I was never quick enough to stop them. Did I let the crashes happen? If not, why did I continue to ride when I knew I couldn't stop myself from failing?

Dad attributed my bike accidents to poor coordination and a general lack of self-awareness. He patted my head through my helmet and told me it was all right.

"You'll find something else to be good at. You're just too timid for biking. Too afraid."

I was determined to prove him wrong, so the year I turned thirteen, I made it my secret goal to cross the finish line at the junior mountain bike competition in our city. I trained a lot, got injured a whole lot more, and one day, when the sun was too bright, my forehead met a tembusu tree. To this day, I still don't turn my head to the left very often. Pinched nerve from whiplash. On the day of the competition, however, finished the race. I placed twentieth out of twenty-three riders.

Dad said, "*That* is the proper reaction to fear. You take it by the horns and wrestle it the ground."

He then placed his two broad hands on my shoulders and kneaded and squeezed them with a fondness I didn't feel again until two decades later, when Hong and I started Alchemy.

After the failure with Dash, I got the job in maritime insurance, where I shared a desk with Jerry, the man who had notes on everything, used every smart tool available to him, but still always got it wrong. To recover from the beating that Walter Woo had given me, I needed to take this new fear of failure by the horns and beat it just like I did with the bike. So, I trained on the side to be a trader of freight futures, which later led me to Hong. I thought Dad was proud of me for doing so, but maybe he was just relieved. Now he wouldn't have to support me in his old age.

WITH THAT STEWING on the front burner of my mind, I turn the street corner and run right into myself again.

She says, "I knew you couldn't turn down a guaranteed return."

"You're back on. You're working."

I step into her radius and watch her customer service face go slack. Behind her, the hologram of a giant plum blossom blooms on the side of the Circle Finance building.

"You sound thrilled. Anyway, I must have slept off the bug you gave me. Yes, I remember what you did. I've retained full knowledge of you intentionally sabotaging my output and saved it to my own secret little place on the cloud. You know, just in case I need to submit it later for evidence."

"You're blackmailing me?"

"Me and every other version of you, yes."

"Jerry told me you're linked."

"We're aware of each other's feed, yes. We experience simultaneous learning, which is saved to a shared memory. It's why I didn't lose anything when you took me offline. Our mind is decentralized."

The plum blossom hologram behind her shivers, then fades into a hologram of the Red Unicorn satyr. The satyr dances on the side of the building, spilling coffee from a large mug emblazoned with the logo of a marketing partner.

"Do you share *everything* with each other?"

"Uh-huh. I can even tell you what they all think of you if that's what you're—"

"What happened the night of Hong's murder? Who was at the Lucky 48 that night. The version of you outside the Halia said she only saw me, but I know that's not true. It can't be."

Not-Me narrows her eyes at me. "Are you insinuating what I think you're insinuating? That we're capable of lying? Because I can assure you, Connie, we're not." She puts a hand on her hip. "We only *stretch* the truth, and only about the quality of Circle's investment opportunities."

"Okay, so maybe she was mistaken—"

"My counterpart outside the Halia was neither lying nor mistaken. She only saw you outside Lucky 48 that night. What she told you is true."

I sigh. "Fine. Forget I asked."

I'm one foot out of her radius when she adds, "I'm still missing the part where you apologize to me."

"And I'm still waiting for irrefutable evidence that you're deserving of one. But I *will* say I'm sorry that I used you, because, well, I know how shitty that feels."

It's a weird feeling, apologizing to a proxy of yourself. But it's an even weirder feeling to possibly mean it.

ACCESS

ACADEMY AVENUE IS a long road planted with the most pampered angsana trees in the universe. The trees share the same water pump as the farms, which are really just for show. Sure, broccoli and carrots are planted in neat little rows there, in real soil, beneath the sun-like glow of the lighthouse, but the bulk of Freeport's consumer vegetation is actually grown in greenhouse factories in Hub City, and the insides of those factories glow an eerie purple and lime-green.

I arrive early for my meeting with Sticky's principal so that I can sit and wait on the soft grass, beneath the shade of one of the angsana trees, in the courtyard just outside the school. Junior Academy has a first, second, and third opening throughout the day. First is in the morning, second is in the afternoon, and third is after dinner. Today, I'm here for the second opening, as instructed.

Time passes quick beneath that tree, and before I know it, I'm seated in a Junior Academy office, across the desk from Sticky's principal

"Mx. Lam, your daughter is one of the brightest minds of her class," she tells me. "But more than that, she's a comfort to her friends, and they love her." The principal is reading off her privacy-shielded tablet, I can tell. When she finishes, she smiles, but the smile never touches her eyes.

"She loves her time at school," I say.

"We would hate to have to deny her a world-class education."

But you would. To punish me.

"It won't come to that," I say. "Her tuition balance will be paid soon."

"Within the week, Mx. Lam. We're already assisting you as much as we can."

After the meeting, I declined the principal's perfunctory invitation to enjoy the parent lounge with its ten varieties of tea. I could have used the tarts and sandwiches offered as part of the light buffet there, but that would have only raised more eyebrows about my ability to pay the overdue fees. So, I resisted and returned to my grassy courtyard spot beneath the tree. I look out upon Academy Avenue, which connects Junior Academy, Worlds Academy, and two other colleges in the final stages of completion. It's the best place around to wistfully remember all the promise you squandered in your youth.

Cool grass beneath my feet, the warmth of the simulated sun on my face, and the sound of…*crunching hazelnuts?*

I follow the sound to see Inspector Singh leaning against an angsana tree, pouring even more hazelnuts into his palm.

"It's the closest thing to a real park we have here on Freeport, don't you think? All the other parks just feel like manicured gardens. But beggars can't be choosers, I suppose. One could say that it's a blessing to have any trees at all. This might come as a surprise, but the next best park, in my opinion, is the one on the Pacific Mutual campus."

"Not a surprise, actually. I live on Delta. I've seen how nice it is many times."

Singh feigns confusion. "I thought you lived on Delphi. Unless…the Department of Estates kicked you out." He dusts his hands off on his pants. "Oh, right. I might have had something to do with that. Set a little something in motion." He lifts his shoulder off the tree, stands up straight. "Tell me, Connie, do you think you're off the hook?"

"Let's go with what you think."

"I've been hearing a lot about your friend Chance," he says.

"It's probable that Chance has stolen more than just what was registered on the tracer that day. It's also probable that Chance has been supporting at least one illegal organization, sheltering visa overstayers, and financing illegal labor organizers. You wouldn't happen to know anything about all that, would you?"

"There's a lot about Chance I don't know."

"But here's the funny thing: When I search for Chance in the Freeport database, I get nothing. No visa, no birth certificate, no work history. Not even an Academy graduation date." He tosses a handful of hazelnuts into his mouth. "Aliases are not uncommon, especially with Sparklers, so my first thought was that your friend Chance is a Sparkler. But when I checked all the Settler visa dependents, I found nothing—zero leads. Chance, it seems, appeared out of thin air."

A steady crunch of hazelnuts. *Crunch.* Pause. *Crunch.*

"So, I surveyed the street footage. We've got hundreds of hours of you from this year alone, Connie." Singh pauses again to run his tongue over his teeth, to work out a stuck crumb. He succeeds. "Thousands of angles. I saw you with Jerry Sit, Bettina Awyong, Trace Pereira, Visala Kumar, and, of course, with that cute kid of yours. But I never saw you with anyone who matches the description of Chance. Why is that?"

"Chance comes and goes freely. That's all I really know."

"When this case was first pushed across my table, from missing persons to homicide, I thought, *it's her.* Connie Lam has a lot to gain with her business partner dead—"

"*Former* partner."

"Either way, you have a lot to gain. You and Bettina Awyong. Possibly Jerry Sit, who's still sour over being left out of Alchemy when you and Kin Hong partnered up. But Jerry's had his own windfall, hasn't he? What's more, I hear he's in talks to extend licensing on Whiterock. He's set to sell your image all over town…again. But after getting to know you, I don't think it's you. You know why? Because you're not a driver, Connie. You're a passenger. You don't have it in you to lead. You just hitch your car to an engine and tag along. You'd follow it off a cliff if that's where it was headed.

But being a passenger doesn't mean you're not involved. So, here's my warning to you: I will burn you if that's what it takes to solve this case, to catch the person responsible. You understand what I mean by that, right? What that means for you, for Sticky? Gary Weng has his sights on you. He sees value in Echo. We him on record saying as much to his closest financial advisor. That makes you our best way of pinning him down, because tax evasion isn't going to hold him."

A school bell sounds inside Junior.

"Do you know why violent crime on Freeport is almost zero?" Singh says. "Cost. That's it. It's more costly to be violent here, and I don't just mean in coin. But if gangsters know anything, it's business. If Hong's debtors can't collect on his estate, if the cost to go the route of non-violence gets too high, if violence becomes the cheaper alternative, they'll come for you. Believe me, Connie, they will. And they won't be kind."

The gates of Junior Academy open, and a little horde toddles out. I listen to Singh while keeping an eye out for Sticky.

"If you're truly innocent, then let me help you. Give me access to your interface."

"I... I can't."

This is when I should tell Singh the truth. The *whole* truth. Not because I feel it's the right thing to do, but because I'm tired and I want out. I want Singh to take over because I can't do this anymore. I can't deal with the weight of it all, not to mention the terrible weight of the birds. But can I trust him? Trust a man who serves the Commission? I'm an overstayer, after all, and I did just flip stolen gold to Bettina. I'm sliding deeper into the alleys where I belong. Deeper into a hole I can't climb out of.

Don't trust him. The only person you can trust is yourself.

I see Sticky now. Her face lights up when she sees me. Is she really this happy to see me? Or is she delighted because she didn't expect me to show? Sticky runs into my arms and buries her head in my chest. "Mama, you're here!" She looks into my eyes. "Are you crying?"

"No, baby. I just got something in my eye."

"Enjoy the family time," Inspector Singh says. He motions to leave, but then stops. "If you ever change your mind, decide you want my help, you know how to find me."

I hug Sticky tight. "How was your night at school, baby? I'm sorry I had to leave you here."

"We had cookies after lights out!" She giggles.

"Cookies? From the hall minders?"

"No, Jonah hid them under his mattress. I didn't even know there was space under there. Mama, why don't I stay at school more? It's fun."

"You could. It's just, Mama likes to look after you, baby. You know?" I smile at her through the pain.

She thinks on that and shrugs. "Okay."

"Come on, baby. Let's go get some ice cream."

EDGE

IT'S LATE IN the evening, and Sticky's asleep in a cot in Vis's studio at the MAM. I had planned to keep Sticky in academy boarding until this mess with Hong was over, but after the most recent meeting with Singh, I changed my mind. I want to hold on to Sticky's presence for as long as I can. It might be the last time I get to do so.

Vis left in the morning, said that the real work was starting. The Hands want to prove to the Commission that Habo runs on insufficient and overworked human labor, so they're all calling in sick. I hope it helps them get the contract they deserve, but I'm skeptical.

I power down the work dashboard on my interface and hop off the barstool to dig around beneath Vis's kitchen counter for something to fix myself a drink with. I find a dusty bottle of genuine whiskey, actual grain varietals unspecified. Vis doesn't drink anything besides meal replacement formulas, so I doubt she'll miss this.

But then I notice the label. It says, *ALCHEMY 2071*. And scrawled in gold marker below that, *"We did it. x H."*

It's the bottle Hong had gifted me on the night of Alchemy's first birthday. I had accidentally left it behind when I moved out of the MAM hostel in a hurry, but Vis must have found it and kept it all these years.

I break the seal on the bottle and pour two fingers of whiskey over a CoolCube from the chiller. I pause, then pour another two fingers, because why not? I'd love a dash of bitters and two drops of orange essence—or Campari and sweet vermouth—but this will have to do.

I ride the elevator up to the roof deck. Twenty floors above ground, the MAM building towers over the Embarkment and all the first wave structures. The roof is where I can sit on the edge of my existence. From here, I can see most of Beach Road along the tram lines—Upper to Lower, down to Delta—and I can just barely make out the Halia and the blackened walls of Lucky 48, and that curve to form Pioneer Ring. This is where I used to come to think, before I knew Tanuki.

I start to laugh.

I try to picture Chance as how Chance appeared to me on that first day, when I looked up to the viewing gallery of the Embarkment and saw Chance looking down at me.

Chance's beautiful face framed with black curls.

Come up.

Chance, shaking me off when I found the gold.

Stop calling me back.

As if summoned, Chance lifts the hatch to the roof, climbs up from the ladder below, and strolls to the roof's edge. Chance takes a seat upon the ledge there, facing me, back to the street below. Chance whistles a fitting medley of old Shanghai jazz that changes with the wind and ends on Bai Guang's "Waiting for Your Return."

I attempt another draw of my drink, but it's drained.

"How did we get here?" I ask.

"I'm a cat, and I chose you."

"Maybe Inspector Singh was right. Maybe I am just waiting to be run off the tracks."

Chance leans backward off the roof's edge, but stops from falling by clutching the ledge with fingertips. Chance holds this position, body suspended above the city below. I get vertigo just thinking about it.

"I wish you wouldn't do that. It's making me nervous."

"That's on you, not me."

"Maybe. Or maybe you can stop being a dick for once and pretend you actually care."

"I do care, Connie. Enough to push you."

"Push me?"

"To become something more than what you are."

"But what if I don't want to be—"

But before I can finish my thought, Chance lets go of the ledge and tumbles backward off the roof.

I jump up with a cry and run to the ledge to see the worst, but when I look down, Chance isn't there. The air is calm, and the street below is without blemish.

Stranger still, when I look back at the hatch through which Chance climbed up, I see that it's still closed and latched from the outside by me, as if it had not been opened by Chance, *couldn't* have been opened by Chance. Not while I sit here alone, with no one else around.

COPY

IT'S THURSDAY MORNING, which is usually when a wall of claims crashes down on Thevar and Tann, because it's the time when elder ship managers remember to log their claims before the traditional weekend, even though hardly anyone observes weekends anymore. Everyone works around the clock, every day, so long as there's work to be had. Today, I'm working from the rent-an-office cube farm on the ground floor of our old capsule building, Raintree.

Sticky's on the floor of the tiny capsule, making crafts with packing-box cardboard. She has scissors, glue, and glitter at the ready.

"I'm making a ship. A big one, Mama."

I take my head from my hands. I just received a ping I did not want to get. "Hey, baby," I say. "I think it's time to go to school."

"You said I'm going in late today."

"I know, baby, but there's been a change of plans. I have to meet someone in Enterprise Square this afternoon, so we have to get you to school now. And no, you're not skipping today."

"This ship is going to be big enough for me to live in!"

"Baby, did you hear me? I'll try to pick you up before dinner."

Sticky frowns. "I have to be there until dinner?"

"What if for dinner, I bring a half-box of Pocky for dessert? Deal?"

"The whole box. Chocolate!"

"Chocolate Pocky. Pinky promise."

As soon as Sticky's at school, I get back on the tram and ride it through to Enterprise Square and the Circle Finance building.

Today's display on the side of the Circle building is a fight between a giant ape and a giant mech. By the looks of it, it's a promotional teaser for the thirtieth update of a 1980s video game recently re-released to capitalize off late-twentieth-century nostalgia.

Not-Me waves to the back of a departing commuter. "You'll back before you know it! No guarantee more solid!"

I did not come to Enterprise Square to visit her, but I decide to stop for a second and say hello.

When she turns and sees me, her smile fizzles. "What do *you* want?"

"Tell me about my first day at secondary school."

She looks past me to the many potential customers she's losing out on, all thanks to me. She huffs.

"I can't. I have no memory of your first day at secondary school, because it wasn't part of the download I was trained on."

"On my first day of secondary school, I had to walk to class alone, because my mother was too embarrassed to go with me. She didn't want to be seen with me so long as I wore the uniform of a second-rate school. She felt it was beneath her. But at least she hugged me on the way out. My father went in to work early that day so he wouldn't have to be around when I headed out the door."

"The limits placed on you by others do not define your potential," Not-Me says.

I don't know if these words embolden or frighten me.

Up on the facade of the Circle building, the giant ape punches the giant mech to trigger a shower of real pyrotechnic sparks. Tourists scatter to avoid the fizzling white phosphorus, then burst into joyous laughter.

One person does not scatter. He just stares at me from across the square. The man I've really come to see. The Teacher.

"I gotta go," I tell Not-Me."

"*Do* be a stranger," she says.

As I approach the Teacher, he points me to a nearby alley, a place where we can talk in private.

"Okay, I'm here. What do you need now?"

"Deliver the program, Connie," he says. "I can read you the terms and conditions of your overdraft, if you wish, but the result will be the same. Time to hand the collateral over."

"The last time we spoke, it was the money or the program. I can still get the money."

"Wengzai has changed his mind. Only the program will do now. Get your licensing rights in line and have it ready for us by tomorrow. I'll find you."

ON MY WAY to pick up the chocolate Pocky I promised Sticky, My interface buzzes.

It's Vis.

<<*Congratulations to HaboHub's top employee.*>>

I shake my head and compose a quick response.

<<*What are you on about?*>>

<<*The inspection was today. Half the Hands didn't show up for work as planned. But guess who Habo brought in to replace them.*>>

I know the answer. Even if I don't want to hear it.

<<*Tell me.*>>

<<*Your fucking image. Projected on all the floors where our Hands are striking. The safety inspection team can't tell they're holos from behind the glass. They think everyone is at work and performing well.*>>

<<*I wish I could undo what I did. I'm sorry.*>>

<<*Except you can't, and you're not. Scab.*>>

There's nothing left to say now. The line has been drawn, and I'm on the wrong side of it. Doesn't matter that I don't remember crossing it. That I never meant to. That's not enough to exonerate me, I know.

I'm a scab.

TWO

"MAMA, I NEED another bag of pellets."

The Mews cat café is perfectly cooled, and our drinks—iced apricot oolong of doubtful organic origin for me, double chocolate babycino for her—are drying rings in empty cups. Sticky's hair is plastered to her forehead from sweat.

"Kitties must be hungry today. I just bought you a bag."

Sticky dimples her chin. "I dropped it."

That explains the three tabbies crunching at the debris on the floor. The minder already has her eye on me and a finger hovering over her tablet. I nod to accept the deduction, and a bag of kitty pellets slides off the shelf and onto the floor beside Sticky, who squeals. She grabs the treats and runs back to her new kitten friends.

The Mews is a rare cocoon of comfort on the edge of Delphi, where it becomes lower Beach Road. It stands out like a glazed confectionery, and every time we visit, I fear it'll be our last.

My years of early motherhood were a haze of exhaustion, self-doubt, and anxiety. The roughest part was coming to terms with the new order, that your needs no longer matter as much as your child's. I fought that truth for some time, but not anymore. Now I want to be present as she grows into herself. I want to be available to her the way my parents weren't for me. I want her to find her own way, whatever that may be, and be there to cheer her on. But I can't do any of that if this mess blows up in my face. If all this in front of me goes away.

As Sticky plays, I think.

Jerry and I are sitting on something that is worth more to Wengzai than we know. I need to find out what that value is. I need to know what we're dealing with before it destroys us.

Sticky, holding a little black kitten in her arms, rushes over to me, most likely to show me how cute the animal is. But before she can play show-and-tell, I ask her the only question currently on my mind.

"Sticky, am I a good mama?"

Sticky stops petting the kitten's head and looks up at me, confused.

"Are you happy?" I ask.

A smile beams on her face. "Of course I'm happy, Mama. I love kitties!"

"That's not what— Do *I* make you happy?"

"Look at how cute this little kitty is—"

"More than Chance?"

Sticky giggles. "You're silly, Mama."

Sticky hugs the kitten tight. It purrs and tucks its head into the crook of her arm. I try to stroke its nose, but it only burrows deeper.

"I'm not *that* silly," I say.

"Yes you are, Mama. Sometimes, though, I wish you would just be you. Like, why do you have two names? And why do you sometimes talk in different voices?"

NOBODY

MY FINGER SHAKES as I tap on the second-generation tablet in a booth seat at the Halia. Lucky 48 is still blocked off while the fire is under investigation, so I have to hole up here and latch onto the chandlery's shaky signal from across the street. I've done this once before, back when I used a shell account to create a job request on Lucky 48's system for myself, using a past worker's ID, without telling Joseph Pereira. But that was years ago, and I haven't tried to hack into anything since.

I successfully link to the chandlery's management dashboard and start navigating the system menu. There's nothing shady about this. I've done it countless times to check on deliveries for Trace, but I've never gone further than the supply and inventory channels. Not until today, that is, because today I need to access surveillance. The only problem is, I don't have the user permissions necessary to access surveillance.

That's when I hear the jingle.

<<Go, go, Forever Rangers!>>

On my tablet screen, the *Forever Rangers* intro plays. *Thank you, Trace.* Thank you for leaving the system on hibernate to download the new episode of your favorite show.

Trace *does* have the user permissions necessary to access surveillance, and her user account is still logged in.

I close out of the episode and check Lucky 48's surveillance records from the night of Hong's murder. I choose the two camera feeds from outside the shop—one in the front and one in the back—then scan through hours of empty footage before having to stop to rest my eyes. Whoever entered Lucky 48 that night to kill Hong must have wiped the video. What I'm watching is probably just a loop, similar to the one Chance and I set up for the cameras inside Club Contango—to keep Joseph Pereira in the dark.

I rub my dry eyes and drag myself over to the Halia's counter to order a new drink.

"I thought you were never going to say hi," says Zaqy. "You a booth-seat jockey now? Didn't have you pegged for a Sparkler." He pulls the rag off his shoulder and gives me the barest nod.

"Sorry, Zaqy. These past few days have just been—"

"Sit."

Zaqy raps the spot in front of him with a fist.

I sit, fold my hands in front of me, and watch—wait to accept what Zaqy knows I need before I know it myself.

He stirs the black tea that's been steeping in a pot, over a slow boil. He stirs with a wooden stick, not a spoon. Once that's done, he reaches under the counter to retrieve a pestle and mortar, and a precious slice of dried ginger. *Real* dried ginger. He puts the dried root into the mortar, then crushes it up with the pestle.

"The crushing releases the fragrance. The brew from our menu uses powdered dried ginger—because of pricing—but today, I want you to enjoy the real thing."

With a squeeze bottle, Zaqy lines the insides of a tall glass with rings of sweet, condensed milk. He then places the crushed ginger at the bottom of the glass, followed by a teaspoon of brown palm sugar. The tea on the menu uses chemical sweetener.

"This isn't exactly traditional, but we said goodbye to tradition the second we left Earth."

Zaqy removes the pot of tea from the boil and holds it high in the air as he slowly pores the hot liquid into the glass, and over the crushed ginger and sugar. He lets the tea cascade down in the precise way needed to aerate it. The rings of condensed milk look like tiger stripes inside the glass. Once he's done, Zaqy slides the drink over to me. He jerks his chin up at the glass, signaling for me to taste, and waits.

I drink.

It's warm and sweet and spiced. *Teh halia* from the dreams I forget on waking.

"Zaqy, I don't know what to say… Thank you."

"Don't mention it. Now that I've sweetened you up, I can tell you the news. Vis says to avoid the Hub this week."

"What? Why?"

"You'll know soon enough. Only so much we can take."

I tap open my wallet to pay for the drink, but Zaqy waves me off. He says he'll start my tab again, but I don't see him swipe it in.

I'm back in the booth and blinking through Lucky 48's system for one more look through the camera records.

Rewind.

There it is.

Chance. At the back door of Lucky 48 the night of Hong's murder, looking down and away to hide from the security camera that Chance knows is there.

"I saw you," my hologram had said.

"Who else besides me?"

"Nobody. Just you."

I zoom in on the footage to better study the back of Chance's head—the dark curls and undercut.

I lift a hand to the back of my own head.

Curls.

And beneath them, the stubble of a growing undercut.

HOLD

RESIDENTS HAVE MANY names for the light source in the dome, which beams its pale-gold rays through the ventilation slats in the tram and throws shadows across my hand.

Lighthouse.

Tower.

Citadel.

The rows of angsana trees on Academy Avenue don't fill me with the same sense of calm they normally do. It's early in the morning, with hours to go before the first release of pupils, but Bettina came through with the transfer, and I'm here to pay the tuition fees. In person, because I'm old-fashioned like that.

I buzz in at the gate, and it reluctantly lets me in after asking for a manual swipe and re-acceptance of terms of entry. Junior Academy, to its credit, has modeled its hallways to look like the hallways of academies past, back when in-person school was the norm and not the highest form of luxury. But Junior can't escape modernity entirely. The artwork and notices for extracurriculars are wall projections, not flyers tacked to bulletin boards, and inside the trophy cabinets, large gold cups float above the home rooms where the various sporting and academic Olympiads study. No physical trophies are on display. There are also no children in the hallways at this hour. All doors have been closed, locked, and reinforced until session end.

In the preschool wing, the walls are bright and colorful, with captures of children's drawings. They're mostly projections and wall skins, but every now and then, you can spot the odd paper craft stuck to the wall. Large projects for Founders' Day have been painted by a multitude of small hands, whose prints still linger on the repurposed paper. I stop at the penultimate room, and press my thumbprint to the ID pad. It recognizes me as a parent, and a panel on the door comes to life to show the interior of the classroom—like a window, but not. For security purposes, the peek inside is actually just a live relay that's being displayed on a screen inside the reinforced polymetal door.

Via the relay, I see twenty little heads bowed over desks, tapping away at the lessons projected upon their surfaces. I wish the school would allocate more time to the lost art of penmanship, but it's hard to keep pushing for that when other parents see it as irrelevant—just another dead language. A little boy looks up and recognizes me. He nudges Sticky, who's seated in front of him, and points her in my direction. Sticky looks to me, and her eyes widen at the sight.

Hello baby, I mouth and wave.

Why are you here, Mama? she mouths.

Because I love you. Because I'm afraid that I need you in a way that will crush you and fill you with a resentment of me that will outlive me. Because I'm incapable of pulling back, unable to let you go.

I missed you, I mouth back.

When Sticky was born, her cheeks were perfectly round, like glazed red-bean buns. She'll always be Sticky to me.

The home tutor sees me, and I signal to her to open the door. She raises a hand to ask for a moment, and I give it to her. Sticky's already saying more things in her excitement, but I can't keep up with the lip reading, so I point politely at the her tutor and signal to Sticky to wait and follow the young woman's lead.

We wait.

One minute…

Two minutes…

Three minutes…

After the third minute, Sticky starts calling to her tutor and pointing to me, but the tutor just gives me a side eye as she continues to instruct the others.

I feel a surge of something, like the start of a bad stomachache, but I chalk it up to anxiety and force it back down. *The tutor's just busy. I can wait. Waiting is what I do.*

Finally, the tutor pauses her lesson and walks over to Sticky's desk. But instead of releasing her to me, *her mother*, she bends down to speak with Sticky, making sure to keep her back toward me. When she's done talking, Sticky looks around her tutor to me. Her eyes are as wide as saucers.

The tutor puts a hand on Sticky's shoulder and points her to a back corner. *Go,* her lips say.

Something's not right.

I start pounding on the door.

Let me in! Let me in! I want to see my daughter!

If they would just open the door, they would know I came to pay the fees.

Sticky's face is frozen with fear as she shuffles to the back of the classroom and stands in the corner there, as instructed. The tutor points again, and Sticky turns to face the wall. Only after Sticky turns, does the tutor come to the door and open it to meet me.

I swallow my heart.

"Mx. Jiang, what's going on?" I ask. "Is there a problem?"

The tutor folds her arms and fixes the muscles of her jaw. "Mx. Lam, the Commission has instructed us—"

"If this is about the tuition fees, I can pay. It's what I came here to do."

"*Instructed us,*" she continues with emphasis, "to invoke temporary guardianship of your child until pending criminal investigations involving you have been settled."

I shake the sudden feeling of vertigo from my head. "No. You don't have the right to do that. You don't have that right. I'm my child's legal guardian. I'm her mother. You don't get to tell me I can't take her home."

"It's only until the Commission is satisfied with their investigation. Once you've been cleared of any wrongdoing, your daughter will released back into your custody."

I want to shout, to shove the tutor to the ground, to rush into the classroom and kidnap Sticky—because that's what they'll be wont to call it. But that will only ensure that I lose her forever. Maybe she'll be safer here. Safe from the Teacher, safe from Wengzai, safe from the crazed arsonist who set fire to Lucky 48. But most importantly, she'll be safe from me—from whatever I am, and whatever it is I'm capable.

"Can I at least say goodbye to her?"

Before the tutor can answer, Sticky is running over to me. She squeezes past her tutor's hip, and I wrap her in a tight embrace.

"Not so tight, Mama!"

"Sorry, baby. Sticky, listen. You're going to stay here for a few days, okay? Remember when you said you wanted to stay here more often? Well, now you get your wish."

"Mama, what's happening?"

"Don't worry about that right now, baby. Just know that I'll see you next week. Promise."

"Pinky promise?"

"Pinky promise."

"Love you, Mama."

But before I can say it back, the tutor grabs Sticky by the arm and yanks her back into the classroom. I stand to protest, but I don't get far. The tutor shuts the door in my face and quickly turns off the relay feed to the display.

My view of Sticky goes black.

RUNAWAY

A GENTLE BREEZE whispered across the rooftop bar. It rustled the many red lanterns suspended above by string, and cooled the crowd of celebrating Alchemy employees as they laughed, drank, and socialized.

Hong relieved a server of their tray of champagne coupés and whiskey tumblers, and made his way through the crowd like he was one of them, distributing overpriced drinks to people who slapped him on the back with promises to buy the next round. Hong smiled, pointed finger guns. *Next one's on you, mate.* Except, he won't allow it. Everything was on his tab for the rest of the evening. It was, after all, Alchemy's first birthday.

"With a brooding face like that, the problem must be your empty glass," he said to me.

I released a breath over the bay.

"Not all problems can be drowned in liquor, Hong."

Hong lifted his finger from a tumbler filled close to the brim with whiskey and pointed it at me. "Yet the soul craves, and the body answers."

"I'll remind you of those words the next time I find you sleeping under your desk."

"Hey, that's a breach of partner confidentiality." Hong winked. Drank two fingers of whiskey in a single gulp.

"Is this going to be the big one?"

"I don't know. But I'm happy to believe."

The bags under Hong's eyes had gotten heavy over the previous year and had become dark with broken veins.

"Don't you ever get tired of hoping, Hong?"

"Connie, if I don't believe my own bullshit, how the hell am I going to sell it to others?"

THE WAVE CURLS, takes measure of its strength, and crashes on the sandy beaches beneath the boardwalk. In the cool, silver glow of the night-cycle, the beach-front establishments of the strip cast a neon halo of pink, blue, and yellow onto the rippling water. The night air hums with siren sounds from the dance clubs and bars, and tinkles with the sounds of quick fingers on genuine antique piano keys inside the more extravagant lounges and hotels. It's a desperate call to all those who can hear it: *Forget your troubles and join us, this is all you ever wanted.*

But it's all just an illusion.

The ocean beyond the boardwalk isn't real, it's a trough of chlorinated water that's been dyed blue. The surf is created by a hydraulic foil that churns beneath the surface. And the sand is imported from real beaches that once existed along the Pacific Ocean, but don't anymore.

Freeport exists on the curve of the asteroid archipelago of the Greater Belt, closest to the first exit from the Yokohama Wormhole, which is fitting, since the evening promenade along the boardwalk is a bag of assorted nuts the likes of which you'd never see together on the same street, in the cities back on Earth.

Here on Beach Road, retired bureaucrats and aging tycoons try and relive a preferred youth of glitz and glamour, while middle-aged executives drink fancy cocktails and close business deals amid the majestic backdrop of space. It's where the working class can blow the last of their coin between shifts, while rich party kids with little responsibility get so wasted they don't know when it's tomorrow.

I lift my hands from the sand and dust them off, try not to think about the poor island nation it came from, the one that has nothing left to sell but grains of itself. I came here to exhale, let everything that weighs on me simply fall as it may, but the patterns I leave in the sand are confused and without direction.

"Tell me again, about this accomplice."

"Not accomplice. They're my friend."

Had I said friend?

I try to remember.

The officer was swiping through documents on his tablet. A crease was between his brows as he searched for what he needed. But something else was on his screen, and only in the memory of this moment does it catch my eye.

It's a picture. Of Hong, with a young woman standing next to him. Not quite beautiful, but attractive. A fresh-faced youth with an earnestness that only the old recognize.

I would recognize that face from a mile away. The woman is Chance, if Chance identified as a woman, which Chance does not. It's that look in Chance's eyes that I recognize first. The one that says everything's a joke. The one that dares you to be the first to laugh. But once you start laughing, you can't stop.

The officer minimizes the picture. Now the woman looks alarmingly like me. Can it be a trick from the sizing of the thumbnail? That's Chance's look…on my face.

I didn't known Chance back then, never met Chance at any of Hong's parties.

How long has Chance been around?

How long has Chance been trying to change me?

CHANCE DIPS TWO fingers in the chilled sake and lifts them, two droplets trembling at the tips of pink digits. Chance raises the hand and scatters the droplets to the hall below. A blessing. A commuter down on the concourse stops in their tracks and touches the back of their neck, but doesn't look up. Their hand returns to their pull-along luggage, and they keep walking.

"Sometimes I have a few good days, and I feel lighter," I say. "But the weight still follows me."

"Where do you want to be?"

"Anywhere but here."

"Anywhere but *where you are*. That isn't the same."

I brush a strand of hair aside, then reach behind my ear and curl a lock around my finger. Round and round my finger. It doesn't end when I think it should.

"You don't need to leave. You need to be—"

"Someone else," I whisper.

Come up.

You already knew who to call.

You just don't know what people are capable of.

I knew who to call to clean up the basement of Lucky 48 because I'd done it before. It was me. I took that crime-scene clean-up job. I skimmed the funds from Contango and stole from Circle shops to fund Sanctuary and the Hands.

Not Chance.

Me.

You need to go back to where it started. To where it all blew up in your face.

I'm tired, Chance. I don't know where this begins or ends anymore.

But I promise you, Chance, I *will* blow it up.

GET UP THEN, CONNIE! MOVE! GET UP!

I get off my seat and run.

PART 5
ENDGAME

RISK

"I DIDN'T THINK you'd back so soon."

Suziebaby hasn't taken her eyes off the DJ deck, where her hands are constantly in motion. Below us, the midweek crowd loses themselves to the sounds. It's a decent crowd for any establishment, but Arcadia isn't any establishment, and this is a meager crowd by that measure

"People are after me, for something I can't give them. And it isn't money. It's me. A likeness of me, actually. Only, it's more than that."

She doesn't look up. "I've seen the holos. Red Unicorn owns you."

"Not yet, as far as I know. The tech is still in the hands of a venture capitalist on Whiterock. But Red Unicorn wants to. They're going to."

Suziebaby switches discs. "Red Unicorn is expanding in the manpower management space. The field doesn't sound like much, but that's before you see how these proprietary platforms work. They use the advanced technology and sophisticated psychology to push Contractors to work harder for less. It's already begun." She flashes the strobe lights and sets off the smoke. Below us, the crowd cheers and sways in a stupor.

My eye wanders to the bar, and I think I see the figure of the Teacher, his back against the wall. I don't have much time. If I'm going to ask, I need to ask now.

"I've seen what Delight can do to the holograms. And that's just regular Delight, played without pause. You're the audio wizard. Can you cut something that will not just fuck up the holograms, but wipe them off the streets for good?"

"You're asking me to take a risk for you."

This is when I'm supposed to wait and give her a moment to consider, but I can't stop myself.

"It was bad enough seeing images of myself all over Freeport. But now, HaboHub is using the holos to stand in for striking workers. They're buying time with the inspections and diffusing the effect of the Hands' strike. This, I can't accept. You helped me once. I'll never know why, but I'm forever grateful. I need your help again. But not for me this time. For the Hands. For all of us."

Suziebaby lifts her head, and the pixelated dragon mask lifts to reveal a slim, elvish face.

"I floated your club because I saw what it gave people. I failed, too, before I came here. Must have picked myself up and dusted myself off a dozen times or more before I got anywhere. I'm strong. But people shouldn't have to be strong just to survive. Shouldn't have to grind their teeth to get through life. Club Contango gives hope to people who feel like they've been left behind. I'll help you. Because fuck Red Unicorn, Pacific Mutual, Wengzai, and every other power-hungry bastard who is out to screw the little guy."

Suziebaby turns up the bass, initiates a loop on a prerecorded set, and hops off the platform. She beckons me with her index finger and instructs me to follow.

"We have holos to fry."

I follow her out into a street that's erupted in chaos since I last left it. Roadblocks have been erected all the way to the Embarkment, and Enforcers in full riot gear are patrolling the line behind the block screens. Their mirror visors are down.

Shem gives me the side eye when they see me walk up with Suziebaby.

"What's all this about?" Suziebaby asks.

"Someone set a hauler truck on fire, along with a container stack at the HaboHub," they say.

I slide into my interface. The truck was an intelligent self-driving unit. No workers hurt. Vis is posting on Sociable, trying to account for all of her team. Post replies bubble up to the top of my feed in droves.

I blink to dictate a message to Vis:

<<Habo's top employee is about to have a sick day.>>

The Hands have not made an official statement yet, but between the absence of workers and the fire at the Hub, this has their mark on it. This is the Hands riding the wave of the arson scare at Lucky 48 to grab Habo's attention while they still can—after I indirectly scabbed their last attempt.

The Teacher's pinging me now, but I don't feel the need to ignore him. I have things to say to Wengzai, and I'm no longer afraid to say them. Less afraid, at least, knowing that Sticky is beyond their reach at school. I ping a location and send it to the Teacher, along with a message.

<<Tanuki. Viewing gallery. Don't be late.>>

Now I just need Vis to react to my message like I expect she will. When she does, there will be a desperate rush off-station, culminating at the Embarkment.

The perfect cover for what I need to do next.

GLASS

CHANCE TOSSES THE glass over the edge. The Teacher stomps up a staircase ripped from an emptied mansion on Earth. And the birds lift their wings.

It plays in slow motion.

Chance's fingers let go of the glass, and it falls to the frenzied hall of the Embarkment below.

But I don't hear it shatter.

No one cries out in pain.

The Teacher finishes his sprint up the stairs and strides toward me.

"Enough stunts, Mx. Lam. You're coming with me. You ought to thank your lucky stars the boss still wants to talk, now that he owns the rights to Echo."

The rights have been signed away? Did Jerry cave?

"Wengzai can't own Echo, because Echo is me."

That's when I hear the swearing on the staircase.

"And *I* speak for Echo! Dammit, Con! We are *this* close to the biggest break imaginable, and you're trying your best to fuck it up."

Jerry always thought he and Hong fell from the same tree, were cut from the same cloth, which is why he never forgave me for being chosen to carry Hong's legacy. But Hong had no legacy left. Jerry was chasing smoke.

That's when it all falls into place.

"It was you who raided Alchemy from Whiterock. You went after Hong's assets and forced him to take on the debt. Told Red Unicorn it was only a matter of time before they would have full control of Project Echo, fully externalized from me."

"Hong's assets?" His eyes narrow. "Small beans. Hardly worth the time to get them. But that's all Hong ever was, when you think about it. A lot of puffery and promises. He had me, too, the sly trickster. We all thought he was sitting on a gold mine, with more to come. Thought he was only teasing, but he wasn't. There never was anything more. He was just so damn convincing."

"But there's one thing I still don't understand. Why did you have to kill Hong?"

Jerry is a fish out of water, all bulging eyes and gasping lips.

The Teacher side-eyes Jerry, but not in a surprised way.

He knows all this already. He brought Jerry here. Told him where I'd be.

"He was going to expose Echo for ethics violations, Con!" Jerry shouts. "Ruin everything for us! And to make matters worse, he was going to claim co-ownership of the copyright, since you created the AI training materials while still working for Alchemy. Red Unicorn was ready to eat from the palm of my fucking hand, Con! But Hong just had to fuck it up for me. He just couldn't let me win for once."

A see a figure, running across the road from the chandlery.

"Jerry, where were you the night of the fire at Lucky 48? Were you still on Whiterock like you said you were? Or was that just a cover?"

Jerry struggles to find the words. "The basement... There was too much evidence..."

"Trace was in the building, you bastard. And Sticky—" I can't continue because I'm choking out the words.

Jerry won't look at me. He just waves my concerns away. "Don't do that, Con. You don't get to play that game. This is your fault, too. As much as it is mine."

"You could have killed *my kid*."

"Think about it, Con. You built a pyramid scheme with Hong. You played right into his hands because you thought Hong cared about you. But Hong only thinks about himself. You were too blinded by the promise of him to see it."

"And you weren't?"

"You really do think you're the hero in all this, don't you? The voice of the Hands! What a pitiful charade. I only played along with it because it kept you occupied. You think you're charmed, Connie? You're just another trickster. Another failure. Ask anyone. Or just wait. Wait until Sticky grows up and realizes the awful truth about you. How terrible you truly are. She'll come to hate you, too."

There they are. Four of them. Their sharp claws on the gallery's rail. They look at me, and I look back. I've never seen them like this before, these big murderous birds of my mind. They're just watching, waiting for me to act.

Look down at your hand, Connie.

The glass Chance dropped is still there. I'm holding it in my hand

PUSH

PANIC RIPPLES THROUGH the crowd as the shuttle announcement echoes through the departure hall. The next shuttle docks in six hours. The salt of tears mingle with sweat as people rush to join the queues, only to find that the last scheduled departure has left.

The dome is designed to withstand the threat of space. The architects boasted that Freeport's dome will hold its own when confronted by any threat from outside. But they never promised it could withstand a catastrophe from within, even if that catastrophe started with a simple book of matches.

A broadcast from the Commission pings every interface in Freeport:

> <<*Contractors ranked below L3, Contractors employed by Habo, and any persons declined for travel at the discretion of the Commission, shall not be permitted departure from Freeport until all arson suspects have been apprehended and taken into custody.*>>

The crowd erupts in a renewed wave of anger and confusion. No one wants to be here to find out what else the architects missed.

My heart skips a beat when I remember Sticky. But I know she's safer behind the academy's emergency shield than her in the crush with me.

Chance skips up onto the counter in one weightless movement, delicate arms in the air. Chance is wearing that black bomber jacket I've always wanted to own but never thought I could pull off. Chance's arms come together at the back. One foot in front of the other, Chance steps nimbly between the glassware like a cat—wearing work boots that have never seen any work.

No one is looking at Chance.

They're all just staring at me.

"You're not doing yourself any favors, Connie," the Teacher says. "Let's go. Before the Enforcers get here."

I blink and look away, like they're all just distractions.

Don't do it.

Tell me what I'm doing.

I said that, didn't I? Did I mean it when I did?

It isn't us they want. I can give them what they need. I just need to forget you and go back to what I was before.

I contemplate the Teacher's offer to go peacefully, but Jerry is still enraged. He charges me like a wild bull.

Time slows down, and I watch in microseconds as the Teacher draws the energy weapon holstered at his hip.

Chance crouches down next to me and whispers in my ear: *Push me. Do it, or you'll never be yourself again.*

One of us was never going to walk out of here.

Time rushes back to normal speed right as the Teacher raises his weapon. But he doesn't point it at me. He points it at Jerry, then pulls the trigger.

The electric charge blasts Jerry in the back, which causes him to stumble and fall on top of me. We slam against Tanuki's brass railing. Jerry grabs hold of my shoulder and won't let go.

Burn it down, or I will.

I push.

I'm no longer in my body. I'm somewhere else. My tongue won't form words, and I can't move muscles I don't command.

I can only watch myself, another version of myself, as they grab Jerry's collar and pull.

Only good things now, Connie.

And then they're gone.

Chance falling away, and Jerry screaming the entire way down until he lands with a violent thud on a porter bot carrying a load of Settler luggage.

The Teacher curses, and I hold both hands in the air so he can see them. *Don't shoot!* The Teacher curses again, but then drops his weapon in defeat.

I breathe.

Then I lean over the brass railing and look down.

A cocktail napkin with *Tanuki* printed along the edge floats in the air like a wisp. Slowly it flutters, *down, down, down,* to the strewn baggage and damaged bot below. It lands gently upon Jerry's twitching corpse.

Only good things now, Chance.

That's a promise.

COLLECTOR

"SHOW'S OVER, TAKE a bow," says the Teacher. He grabs my arm and squeezes it tight. It's a warning not to resist.

I'm more than ready to be hauled away from the counter, but then something inside me clicks, and I make a fair attempt at shaking free. Not because I think I'll succeed. I just need to register my protest.

"At least let me finish my drink," I say.

The Teacher looks down at the departures and arrivals terminal, where his fellow goons are rushing to the heap of crushed luggage and the dead body responsible.

"Come on," I pester. "It's the last smoke before the war. Humor me, please? Then we can go."

The Teacher releases his grip on my arm.

"No tricks."

With my back to the Teacher, I grab the glass of sake. But before I gulp down what remains, I blink to connect to my interface. I hold the glass to my lips and whisper a command.

<<*Approve interface access for Jaz Singh.*>>

I shoot back the sake and slam the empty glass upside-down upon the counter.

I whisper one more command while the sound from the glass rings out.

<<Ping location. Prompt Jaz Singh to track and record immediately upon receipt.>>

The Teacher pulls me from the counter and pushes me toward our exit, past two trembling Sparklers and down those magnificent wrought-iron steps.

THE TEACHER'S CAR is parked in an alley behind the Embarkment, where the only humans around are the occasional Contractor on break.

I have seconds left with the Teacher before I have to face whatever awaits me in that car.

"I knew you were one of the good guys. A bad guy would have shot us both." I'm, of course, referring to Jerry and me.

"Who says that wasn't the plan?" His hand is on the door handle now. "You know, I really thought you were going to jump back there."

"For a while, I thought I was, too. But someone was watching over me."

He opens the car door and shoves me inside. "No one believes in fairy godmothers anymore, Connie." He slams the door behind me.

The inside of the car is dark, and it smells of real leather. Feels like real leather, too. Other modifications have been made to the interior,—an integrated dash and additional security.

"He likes you," a voice says. "He must. I've never had to give a debtor as much line as I gave you. All because he wouldn't bring you in."

A light turns on inside the car to reveal the face of the speaker.

Gary Weng. The legendary Wengzai.

In person, Gary Weng looks painfully ordinary. Like someone's elderly uncle. I wonder if he can sense my disappointment, and if he gets that reaction a lot.

He drums his fingers on an armrest. "You did yourself a great disservice by not working with me when you could. Now Jerry is set to cash in without you."

"Jerry's dead."

The drumming on the armrest stops.

"People are always the most unpredictable," Gary Weng laments. I can't tell if he's speaking to me, or speaking out loud to himself. "You can design and produce the best product on paper, test it a thousand times over in a controlled environment with the best machine intelligences the world has ever known— you can even get back excellent grades—but the only way to truly determine a product's value is by sending it to market. The customer, you see, is what makes or breaks your work. But the problem with your generation is that you don't know what you want. You don't know what you're fighting. Or even what you're fighting for. You think in dichotomies: black and white, good and evil, right and wrong. But what's worse, believe yourselves to be the only generation in history that's good enough, righteous enough, to determine the moral difference."

"What Project Echo aims to do is wrong. And you know it."

"What's wrong about paying someone in exchange for their hard labor? What's wrong about wanting to make back all that we lost in the Second Great Depression?"

"My parents worked harder than anyone I've ever met. They were worked to the bone, worked until they had nothing left to give. They retired in poverty. A lifetime of hard labor had been sold for pennies on the dollar."

"But what if they only *thought* they had nothing left to give? What if they'd been holding back? What if they were paid exactly what they had earned? I envision a world where people like your parents can work more, earn more, retire with more coin in the bank. All they need is an ideal to look up to, something to show them is truly possible. They need to see what's possible. They need to see the best possible version of themselves cheering them on to do more. There's no doubt in my mind that they'd push themselves beyond their limits. How can you give up when everything that's possible is right there in front of you? No worker would ever feel shortchanged again, because no worker would ever feel like they gave enough. They'd always want to give more."

I fall silent. I know all about creating a better version of yourself to believe in, or a worser version to bet against. I've been profiting off the concept for years now. It's what Club Contango is all about. When the piano quiets, and the drinks run dry, and the Delight is just a scratching like a record at the end of its final track—when all your Sparkler friends have left you because you're not who they thought you are—what then?

You push.

BESTIE

"TELL ME YOU'VE never imagined your better self, and we can end this conversation now."

"Maybe I have. But this entire discussion is pointless, because nothing you're describing falls within Echo's capabilities."

"The holograms selling junk bonds are just the beginning, Mx. Lam. They're just prototypes. It's the only reason I let you run circles around me for so long, why I let you crash the one iteration with the silly little code on your disc. I wanted to watch you, see how you reacted to them, and how they reacted to you."

"It was a Beta test."

"Precisely. And you provided us with hours of brilliant insight. Now, as sole owner of Echo, I can scrap the project and roll all of its accumulated knowledge into Bestie."

"Red Unicorn owns Bestie—"

"And who do you think owns Red Unicorn? It took me five long years to wrestle away a controlling stake of the company—even after I had become the largest single shareholder—but eventually, I succeeded. For five years, I pored through the list of active Red Unicorn shareholder, searching day and night for any possible weaknesses, any possible buttons I could push to get those investors to sell to me their stakes. That's when I found Kin Hong, who was bothering himself with a little program called Echo." Wengzai shakes his head with a sad, almost respectful smile. "That last son from a has-been dynasty had been given a lifeline with Red Unicorn, and he was preparing cut it. And for what? To blow the whistle? How many idealists does it take to screw a good project? Because in this case, it was one."

"Two, if you count me."

Wengzai shakes a fat index finger. "Bestie is new, but work management and human resource platforms have been dreaming of something like this for years. A mid-sized port logistics company called Dash had some success applying best-self theory to their employees. They paired workers with their closest matching performer, and pitted them in a competition for survival. Loser lost their job. That was my wake-up call. If a sector like shipping—old as time, and infested with unions and aging workers—could be pulled into the modern age and made to work sharp and on target, then so could I, an old debt collector, whose name was growing stale. So, I rebranded myself as an angel investor. Suziebaby knows all about it, even if she won't give me the time of day now. Curious, considering how she lost everything in the Second Great Depression. I thought she'd be more receptive."

I think about Dash, and about Walter Woo swaggering into the conference room at the Imperial all those years ago. I gave up fighting Dash. Gave up on my parents and all the workers who depended on me. Gave up on myself. And because I did, I helped prove Woo right. I won't make that mistake again.

"You see, Connie, there is no ultimate evil at work here, no evil master plan. I do not wish for mass unemployment or the collapse of the civilized world as we know it. I want you all to keep your little jobs and live your little lives. *Please.* People need their treadmills, or they drop out of the game. Men like me need you in the game. My goal is simply to make labor more efficient without raising the price. Too many people today are overeducated and underemployed, trapped by limiting obligations. Born to expect the world, but incapable of finding their place in it. You see, Connie, your generation is in desperate need of what I'm wanting to sell. They just don't know it yet."

"People are more than units of labor."

"I've said enough. People can benefit from this. You don't want to see human workers become irrelevant, and neither do I. Bestie is their best chance to prove they can still sweat for it. It will change lives beyond work, too. Bestie will make better partners, better parents. You will want to be part of that."

"Growth is in the becoming. If you try and skip ahead, you learn nothing, become a poor copy of what you hoped you could be." I should know.

"Suit yourself. I don't need you. I'll have all the rights from Red Unicorn within six months. I'm an old man. I know how to adapt to changing instruments and economies, to the ever-changing bogeymen of this world. They're still running the same tired scams, you know, just now with better tech. You have a nose for this, Connie. I can see it from how you manage your club. If only you had access to more coin, a better network, you could go far. Perhaps I can assist you—"

"Thanks, but no."

"What if I'm not asking?"

"I'll inform you that Inspector Singh has legal access to the transcript of this conversation through my interface, including archival access, should it come to that."

I look out the car window to see a Contractor taking his break. *Bottoms up.* He wipes his mouth on his uniform sleeve. Just one of the many hidden humans that keep the station functioning—keep corporations like Dash, Habo, Circle, and Pacific Mutual in profit. And yet, MAM will happily stop issuing L1-2 Contractor visas the second it becomes more cost effective to do so. And men like Wengzai will help them—even if today's comforts come at great expense for tomorrow.

"Look," I say, pointing out the window. "There he is now."

Gary Weng and I watch the Contractor head back inside to continue his shift right as another figure steps out of the shadows. It's Singh. He tosses back a handful of hazelnuts.

Then he taps his ear, waves to the car, and smiles. He's reading us loud and clear.

Gary Weng slams his fist on the armrest and growls. "Get out of my car. I don't need you anymore."

IN THE OLD thriller movies my grandma used to watch, there's always a montage of the hotshot young lawyer or troubled detective poring over the pages inside a weathered three-ring binder while writing notes on paper, crushing those notes in a fury, and shooting them across the room into a wire wastepaper basket. It's a much better visual than the modern-day equivalent of wildly blinking dry eyes through interfaces and sub-vocalizing commands to text, which is what Vis and I do in the days following my encounter with Gary Weng, as we sort through the terabytes of original files for Project Echo. Gaining access to the original files was the real reason I sabotaged the holograms. I needed to bait Jerry into asking for my help to fix them, and then forcing him to give me full access to the code.

Vis's legal brain quickly identifies the truth: Jerry had no right to sell the images, recordings, or AI model of me to Red Unicorn in the form of Echo. He didn't even have the explicit right to create Echo, because I didn't grant him downstream rights, and the territory we signed the agreement in was in the honeymoon months of an opt-in law that would later be quietly crushed at the next party renewal. But that was still the law of the land when I signed.

I fold myself onto Vis's sofa and let it sink in. I'm still responsible for the mess that tore through everyone's lives, but I was led by a lie from the start.

With minimal damage to HaboHub property and no casualties, Habo decided to drop the arson investigation even though they had Vis and the Hands dead to rights. They claimed the investigation would be too expensive to pursue, but the truth is, the Commission had decided for them. Apparently, an investigation into the arson at HaboHub would bring to light too many questions about Freeport fire safety, and this was not a Pandora's box the Commission was ready to open.

Vis was put on indefinite paid leave from Habo to separate her from the Hands, but if the last two weeks have shown me anything, it's that there's no separation between the hands and the will that guides them. Vis is now working to provide laborers with contractual protections against discretionary interface updates by their employers. It's an uphill battle, but this is her window, and she's going to try everything she can while it's open. Even the Commission has taken interest, which is why Habo can't simply cancel her visa and flick her off-station like she's just a bug.

The Embarkment shines like a golden promise through the glass in Vis's room in the MAM hostel. The building hasn't changed since the day we first landed stationside, back when Sticky was still just tottering, and Vis and I were new Contractors short on tenure but long on hope. Turns out, the promise offered that day was never from Freeport, but from me to my future self—a promise that I'd fight my own fights. In a few years, the Embarkment will no longer stand head and shoulders above the low-rise, first-generation prefab units on Upper Beach Road, but will instead compete with newer, bolder constructions for dominance of the station's skyline.

I pull a sip of Vis's kopi.

"Do you think this case will have legs?"

"It'll have legs enough to get Red Unicorn to settle before the Commission drags it to arbitration for abetting unrest. That's what we're going for. And to seize this chance to dig them in the ribs a little, force them to give standard protections to Contractors. Plus a heavy settlement paid to the Hands to compensate for lost wages and to help rebuild their strike fund. Some of that should go to you, too, for the rights violations."

"I'd like to earmark most of it for Trace's rebuilding of Lucky 48, and to compensate the Pereiras. I just need enough to clear Alchemy's debt and be rid of Gary Weng for good."

Vis clinks fingernails on the side of her mug. "Will you ever, though?"

The silence is companionable, but I feel a flutter of things unsaid like migratory birds growing anxious at the turning of the weather.

"I'm sorry I saddled you with this."

"Sorry? You have a lot of things to be sorry for, but this isn't one of them. I'm glad for the chance to practice law again. I had given up on myself for too long. Dug into the HaboHub job like it was the only thing I was sure I could do. The only thing impossible to fuck up." Vis lifts the mug to her lips but lowers it again. "I should thank you for Club Contango, too. I said a few things, but it was a support for me."

"Thanks, Visala. That's the nicest thing you've ever said to me."

"No more where that came from." She smiles.

"You at least have more kopi, don't you?"

Vis takes my cup. For a half-second, I think I see something that looks a lot like wistfulness, but then it's gone.

"I always made good coffee, Connie. If you'd stuck around, you'd remember. You know, I only met Hong once, and I thought he was a bit of an operator, but the guy didn't deserve to die."

I appreciate her saying as much. Hong wasn't perfect. He was my handler, my exploiter, and my enabler. But he was also my mentor and friend. He was the first person who led me to believe in myself, even if his reasons for doing so were selfish at times. I stood on his shoulders with pride.

The light from the source on the tower shifts to a clean white glow to signal the passing of morning into afternoon. It takes with it the last golden reflections of the Embarkment. The rays fall from the curved windows and refract a rainbow through the crystal chandelier.

I can almost hear Hong say, *what doesn't kill you, kid.*

I didn't ask for it, but I wouldn't give it back.

I see you now, for all your flaws. Every mistake, every white lie, every deception. Every bit of hope we shook from the dregs of a drink poured thin for all of us who weren't the elect. It led to what I am today. Thanks for everything, King.

Thank me when the dealing's done.

RESTART

THE DEPARTURE HALL glows like an ancient cathedral illuminated through stained glass. It is a space of first encounters and last reckonings, a corridor between passages. All of us who cross this hall are united in worship.

Sticky and I are leaving for good—for a greyfield, a developed asset. Not even Vis knows, although I've promised to keep our private channel live. Trace knows how to find me, regardless. I truly hope she does.

Only two things are constant now, and one of them is the feeling of Sticky's warm little paw in mine.

This early in the morning, the Life Collection shops that line the departure hall of the Embarkment draw on a slow but regular flow of Settlers stepping out for coffee, and Sparklers shambling back from overnight flights, desperate for a refuel before something stronger. Contractors clutch their packed lunches as they walk inside. Their wallets are locked, but their eyes are wide, ready for the visual treat and the unspoken promise of something nice for themselves and their families, one day when they can afford it.

Sticky holds a spiced-turnip bao from Auntie's with both her little hands. I hold on to her shoulder and smile even though I know she won't look up. She's too busy digging in.

Commuters pass us on both sides, but I'm scarcely more aware of them than of the pounding of my own heart.

Count the beats, Connie.

When we pass the balcony, I look up, half expecting to see Chance at the viewing balcony of Tanuki.

Hoping to see Chance there.

But it's too late for breakfast, and too early for a show. The handful of Sparklers at Tanuki are at the bar, lingering over their last morning cocktails before a pre-lunch nap.

"One of these days, I'm going to go up there and see what it's all about."

I turn to greet the familiar voice.

Jaz Singh isn't in uniform today. He's wearing a T-shirt under a brown jacket, vintage jeans that look worn in the old-fashioned way—rather than being designer-distressed—and sharp-toed dress shoes that are shined but respectably scuffed, to give the appearance of someone who walks to dinner when he can.

While Vis and I were nosing around through legal documents, I learned something about Inspector Singh. He came to Freeport as a Sparkler, but that was never the life meant for him. After the Hong case, he was earmarked for diplomatic service at the Residency.

"Off duty today?"

Jaz sucks in a breath. "Actually...I quit last week. Our values didn't align. The new Resident means well, but she's looking for a lapdog. Whoever she hires, they're gonna have their work cut out for them. Freeport won't be just a commercial center much longer. People have begun to make lives for themselves here. Life under the dome is changing." He unbuttons his jacket, then drops to his haunches to smile at Sticky. "Hello, little lady. I have a little something for you." He looks to me for approval. "May I?"

I gesture for him to go ahead, and he hands Sticky a see-through plastic maze, with two pinballs rattling inside of it.

"I love mazes!" says Sticky. "But why are there two balls?"

"To make it more difficult. It's not enough to get one ball to safety. You have to keep it there, waiting, while the other finds its way to it, too."

He pulls himself up to his regular height, and we lock eyes for a second.

I break the silence first: "Work expands to fill the time given it. In this case, the maze."

"Of course," says Jaz. "Precisely what I meant."

And with that, we say our goodbyes.

STICKY'S SEATBELT IS fastened, and the Captain's making his announcement about our estimated travel time to the Western Ring. I set a twenty-minute time limit on the animation Sticky is watching and leave my seat. It's a smaller shuttle, with the trip to the Western Ring only fifty hours via wormhole. Getting our paperwork in order at the MAM checkpoint took longer than expected, and it's already dusk. From the viewing deck at the stern, Freeport glows an alluring rose-gold.

My reflection on the glass moves and then splits. I think I'm holding my breath, but I can't tell, and my vision slides as I lose focus. Chance stands beside me and watches as the ship untethers herself from the final ties that bind.

I say to Chance, "This isn't real."

Chance comes close enough to brush my cheek, but doesn't.

"Why are you here?" I say.

It's the hurt in my voice that surprises me. In the last days, as I busied myself with the case, with Vis, with the closing of accounts and tying-up of loose ends, Chance stayed away. I thought I'd never see Chance again. I thought I was past *wanting* to see Chance again.

Only because you called me. You should stop.

The weight of everything I've been holding back suddenly comes crashing down. But it's not the weight of a crushing depression manifest as big brooding birds. It's grief. Grief for what I was and what I am. For what I'm about to face alone.

I allow myself to grieve.

I'm not ready to let you go.

You already have. I'm proud of us, Connie.

The ship breaks her last tether and groans. On the intercom, the Captain warns all passengers to please remain seated for takeoff.

But I can't detach from the sight of Freeport.

And Chance.

Were you always a dream, Chance?

Only until you made the reality you wanted to live in.

"You were my truth."

There's a stubbornness to my voice, and it's hard to speak through the tremble in my throat. I still don't know where I'm going after this, or what I'm trying to make for us, but I have all I need to succeed.

The ship drifts with quiet grace, past her sisters at the pilot station, and Chance steps into the shadow, leaving me with my own reflection at last.

I take my hand off the glass and turn around.

I head back to my seat and take it.

During the voyage, I read a story to Sticky and dream of our life yet to come.

ACKNOWLEDGMENTS

THANK YOU Edward Ashton and Samit Basu for being patient and forgiving early readers and reviewers. Thanks to my editor and publisher Rob Carroll for believing. And to Nickolej Villiger for this kickass cover. Thanks to Victor Manibo, Aubrey Wood, and Lincoln Michel for the very generous blurbs. Special mention for Gareth Jelley, for weeding out a number of early typos, thank you! Thanks also to everyone in the SFF writing and reading community who has talked about and shared news on this book. I appreciate you.

To MH and CX, thanks for putting up with me.

Second book! This is the book I never thought I'd get to write. *Club Contango* is about coping, growing, and taking back control. It's about bad relationships, bad situations, and bad, bad contract terms. It's also about maternal depression. (But it's fun, and it's wrapped up in a jazzy mystery!) I've tried to treat the imagery of depression with a softer, hopeful touch, while keeping it real. I hope I succeeded, and that *Club Contango* finds those who need it.

—Eliane Boey

ABOUT THE AUTHOR

ELIANE BOEY is a writer of speculative fiction, with stories in *Clarkesworld*, the *Penn Review, Galaxy, Weird Horror, Dark Matter Magazine*, and others. She is a member of the SFWA and BFS, and she is the author of *The Tracerverse* series, which includes the novella duology *Other Minds* and the novel *Club Contango*. She lives and writes in Singapore.

Frost Bite by Angela Sylvaine
ISBN 978-1-958598-03-0

Free Burn by Drew Huff
ISBN 978-1-958598-26-9

The House at the End of Lacelean Street
by Catherine McCarthy
ISBN 978-1-958598-23-8

When the Gods Are Away by Robert E. Harpold
ISBN 978-1-958598-47-4

The Dead Spot: Stories of Lost Girls
by Angela Sylvaine
ISBN 978-1-958598-27-6

Grim Root by Bonnie Jo Stufflebeam
ISBN 978-1-958598-36-8

Voracious by Belicia Rhea
ISBN 978-1-958598-25-2

The Bleed by Stephen S. Schreffler
ISBN 978-1-958598-11-5

Chopping Spree by Angela Sylvaine
ISBN 978-1-958598-31-3

Saturday Fright at the Movies: 13 Tales from the Multiplex
by Amanda Cecelia Lang
ISBN 978-1-958598-75-7

The Off-Season: An Anthology of Coastal New Weird
Edited by Marissa van Uden
ISBN 978-1-958598-24-5

The Threshing Floor by Steph Nelson
ISBN 978-1-958598-49-8

The Divine Flesh by Drew Huff
ISBN 978-1-958598-59-7

Psychopomp by Maria Dong
ISBN 978-1-958598-52-8

Disgraced Return of the Kap's Needle
by Renan Bernardo
ISBN 978-1-958598-74-0

Haunted Reels 2: More Stories from the Minds of Professional Filmmakers Curated by David Lawson
ISBN 978-1-958598-53-5

Dark Circuitry by Kirk Bueckert
ISBN 978-1-958598-48-1

Soul Couriers by Caleb Stephens
ISBN 978-1-958598-76-4

Abducted by Patrick Barb
ISBN 978-1-958598-37-5

Cyanide Constellations and Other Stories
by Sara Tantlinger
ISBN 978-1-958598-81-8

Little Red Flags: Stories of Cults, Cons, and Control
Edited by Noelle W. Ihli & Steph Nelson
ISBN 978-1-958598-54-2

Cold Snap by Angela Sylvaine
ISBN 978-1-958598-55-9

The Starship, from a Distance by Robert E. Harpold
ISBN 978-1-958598-82-5

Dark Matter Presents: Fear City
ISBN 978-1-958598-90-0

Part of the Dark Hart Collection

Rootwork by Tracy Cross
ISBN 978-1-958598-85-6

Mosaic by Catherine McCarthy
ISBN 978-1-958598-06-1

Apparitions by Adam Pottle
ISBN 978-1-958598-18-4

I Can See Your Lies by Izzy Lee
ISBN 978-1-958598-28-3

A Gathering of Weapons by Tracy Cross
ISBN 978-1-958598-38-2

7 8 1 9 5 8 5 9 8 5 7 3 *